PRAISE FOR DAVID ROSENFELT'S NOVELS

BURY THE LEAD

"Exudes charm and off beat humor, sophistication, and personable characters."

—*Dallas Morning News*

"If you want a little edge, try this."

—*Santa Fe New Mexican*

"Well-plotted . . . enjoyable."

—*Kansas City Star*

"A+ . . . It's always a pleasure to read a Rosenfelt book."

—*Deadly Pleasures*

"There are many surprising twists in this exciting legal thriller . . . The ending is a surprise readers will think about for a long time."

—*I Love a Mystery*

"Rosenfelt is talented."

—*Publishers Weekly*

"The running observations of self-deprecating hero Andy Carpenter elicit a smile, if not an out-loud laugh, on practically every page."

—*Star-Ledger* (NJ)

more . . .

FIRST DEGREE

SELECTED AS ONE OF THE BEST MYSTERIES OF 2003 BY *PUBLISHERS WEEKLY*

"Suspense just where you want it and humor just when you need it."
—Entertainment Weekly

"Entertaining . . . fast-paced . . . sophisticated."
—Marilyn Stasio, *New York Times Book Review*

"Rosenfelt's got it all—canny invention, snappy dialogue, deftly managed legal conflicts, startling surprises—and he displays it all with an economy that should make his courtroom brethren hang their heads in shame."
—Kirkus Reviews (starred review)

"Entertaining . . . Rosenfelt writes with exceeding charm and humor."
—San Antonio Express-News

"This novel confirms that Rosenfelt will be a force in the legal-thriller world for a long time to come."
—Booklist

"Genuinely delightful . . . Clever plot twists, deft legal maneuverings, and keen wit boost Rosenfelt's accomplished follow-up to his Edgar-nominated debut . . . The author adroitly maintains a fast pace while switching gears effortlessly . . . Rosenfelt should win a unanimous verdict: first–rate."
—Publishers Weekly (starred review)

"Engaging . . . Rosenfelt has another winner."
—Orlando Sentinel

"Entertaining." —*Cleveland Plain Dealer*

"Rosenfelt keeps the plot roaring along . . . while keeping the reader chuckling and turning pages."
—*Library Journal*

"A tremendous thriller . . . fast-paced . . . a winner."
—*Midwest Book Review*

"The fun part about Rosenfelt's legal thrillers . . . is the dry wit and self-deprecating humor of his hero."
—*Star-Ledger* (NJ)

OPEN AND SHUT

"A very assured first novel . . . packed with cleverly sarcastic wit." —*New York Times*

"Splendid . . . intricate plotting."
—*Cleveland Plain Dealer*

"A great book . . . one part gripping legal thriller, one part smart-mouth wise-guy detective story, and all around terrific." —Harlan Coben, author of *No Second Chance*

"Rosenfelt has a knack for pacing, plotting, and narration . . . This new guy just may have what it takes."
—*St. Petersburg Times*

"Engaging and likable . . . The action is brisk."
—*San Francisco Chronicle*

"Written with the skill of a veteran, Rosenfelt's debut legal thriller boasts fresh characters, an engaging narrator, and a plot that forces readers to keep flipping the pages."
—*Booklist* (starred review)

BURY THE
LEAD

DAVID
ROSENFELT

WARNER BOOKS

NEW YORK   BOSTON

Copyright © 2004 by David Rosenfelt
Excerpt from *Sudden Death* copyright © 2004 by David Rosenfelt
All rights reserved. No part of this book may be reproduced in any form or by any electronic or mechanical means, including information storage and retrieval systems, without permission in writing from the publisher, except by a reviewer who may quote brief passages in a review.

Cover art and design by Shasti O'Leary Soudant

Warner Books

Time Warner Book Group
1271 Avenue of the Americas, New York, NY 10020
Visit our Web site at www.twbookmark.com

The Mysterious Press name and logo are registered trademarks of Warner Books.

Printed in the United States of America

Originally published in hardcover by Mysterious Press
First Paperback Printing: April 2005

10 9 8 7 6 5 4 3 2 1

ATTENTION CORPORATIONS AND ORGANIZATIONS:
Most WARNER books are available at quantity discounts with bulk purchase for educational, business, or sales promotional use. For information, please call or write: Special Markets Department, Warner Books, Inc. 135 W. 50th Street, New York, NY 10020-1393.
Telephone: 1-800-222-6747 Fax: 1-800-477-5925.

To Sara Ann Freed.

I am not a good enough writer to create a character with the grace, dignity, generosity, spirit, and courage that came so naturally to Sara Ann.

Acknowledgments

Once again I must face the unplesant task of admitting that I had help with this book. So, in no particular order, I would like to thank:

Robin Rue and Sandy Weinberg, agents extraordinaire.

Jamie Raab, Les Pockell, Kristen Weber, Susan Richman, Martha Otis, Bob Castillo, and everyone else at Warner. They have been consistently supportive and a pleasure to deal with.

George Kentris, for helping with everything legal; Kristen Paxos Mecionis, for helping with everything involving law enforcement; and Susan Brace, for helping with everything psychological. In a never-ending quest for accuracy and realism, I follow everything they say, unless it interferes with the story.

Those who read early drafts and contributed their thoughts, including Ross, Heidi, Rick, Lynn, Mike and Sandi Rosenfelt, Amanda Baron, Emily Kim, Al and Nancy Sarnoff, Stacy Alesi, and Norman Trell. Special thanks to Scott Ryder for sharing his considerable expertise in everything from computers to skydiving.

And to Debbie Myers—paraphrasing Russell Crowe to Jennifer Connelly at the end of *A Beautiful Mind*— "You are the reason I am here today. You are all my reasons."

I continue to be grateful to the many people who have e-mailed me feedback on *Open and Shut* and *First Degree*. Please do so again at <u>dr27712@aol.com</u>. Thank you.

BURY THE
LEAD

• • • • •

As SOON AS I WALK IN, the woman gives me
the eye.

This is not quite as promising a situation as it sounds.
First of all, I'm in a laundromat. The actual name is the
Law-dromat, owned by my associate Kevin Randall.
Kevin uses this business to emotionally, as well as literally, cleanse himself of the rather grimy things we're ex-
posed to in our criminal law practice. In the process he
dispenses free legal advice to customers along with de-
tergent and bleach.

Also, the woman giving me this particular eye is not
exactly a supermodel. She's maybe four feet eleven
inches tall, rather round, and wearing a coat so bulky she
could be hiding a four-gallon jug of Tide under it. Her hair
is stringy and most likely not squeaky clean to the touch.

Truth be told, even if we were in a nightclub and the

woman looked more like Halle than Boysen Berry, I doubt I could accurately gauge the situation. I'm no better than average-looking myself and thus have almost no experience with women giving me the eye. In fact, though I'm not in the habit of counting offered body parts, it's safe to say that over the years I've gotten the finger more than the eye. And I've probably gotten the boot more than both of them combined.

To totally close off any romantic possibilities in this encounter, I remain in love with, and totally faithful to, one Laurie Collins. So no matter how this round stranger tries to tempt me, I'm not about to engage in an early evening bout of tawdry Laundromat sex.

I notice that the woman's eyes start alternating between me and the door, though no one else is entering. And as I move in her general direction, she starts to inch toward that door. This woman is afraid of me.

"Hi," I say, figuring a clever opening like that will put her at ease. Instead, she just nods slightly and seems to draw inward, as if she wants to become invisible. "Kevin around?" I ask.

The woman mutters, "No . . . I don't know . . . ," then gathers her clothes, which she hadn't yet put into the machine, and quickly leaves. In the process she bangs into Kevin's cousin Billy, who is just coming in. Billy runs the place when Kevin is not around.

"Hey, Andy. What's with her?" Billy asks.

"I'm not sure. I think she was afraid she might succumb to my charms."

He nods. "We've been getting a lot of that lately."

"What do you mean?"

Billy just points toward a shelf high up in the corner of the room, and for the first time I realize that there is a television up there. It's turned to local news, though the sound is off. There was a day when that would have been a problem, but now all the stations have that annoying crawl along the bottom of the screen.

The subject of the newscast is the murder of a woman last night in Passaic, the third such murder in the last three weeks. The killer has chosen to communicate and taunt the police through Daniel Cummings, a reporter for a local newspaper, and in the process has created a media furor. The woman who just left is not alone in her fear; the entire community seems gripped by it.

"They making any progress?" I ask, referring to the police.

Billy shrugs. "They're appealing to the guy to give himself up."

I nod. "That should do the trick. Where's Kevin?"

"Doctor."

"Is he sick?" I ask, though I know better. Kevin has as many admirable qualities as anyone I know, but he happens to be a total hypochondriac.

Billy laughs. "Yeah. He thinks his tongue is swollen and turning black. Kept sticking it out for me to look at."

"Was it swollen?"

He shakes his head. "Nope."

"Black?"

"Nope."

"Did you tell him that?" I ask.

"Nope. I told him he should get it checked out, that he might be getting 'fat black tongue' disease." He shrugs and explains, "I'm a little short this month; I needed the hours."

I nod; the more time Kevin spends at the doctor, the more time Billy gets to work here. I hand an envelope to

Billy; it had come to the office for Kevin. "Give this to him, okay?"

"You making deliveries now?" he asks.

"I'm on my way to the foundation."

Billy nods. "Listen, do me a favor? When you see Kevin, tell him his tongue looks like a bowling ball."

"No problem."

• • • • •

NEW JERSEY EXISTS in a sort of twilight zone. That is, if it exists at all. It is a densely populated, diverse collection of cities and towns, yet it has no identity. Half of it is a suburb of New York City, and the other half a suburb of Philadelphia. The Giants and Jets play football in Jersey, yet they deny its existence, referring to themselves as "New York."

The most embarrassing part is that all the major TV stations that cover New Jersey are based in New York. Ottumwa, Iowa, has its own network affiliates, but Jersey doesn't. It should thus come as no surprise that those same stations treat Jerseyites as second-class citizens.

Stories about New Jersey are barely covered, unless they are simply too juicy to overlook. The recent murders have successfully crossed that high-juice threshold, and the networks are all over them. Even more pumped up are the national cable networks, and I've been invited to serve as an uninformed panelist on eleven of the shows that specialize in uninformed panels. I've accepted three of those invitations, and in the process I fit right in by bringing absolutely nothing of value to the public discourse.

My appeal to these shows is based on the fact that I've successfully handled a couple of high-profile murder cases in the last couple of years. I must've gotten on some list that is shared among TV news producers. "Let's see . . . ," I can hear them say as they check that list when a New Jersey crime story comes up. "Here it is . . . Andy Carpenter. Let's get him. That'll fill twenty minutes."

The one question always posed to me on these shows is whether I would be willing to defend the murderer when he is caught. I point out that he wouldn't legally be a murderer until he's been tried and convicted, but this distinction is basically lost on the questioner and, I suspect, the viewing public. I ultimately and lamely say that I would consider it based on the circumstances, and I can almost feel that public recoiling in shock. "How," they collectively wonder, "could you defend that animal?"

I don't really have to worry about any of that, though, because the police don't seem terribly close to catching this particular animal. Instead, I can focus on other animals, specifically dogs. Right now I am on my way to the building that houses the Tara Foundation, a converted kennel that Willie Miller and I have turned into a dog rescue operation. We've self-financed it, which does not represent a major sacrifice. I inherited twenty-two million dollars last year, and about five months ago I secured ten million dollars for Willie in a civil suit against the people who conspired to wrongfully put him on death row for seven years. To put it another way, we are both filthy rich.

The foundation is named after my own golden retriever, Tara, whose official name is Tara, Greatest Living Creature on This or Any Other Planet. Willie is foolish enough to believe that his dog, Cash, is up there in Tara's class. I only occasionally mock this notion, since Willie is my partner, the foundation was his idea, and he does most of the work.

What we do is rescue dogs from animal shelters, where they are about to be put to sleep, and then find them good homes. People come to us at the foundation, meet the dogs, and then have to endure a fairly rigorous application process to determine if we consider them to have a satisfactory home for our dogs.

As I enter the building, Willie is interviewing a forty-ish couple who are interested in adopting Tyler, a three-year-old black Lab mix. Willie introduces me to the couple, Stan and Julie Harrington, and Stan makes it clear that he knows me from my TV appearances.

I take a seat across the room as Willie continues the interview. The Harringtons alternate answering, slightly anxious and clearly trying to ascertain what it is that Willie wants to hear.

"Where would the dog sleep?" Willie asks innocently, as if he's just curious. Tyler, the dog whose sleep location is the subject being discussed, sits alongside Willie, his curiosity piqued as well.

This time Julie, fashionably and therefore incongruously dressed for these surroundings, brightens. "Oh, we've got a wonderful doghouse in the backyard."

Stan nods in vigorous agreement, unaware that his wife has just blown what little chance they had of adopting Tyler. "I built it myself. It's huge. There are *people* who would like to live in it." He chuckles at the thought, then turns to Tyler. "Wouldn't you like a great big dog-house?" He speaks in a form of baby talk.

Maybe it's my imagination, but from my vantage point across the room, Tyler seems to edge closer to Willie, apparently aware that this couple is not going to become his new parents. And that great big outside doghouse that some *people* would like is definitely not going to be the place where he sleeps.

Willie and I have rather rigid ideas of what represents a good home for a dog. Stan and Julie have just demonstrated that, in our eyes, their home doesn't make the cut. It is an unbending rule of the Tara Foundation that dogs must be allowed to sleep in the house.

I expect Willie to immediately terminate the session and send the Harringtons on their way, but for some reason he decides to delay the inevitable. He asks a question that sounds like a challenge. "Why do you guys want a dog?"

I see a quick flash of annoyance on Stan's face. He doesn't think he should have to answer all these questions; he should be able to buy a dog like he can buy anything else. "I had dogs when I was growing up," he allows. "I'm a dog person."

Willie doesn't seem moved by this revelation, and Julie, sensing things are not going well, jumps in. "He'll be like a member of our family. And he can guard—"

Willie interrupts, incredulous. "You want a guard dog?" He points to Tyler, who doesn't seem that offended. "You think he's a guard dog?"

His tone causes me to get up and walk toward them. Willie's generally been on his good behavior, but he can be volatile, and he's a black belt in karate, so there is always the potential for things to get a little ugly.

"Mr. and Mrs. Harrington," I say, "I'm afraid we don't have any guard dogs up for adoption."

Stan is getting frustrated. "We didn't mean a *guard* dog. We just want a dog that will bark if someone enters the property." He holds up a newspaper that is on the desk. "I mean with what's going on . . ."

He is of course referring to the murder last night in Passaic, the third victim of the serial killer who has dominated the news. It is pretty much all anyone is talking about. "Julie's alone in the house all day," he points out.

"Then why don't you adopt a goddamn burglar alarm?" Willie asks, standing and getting a tad hostile. I shoot him a look that says, "I'll handle this," but he disregards it. "Or maybe you can adopt a fucking Secret Service agent." These dogs are like his kids, and he's not about to put them in the line of fire.

Stan gets up. He's not going to confront Willie, since in addition to being a "dog person," he's a "sane person." "I can see this was a mistake," he says. "Come on, Julie." She's a little slow, so he helps her to her feet and guides her toward the door. The last thing I hear her say before they exit is, "But what about the dog?"

Willie shakes his head in disgust. "Losers." Then he turns to me. "You know why losers like that come here? They don't want no dog. They come here because of you, because they think you're hot shit."

Now I get annoyed, an increasingly frequent occurrence of late. "Fine. It's my fault. Okay? Does that make you happy?"

He grins widely; Willie can change moods even faster

than I can. He taps me on the shoulder. "Hey, lighten up, huh? You can't help it if you're hot shit."

Willie is only partially right about why people like the Harringtons come here. The two big cases in the past year have made me a celebrity lawyer of sorts. But one of those cases was Willie's, and as a wrongfully convicted man set free, he's become a big shot in his own right. So people come here because they've heard of both of us and it's a cool thing to do, rather than go to breeders or pet stores or whatever.

"We've placed thirty-one dogs," I say. "That's not bad for five weeks."

He nods. "Damn right. Not bad at all." Then, "You going to the meeting tomorrow?"

He's talking about an informal investment group I made the mistake of organizing. I've regretted it from day one, which was about two months ago.

I nod reluctantly just as the phone rings, which now and always sends the twenty-five dogs at the foundation into a barking frenzy. I pick it up and shout into the receiver, "Hold on!" I then wait the thirty seconds or so that it takes for the dogs to quiet down before I speak into the phone again. "Hello?"

"How can you stand that barking?" It's Vince Sanders, editor of what passes as the local newspaper in Paterson. Vince is always pissed off about something; this time the dogs just happened to have given him a good reason.

"Fine, Vince, how are you?"

"Did you hear what I said?" he snarls.

"I hang on your every word."

"Then hang on these. Come down to my office."

"When?" I ask.

"When? A year from August, bozo."

Although the "when" question didn't go too well, I decide to try another one. "Why?"

"You're still a lawyer, aren't you?"

"You want to hire me?"

He doesn't consider this a question worth answering. "Be here in twenty minutes."

Click.

• • • • •

VINCE SHOULD BE a happy camper these days. His paper's circulation has gone through the roof since the murders began, mainly because Daniel Cummings, through whom the killer has chosen to speak to the public and police, is one of Vince's reporters.

Vince brought Cummings in about six months ago from somewhere in Ohio, I think Cleveland. He made him his top crime reporter, although Cummings can't be more than thirty. I've only met him once, but he's a pretty easy guy for a defense attorney to dislike, a strong law-and-order type who clearly believes in a presumption of guilt.

I've known Vince for about a year. He's cantankerous and obnoxious on the surface, but when you chip that away and dig deeper, you find him to be surly and disagreeable. You probably could say Vince and I have become good friends, if your definition of "friends" isn't too rigid. We're not "Ya-Ya Brotherhood" types, but we

hang out some in sports bars and trade insults, which fits
my definition pretty well.

Vince usually starts off our conversations with five
minutes of complaining, but he doesn't do that when I arrive this time. Instead, he offers me a chair and starts
telling me what's on his mind, almost like a normal
human would do. "I want to hire you," he says.

Since I'm a criminal attorney, I'm surprised. Under all
the bluster, Vince is a straightforward, ethical guy. "Are
you in some kind of trouble?" I ask.

"Of course not. I want you to represent the paper. Not
officially. Like a consultant."

Vince's paper is owned by a newspaper syndicate,
which employs lawyers by the barrelful. "You already
have lawyers. What do you need me for?"

"They're idiots. Besides, you'll be dealing only with
me. They won't even know about you. You'll be my own
private idiot."

I'm not understanding any of this. "So you're going to
pay me?"

"Pay you? Are you out of your mind?"

My friends share two common views about money.
They think they don't have enough, and that I have too
much. "This is what I do for a living, Vince. I'm a lawyer.
I got an A in money grubbing in law school."

He throws up his arms in an exaggerated gesture.
"Fine. You want my money? No problem." He yells out
so he can be heard beyond the closed office door.
"Shirley! Don't mail that check to the Orphans Fund! I
need it to pay the big-time lawyer!" He turns to me, shaking his head in disgust. "It's just as well. Little brats don't
have parents, they think that entitles them to three meals
a day."

I know that Vince is lying; I would know that even if he had a secretary named Shirley. But I'm not going to get any money out of him, and I'm curious as to what is going on, so I accept a jelly donut as a retainer. For the rather rotund Vince, it's a significant payment.

Vince describes his concern about the newspaper's position in the Daniel Cummings matter. He has no idea why the killer has chosen Cummings as his conduit, and though he loves the resulting boost in circulation, as a journalist he's uncomfortable that his newspaper seems to have become part of the story.

"These last couple of weeks there have been more cops in here than reporters," he says.

"But you've been cooperating?"

"Of course. I mean, there's no source to protect, right? Daniel's only source is the killer, and he has no idea who he is."

"So what are you worried about?" I ask.

"I'm not sure. Nothing specific, but who knows where this is gonna go? Who knows what the cops are gonna ask us to do?"

This doesn't seem like Vince; he's usually far more confident and decisive than this. "Okay," I say, "I'll keep an eye on things. I'll have to talk to Cummings."

Vince nods. "I told him you would. Just so you'll know, he's not thrilled about it."

"Why?"

He shrugs. "He seems to think you're a major pain in the ass."

"You told him that?"

"I didn't use the word 'major.' I used the word 'total.' He also doesn't want you interfering with how he does his job."

I nod. "I don't expect to. Is he a good reporter?"

"As good as any I've ever had," he says. "When do you want to talk to him?"

"How's tomorrow morning? Around eleven? And I'll want the stories he's written on the murders to read through tonight. Plus the stories in the other papers."

"Done," he says. "Laurie back yet?"

I shake my head. "No."

"Maybe if you'd take on some clients, she wouldn't have to go work for somebody else. Hey, why don't you put her on this case?"

Laurie is a former police officer whom I employ as my private investigator. There is no way she'd want to work on this. "First of all, this isn't a 'case,'" I say. "Second of all, she likes to be paid in money, not donuts."

He takes a big bite out of a glazed one. "Women don't know what they're missing."

• • • • •

TARA GREETS ME at the door when I get home. She has a tennis ball in her mouth, a not-so-subtle reminder that I haven't taken her to the park in two days. I drop off the stories Vince gave me and we head out.

The place we go to is called Eastside Park, less than five minutes from my house on Forty-second Street in Paterson, New Jersey. It's the house I grew up in, the house that contains every memory worth remembering. I moved back in after my father died, and feel like I'm home, now and forever.

Paterson has always been considered a good place to leave, and getting out was long regarded as a sign of upward economic mobility. For that reason, even though I'm still there, I am in touch with very few of my childhood friends, who have headed for parts wealthier.

Going to Eastside Park always brings back memories of those friends and the times we shared. It's where we played baseball, football, and tennis, where we tried to look cool in the futile hope that the girls would notice us. It's also where I hit my one high school home run. It was against East Paterson High, a city we never had much respect for, mainly because any place that names itself based on its direction from Paterson can't have too much going for it. We were obviously right, since they've since changed their name to Elmwood Park.

But back to the home run. I can still feel the ball hit the bat, can still remember flying around the bases as the left fielder tried to field it. It should have been scored a triple and an error. I knew that then and know it now. But my cousin was the scorekeeper, he ruled it an official home run, and nothing can ever change that.

I didn't have Tara in that distant past, which automatically means the present is a hell of a lot better. We toss the ball around for about fifteen minutes. I don't throw it quite as far as I used to; Tara is eight years old and starting to slow down. Considering the implications of that sends very real spasms of anxiety through my gut. And since I'm not a big fan of self-inflicted gut spasms, I avoid such thoughts at all costs.

When we're done, we stop at a coffee shop with outdoor tables. I get an iced coffee, and Tara has water and a bagel. Her favorite is cinnamon raisin, probably because she knows I don't like them and therefore won't steal any. As we usually do, we hang out for a half hour, which gives Tara enough time to be petted by fifty or so passersby.

We stop off on the way home to pick up a pizza and some beer. The NFL season is opening tonight, and I want to get it started on the right note. I'll just have enough time to go over the papers Vince gave me before kickoff.

Once we get home, I inhale the pizza and plant myself

on the couch with beer, potato chips, and dog biscuits. I
bounce up and down lightly a few times to test out the
couch, making sure it feels right, since I'll be spending the
entire football season here. Tonight's stay will be of relatively short duration; Saturdays and Sundays, on the other
hand, can last for ten straight hours, the only interruptions
being occasional trips to the bathroom. I've considered a
bedpan, or a couchpan if they make them, but I'm not sure
Laurie would fully understand.

With two hours until kickoff, I start reading the material Vince gave me. Cummings's initial story on the murders appeared the day after the first killing. The victim
was Nancy Dempsey, a thirty-four-year-old nurse who left
her house in Paterson on a Monday evening, announcing
to her husband that she was going to the supermarket. Her
naked body was found the next morning in a vacant lot
two miles from her home, strangled from behind. Her
hands were severed and have not been found.

After reading Cummings's piece, I read the coverage of
the same murder in the other two local papers. Cummings
has a quality to his work that comes through in every paragraph, a unique style and ability that his competitors lack.
There is an edge to his words, a scorn for the killer, that
makes his otherwise straightforward reporting come alive,
and is quite compelling.

Cummings's article clearly struck a chord in the killer
as well, as he contacted the reporter that very afternoon.
Thus began a cat and mouse game, chronicled by the arti-
cles, during which the killer has kept a running communication with Cummings, who in turn has been cooperating
with the police. The stories reflect the need to keep the
public informed, while maintaining certain areas of se-
crecy that the police want preserved.

Two more murders have taken place since, with approximately a one-week interval between them. Victim 2 was a sixty-two-year-old grandmother of three, Betty Simonson, intercepted in Ridgewood while returning home from a canasta game. Victim 3 was a twenty-one-year-old prostitute, known only as Rosalie, murdered last night in Passaic. These two women were also found naked and strangled from behind, with both of their hands severed and removed from the scene.

Cummings has been placed in an extraordinarily difficult situation and seems to have responded well. The stories are revealing and riveting without being overly exploitive. He describes his conversations with the killer in great detail, right down to the inflections in the man's voice. If he is uncomfortable in his dual role as journalist and informant, he's hiding it well. In fact, he seems to relish it; in each article he places himself as part of the lead. And through it all comes his intense, though understandable, disdain for the psycho who has chosen him as his messenger.

Tara jumps on the couch, alerting me to the fact that game time is approaching. I call Danny Rollins, my bookmaker, and place a bet on the Falcons plus five points against the Rams.

I know there have been many significant inventors and inventions throughout the course of human history. Alexander Graham Bell, Thomas Alva Edison, the Wright Brothers . . . these are men who had a dream and realized it, and they received justified praise for their work. But the greatest invention of them all goes unappreciated, and its creator remains anonymous. I of course am referring to the point spread.

The point spread turns every football game into an

even match and therefore makes it eminently watchable. The Little Sisters of the Poor could play Nebraska, and if you give them enough points, people will bet on them. It is pure Americana. Every team, no matter how disadvantaged, has an equal opportunity. My eyes fill up with tears as I think about it, and Tara snuggles next to me, obviously caught up in the emotion of the moment as well.

Unfortunately, in this case the point spread isn't quite enough, and the Falcons, and I, lose by seventeen. I'm undaunted, though; it's a long season, and I'm not going to get through it by panicking over a single loss.

I'm in bed within five minutes of the final gun, and maybe ten seconds after that I'm trying to figure out how to fall asleep with this huge pit in my stomach. It's not just the potato chips and pizza, it's the fact that Laurie isn't here.

Laurie is my investigator and my lover and my best friend. We became romantically involved while I was separated from my former wife, which I guess means she got me on the rebound. If that's true, she's the best rebounder this side of Shaquille O'Neal, because I am in a permanent state of smitten.

Though we have separate residences, Laurie and I stay together at least half the time. Unfortunately, she has been in Chicago for ten days, working on a fraud case for an insurance company. It's been a long ten days.

I spoke to her this morning, and she said she was going to be having dinner with some friends tonight, but I try calling her at her hotel anyway. She isn't in her room. It's eleven o'clock in Chicago, and she's still out on the town? Who has dinner at eleven o'clock? And if you do, when do you have a midnight snack? Four in the morning?

What kind of floozy am I involved with?

• • • • •

I SLEEP THROUGH the alarm and then take my time walking Tara in the park, never once looking at my watch. It wouldn't take Sigmund Freud to peer into my subconscious to find out what's going on. I want to be late for the "investors' meeting," called for nine o'clock in my office.

I arrive at ten after and they're all there, eager to get started and staring daggers at me for causing the delay. There's Edna, my dedicated secretary, who normally doesn't come strolling in until past ten; Kevin, my Laundromat-owning associate, who judging by the strewn wrappers appears to be on his fourth apple turnover; and Willie, the death row inmate-turned-Warren-Buffett-wanna-be. Only Laurie is missing, but she is going to participate from Chicago over the speakerphone.

Leading the meeting is Freddie Connors, the stockbro-

ker who happily stepped into this windfall of fresh investment money by having the good fortune to be Edna's
cousin. He smiles at me. "Andy, we were afraid you
weren't going to make it."

"God forbid" is my response.

Kevin, Edna, and Laurie all have money to invest because of me. I received a commission of over a million
dollars from the Willie Miller settlement, and since I have
all the money I could ever need, I split it up among them.
I don't regret doing so, and it is certainly not the reason
that I'm feeling somewhat bitter.

Cousin Freddie's style is to present investment alter-
natives and to encourage us to actively participate in the
decision making. As a group, we have gradually split into
two camps. Willie is the unlikely leader of one of the
camps, and I lead the other. In Willie's camp are Edna,
Kevin, and Laurie. In my camp is me.

If this were camp color war, my team color would be
beige. I study charts, look at the numbers, and make the
logical, safe selection. Willie comes up with off-the-
wall ideas, hatched in that fairy-tale land he calls a mind,
and everything he touches turns to his team color, gold.

My team is getting its beige ass kicked.

Freddie gets Laurie on the speakerphone and then updates us on the status of our investments. In two months
their collective portfolios have gone up almost eleven
percent, while mine has gone down one point five. I hide
my humiliation and nod wisely, as if financial retreat is
all part of my grand plan.

We finally get around to discussing our options, and I
talk about a telecommunications company well positioned to take advantage of a growing market, relatively

debt-free, and possessing a favorable price-earnings ratio.

"An interesting idea," Freddie concedes. "Good fundamentals . . . sound management."

I nod smugly, appreciating the praise but acting as if I expected nothing less.

Willie makes a sound somewhere between a chuckle and a snort. "You have a better idea?" I ask.

He nods, then asks Freddie, "What was that prediction thing you were telling me about?"

Freddie looks puzzled: Willie is not the easiest guy to understand.

Willie says, "You know . . . that thing where you buy up a lot of stuff 'cause you know people are gonna want it in a few months."

"Futures?" says Freddie.

"Yeah, that's it . . . futures. I think we should buy coffee futures."

Laurie's voice comes through the speakerphone. "Why?"

Willie goes on to explain that the Olympics are coming up soon, and many of the events are going to be on late at night or very early in the morning. People will want to watch them and will drink coffee to enable themselves to stay awake. It is as dumb a theory as any I have ever heard.

It is not quite the dumbest theory Edna has ever heard, and she nods in appreciation of Willie's wisdom. "If I don't drink coffee," she breathlessly reveals, "I'm asleep by eight o'clock."

"I'm the same way," Laurie chimes in.

"Then you must have had a gallon of it last night," I say, becoming more and more pathetic by the moment.

"Come on, people, this is ridiculous. You think the whole country is going to drink coffee to stay awake?"

"Of course not, but anybody who wants to sleep can drink that decaf stuff," says Willie. "That's part of the futures thing, right?"

Freddie nods. "Sure."

Willie smiles triumphantly. "So we got everybody covered."

The discussion goes on for a while longer, but everyone jumps on Willie's bandwagon, leaving me alone with my price-earnings ratio. Kevin comes over and patronizingly tries to cushion the blow. "I think your reasoning is sound, Andy, but Willie's on a hot streak, and I believe in riding hot streaks."

"I hope you and your fat black tongue make a fortune," I say, hitting a new low. I stand up. "Well, it's really been fun, but I've got to go see a client."

"We've got a client?" Edna asks, surprise evident in her voice.

"We've got a client?" Kevin asks simultaneously, shock evident in his.

"Yes," I say. "We're a law office. That's what we do. We represent clients."

The truth is, that's not what we've been doing lately. I've been a little burned-out since my last major trial, when I defended Laurie against a murder charge. It was intense because of how much was personally at stake. Since then I've pretty much found a reason to turn down prospective clients, many of them because I thought they were guilty, but some because the cases just didn't seem challenging or interesting enough.

People who don't know any better are always comparing me to my father, viewing us both as hardworking, high-powered attorneys. Even putting aside the glaring difference that he was the district attorney and I am on the defense side, there is still little comparison. I can't recall him ever missing a day of work; he often likened it to working on an assembly line where the products coming through were accused criminals. I pick and choose my cases and show up when I please.

You might say I couldn't carry my father's briefcase, but you'd be wrong. The truth is, I'm too lazy to carry it. And I offer as proof the shock on the part of my staff on hearing we have a client.

"Who is it?" Edna asks.

"Vince Sanders," I say.

Laurie's voice comes through the speaker. "Well, at least it's not a paying client."

• • • • •

ON THE WAY TO MEET with Daniel Cummings, I reflect on why I've been in a foul mood lately. I'm not big on self-reflection, so I try to get this session over while sitting at one traffic light.

I quickly come up with four possibilities. One, I need to get back to some real work. Two, I'm thirty-seven years old and beginning a midlife crisis, whatever that is. Three, I miss Laurie terribly. And four, Laurie doesn't seem to miss me nearly as much. I don't know which of those is true, but the one I'm rooting against is number four.

The meeting with Cummings is unlikely to bring me back to the ranks of the smiling humans. I have a vague consulting role, in an area of the law that I am neither expert at nor interested in. I'm sorry that I took it on at all, though Vince really didn't give me much of a choice.

Cummings keeps me waiting outside his office for fifteen minutes while he talks on the phone. This is not a good way to start a lawyer-client relationship, but the way I'm feeling it's an excellent way to end one.

He finally comes out to get me, a hint of an insincere, apologetic smile on his face. He holds out his hand. "Daniel Cummings." His tone and manner are such that he might have said "Prince Charles."

I shake it. "Andy Carpenter" is my clever response. We've met once before, but if he doesn't remember it, then I'm not going to give him the satisfaction of revealing that I do.

"We've met before, haven't we?" he asks.

"I don't think so," I say, starting this relationship off on a mature note.

"Come in."

He leads me into his office, points to a chair, and offers me something to drink. I choose a Diet Pepsi, and he has a mineral water. He's about six one, with hair so lightly colored that at first glance it looks like he's going bald, though he isn't. He has chiseled good looks; he'd be a natural as a Russian movie star.

I don't know how much Vince is paying his reporters these days, but there is no way that journalism is Cummings's only revenue source. Sell his suit, shoes, and watch and you could buy something with bucket seats. And he looks comfortable in them, like there are plenty more just like them back home in a walk-in closet the size of North Dakota.

"I don't know if Vince told you," he says, "but I'm not keen on the idea of you getting involved in all this."

I'm not quite ready to share anything Vince told me. "Why is that?" I ask.

"Because I can handle it on my own, and I'm afraid

you'll get in the way. And nothing personal, but defense attorneys are not my favorite group of people."

"That must keep them up nights," I say as dryly as I can manage.

His grin is without humor. "I wouldn't know."

"It'll help me avoid screwing things up by knowing what it is I'm dealing with. So why don't you start at the beginning?"

He gives me a brief rundown of the events, providing little more than I got from reading the stories. The killer contacted him by phone at the office after the first murder, praising the reporter's "understanding" of his work.

"Why did he think that?" I ask.

Cummings shrugs. "I don't know. Maybe I accidentally wrote something that hit him close to home. Maybe he just liked my style. I've made something of a study of the criminal mind, but I can't quite read them."

"But he told you he would be communicating through you exclusively?"

Cummings nods. "His exact words were, 'You will reveal me to the world.'"

"So you went to the police." I already knew that he did, so I'm just trying to move the story along.

He nods. "Of course. The first thing they did was tap my office phone, but they neglected to cover my home phone, which is where he called the next time. Our local police strategists leave something to be desired."

"Any idea how he got your number?"

He shakes his head. "None."

"You said you were afraid I would get in the way. Can you be more specific?"

"If you're looking over my shoulder, it will make it harder for me to do what I want to do."

"Which is?" I ask.

He looks me straight in the eye. "I'm going to catch the son of a bitch."

Just then the phone rings. I see him take a nervous breath before answering it. Every call could be the killer. After a moment he picks up the receiver. "Hello?"

He shakes his head slightly, telling me that this isn't the call. "I'm leaving now," he says into the phone before hanging up. He stands, grabs his jacket, and heads for the door. "There's a press conference in twenty minutes."

I start following him, even though he hasn't asked me along. "Are you covering it or part of it?"

He smiles the first genuine smile I've seen. "Good question."

We take separate cars to state police headquarters in Hackensack. Because the murders have been committed in three different communities, no one department has jurisdiction, and the state cops have taken over. Even though they'd never admit it, the mayors of the towns in question are breathing a sigh of relief. Real pressure is starting to mount to catch this guy, and the intervention of the state cops takes them off the political hook.

I get stuck in some traffic behind Cummings, and by the time I arrive he is already up on the stage with the state police brass. I take a spot along the side of the room, as the press mills about, waiting for the conference to begin.

"This is a new one for you, isn't it, Andy?"

I look up and see Pete Stanton, a Paterson police lieutenant and my closest and only friend in the department.

"What is?" I ask.

"Usually, you wait until we identify and catch the scumbags before you represent them."

I shake my head. "A lawyer can go broke waiting for you idiots to make an arrest. So I've already got myself a client."

"Who?"

I point to the stage. "The intrepid young reporter. And the newspaper he represents."

Pete was the detective assigned to the first murder, before anyone had an idea that there was a serial killer on the loose. Since I'm basically in an information-gathering mode at this point, I might as well start pumping good old Pete.

"You guys making any progress?" I ask.

"There are a number of leads that we're aggressively pursuing along with our colleagues in the state police," he says. "We're very confident."

"So you've got nothing."

"Not a fucking thing."

"You still working the case?" I ask.

He nods. "Barely. Mostly, we just admire the professionals." He points to the brass on the stage. There's a rivalry between the state and local police forces that will last until eternity.

"Piss you off, does it?" I ask.

He shrugs. "Temporarily. As soon as the killer moves into New York or Connecticut, it'll be interstate and the feds will move in. Then the state assholes will be on the outside with us."

"It would be nice if one of you actually caught the bad guy," I say.

"Wouldn't make your client too happy."

"Which means . . . ?"

Pete nods toward Cummings on the stage. "Look at him. He's a star. You think he wants this to be over so he can go back to being just another typist?"

I have to admit that, though Cummings isn't grinning and giggling, it does seem that he'd rather be on that stage than in the gallery down here with his colleagues.

Captain Terry Millen of the New Jersey State Police starts the session with a statement about the latest murder. He then refuses to answer just about everything the media throw at him, expressing his confidence that they'll understand he can't reveal information about this ongoing investigation. With that as the ground rule, there was no reason to have this session at all. Did he think he was going to be asked how the Giants will do on Sunday?

Frustrated by the lack of answers they are getting, two reporters direct questions to Cummings. He toes the party line, claiming that Captain Millen has asked him not to respond. Other than getting some television face time, there was no reason for Cummings to have been here at all, but he certainly doesn't look put off at this total waste of his time.

I would like him a hell of a lot more if he was annoyed. Like I am.

• • • • •

IT'S ONLY BEEN FIVE DAYS, but it's already obvious that working for Vince Sanders is not going to get me out of my funk. Nothing new has come up, the police appear to be nowhere, and basically everyone is in the uncomfortable position of waiting for the killer to make the next move. I remain a figure on the distant periphery, with no real role in any of it.

I start spending more time in the office, though it's not exactly a hub of activity. Most of Edna's efforts are directed toward honing her skills as the world's finest crossword puzzle player, interrupting that endeavor only long enough to check financial prices on the Internet and shriek with glee.

A hurricane has hit South America, destroying some coffee crops and sending coffee futures straight up. I make a silent vow not to drink another drop until the Olympics are over.

Kevin comes in for only an hour or so a day. There's really nothing for him to do, and he has responsibilities running the Laundromat. When he is here, he spends most of his time on the computer, indulging his hypochondria. I looked over his shoulder a few times, and he was in chat rooms on medical Web sites, seeking and giving medical advice, with such noted physicians as LOLA427 and SICKLYONE.

Laurie is coming home tonight, and I'm picking her up at the airport. I've got plenty of time until I have to leave, so I decide to play some sock basketball, a challenging game whereby I shoot a pair of rolled-up socks into a ledge above my door. I am not only the inventor of the game but also its most talented practitioner.

To add some flavor and excitement, I set up grudge matches, and today's game is between the American Heroes and the Al Qaeda Assholes. As captain of the Heroes, I'm in rare form, and we're ahead seventy-eight to nothing when the phone rings, signaling halftime.

It's Vince Sanders, making his daily call to check up on the nonexistent developments. "So where do we stand?" is his opening chitchat.

"It's halftime," I say. "I'm up by seventy-eight, and two of the terrorists are in foul trouble."

"What the hell are you talking about?"

"Sock basketball. You take these rolled-up socks, and—"

He interrupts. "And I ram them down your throat if you don't tell me where we stand on our case."

He keeps calling it a case, which it certainly isn't. "Oh, that?" I say. "I've got it all figured out. It was Mrs. Plum in the library with a candlestick."

Click.

I've probably talked to Vince on the phone a hundred times, and the next time he says goodbye will be the first.

"You might want to take a look at this," Edna says.

She's pointing to a story on her computer. Edna has it set up so that various financial Web sites e-mail her when significant events in her area of interest happen. This one has to do with a merger that has fallen through in the telecommunications industry, sending all similar stocks tumbling in sympathy. Mine is down a point and a half.

"Thanks for sharing that," I say.

She smiles. "Want me to make you some coffee? It might make you feel better. Everybody's drinking it these days, you know."

Stifling my impulse to strangle Edna with my bare hands, I head over to the foundation. I walk in on Willie looking positively giddy; when he sees me, he rushes over and gives me a high five. He's probably heard that my stock went down.

That's not it. "Carrie just walked the fuck out the door!" he screams.

Carrie is a seven-year-old Brittany spaniel, blind in one eye and as sweet as they come. Willie has just color-fully told me that she's been adopted, and he goes on to say that her new parents are an elderly couple who are going to take her to live with them on their boat.

I've learned that there are few feelings better than rescuing a dog facing certain, anonymous death in an animal shelter and then sending that dog off to a happy life. It immediately cheers me up, and not even Willie's question a few moments later can fully detract from that.

"You want some coffee?" he asks. "We've got Colombian roast, vanilla nut, cinnamon, hazelnut, and three kinds of decaf. I ordered one of those machines that make lattes, but it's not here yet." He pronounces "lattes" to rhyme with "fatties."

For some reason, I don't feel like coffee, so I leave for the airport to pick up Laurie, even though I'll probably get there two hours early. My mood is not improved by the fact that I pass two hundred and thirty-seven Starbucks on the way, give or take a couple of hundred.

For years, Newark Airport stood as a monumental tribute to the arrogance of New Yorkers. It has always had great access by highways, ample parking, and not that much air traffic, so planes generally run on time. By comparison, the highways feeding JFK Airport are so jammed that it's almost faster to walk, parking is a total pain, the terminals look like they were positioned by blindfolded dart throwers, and the planes are always late. Yet for a very long time, many upscale Manhattanites wouldn't dream of taking off from or landing in Newark. The mere suggestion of it drew frowns, as if they were afraid they'd get cow dung on their shoes when they left the terminal. These attitudes have changed somewhat, but if you see somebody check the bottom of their shoes when they reach their car, you can still bet they're heading toward Manhattan.

Being from New Jersey, I'm used to cow dung, so I don't even look down as I walk to the terminal. Once I get there, boredom sets in, since the tightened security makes it impossible to get to restaurants or newspaper stands or even chairs, for that matter. All of those things are in that glorious land beyond security.

About twenty minutes before Laurie's flight is scheduled to arrive, my cell phone rings. I think it might be her, calling to say she's landed early and wondering where I'm waiting.

Instead, it's Vince. "Where are you?"

"Newark Airport."

"How fast can you get to Eastside Park?" he asks.

"I hope that's a rhetorical question."

"What?"

"How does a week from Tuesday sound?"

"Andy, I need you down here. There's been another murder."

I'm very sorry to hear that, of course, but there's no way I'm leaving this airport alone. "Vince, I'm a lawyer. I don't go to crime scenes. I hold up photographs of them in court."

"Andy . . ."

It's time to be firm. "I'll have to read about it in the paper, Vince. Laurie is coming in, and—"

He cuts me off. "The victim is Linda Padilla."

I'm outta here.

• • • • •

I'M OUT OF THE AIRPORT in five minutes, leaving Laurie to fend for herself. If Linda Padilla has been murdered, then this case is going to explode. And if Cummings is still in the middle of things, then as his lawyer, I have to make sure it doesn't explode in his face.

Four years ago Linda Padilla was a middle-level bureaucrat working in the State Housing Administration. Having grown up in low-income housing herself, she was aware of the rather large need for improvement in most of these developments.

What she had not been aware of was a conspiracy among some of those above her to embezzle money meant for housing construction. When she discovered it, she feared that it would be swept under the rug, so she went public with the revelations. People went to jail, others turned state's evidence, and she became an instant media star.

Superstar whistle-blowers don't remain in bureaucracies long, and Padilla left to start a watchdog operation. Emboldened by her actions and aware of her reputation, others in different areas of government and the private sector started coming to her with their tales of official and executive wrongdoing. Padilla eagerly and effectively presented them to the world. It wasn't long before people in power were, if not cowering, at least fearful of becoming her next target.

Padilla took advantage of her fame to become very wealthy. She was a highly sought-after figure on the lecture circuit, and the word was, she could command more than fifty thousand dollars per speech. She also wrote a best-selling book on her exploits; she had reinvented herself as a cottage industry and made a fortune in the process.

Three months ago Padilla announced her candidacy for governor in next year's election. The public responded almost instantly, and poll after poll showed that she had the very real potential to turn the state's political landscape upside down.

But Vince's words make all that moot, and her murder is likely to initiate a media earthquake. I listen to the radio on the way there, and the news is sketchy at this point. All that is known is that Linda Padilla has been killed, and there is speculation that she is in fact the latest victim of the serial killer that has been stalking the area.

It takes me almost twenty minutes to get to Eastside Park and another ten minutes to work my way close to the crime scene. If I were a looter anywhere else in New Jersey, I'd be salivating, since there's no doubt that every cop in the state is here in Eastside Park. There are so many car lights and floodlights that it seems like daytime, though it's approaching nine P.M.

Since in the eyes of the police I have no standing in this case, I'm limited as to how close I can get. I'm trying to maneuver around that problem by finding cops I recognize when I see Vince pointing to me and talking to an officer. The officer nods and comes over to get me, bringing me inside the barricades. As I walk toward Vince, I look around but don't see Daniel Cummings.

Vince grabs me by the arm. "Come on."

He starts taking me toward the crime scene, which means we have to navigate through what seems to be five million people.

"Where's Cummings?" I ask.

"With the state police."

"Was he contacted by the killer?"

He laughs a short laugh. "Yeah. You might say that."

A few moments later I understand his cryptic comment. Cummings is leaning back on a chair as a paramedic bandages his head. It appears the bandage is protecting a wound on the left side of his temple.

The medic finishes and nods silently to Captain Millen, the state cop who ran the press conference and who is in charge of what is rapidly becoming a train wreck of a case. Millen walks over to Cummings and starts talking to him.

"So, Mr. Cummings, you feeling okay?" I can tell his concern lacks something in the sincerity department, since he does not wait for a response. "Tell me everything that happened tonight. Leave out nothing."

Cummings frowns his displeasure at this. "Captain, I already told the story to the officer. Can't you—"

"No, I want to hear it from you."

"Captain Millen, my name is Andy Carpenter," I say, my voice deep and powerful so as to convey my authority. "I'm representing Mr. Cummings."

"Good for you." He doesn't seem to be cowed.

"My client is obviously injured."

"And Linda Padilla is obviously dead. So stop interrupting or I'll have you obviously removed."

He's speaking to me as if I am an annoying child. This is unacceptable and demeaning, but I back off, so as to avoid getting sent to my room for a time-out.

Cummings, coherent enough in his injured state to know that he'll get no help from me, begins to tell his story. He had received a phone call on his cell phone while driving on Route 3, about fifteen minutes from here. It was the killer, who told him that the next victim was about to be killed in Eastside Park, near the pavilion.

Millen interrupts. "How did he know you'd be out with your cell phone?"

Cummings shrugs. "For all I know, he tried me at home first."

As the conversation continues, I learn that the police had been tapping all of Cummings's phones except the cell phone that the killer called on. It was not Cummings's personal phone; it was one supplied by the paper, which he kept in the car and rarely used. He hadn't thought to mention it to the police and is baffled as to how the killer could have gotten the number, since he doesn't even know it himself.

"What did you do next?"

"I rushed here, of course. And I tried to keep him on the phone as long as I could. I thought maybe I could save whoever . . . if he was talking to me . . . well, he couldn't do anything." He glances over toward the inside of the pavilion, where Ms. Padilla's body lay covered. "Finally, we got cut off as I reached here. I tried calling you, but there wasn't any cell phone reception. So I went in . . . hoping to stop . . ."

My own cell phone goes off, rather untimely considering what my client has just said.

"Hello?"

It's Laurie, calling from the airport. "Where are you?"

"I'm at Eastside Park . . . there's been a murder."

Millen looks over at me, then back to Cummings. "How come his cell phone works here?"

Cummings has a flash of anger at Millen. "I don't know . . . and I really don't care."

"Who was murdered?" Laurie asks.

"Linda Padilla," I say. "Take a cab home. I'll call you."

I hang up, having smoothly accomplished the difficult feat of making my own client look like a liar.

"Good job" is Vince's sarcastic whisper.

I shrug as Millen questions Cummings in excruciating detail about the phone conversation, seeking to find out every possible nuance, probing for exact words used, tone of voice, et cetera. Finally, Cummings tells Millen that he doesn't remember much more. He was apparently hit on the side of the head by an unseen assailant. He was knocked out, though he doesn't know for how long, and when he came to, he called the police, since the cell phone's reception had somehow been restored.

"Did you see him at all?" Millen asks.

"No."

"His car?"

"No."

Cummings seems to wince in pain and touches the bandage on his head.

"Captain," I say, "he needs to get to a hospital."

Millen seems about to argue, then changes his mind. "We'll be in touch tomorrow."

The paramedics load the reluctant Cummings into the ambulance, which will take him to the hospital for X rays. Once he is gone, Vince and I walk off to talk alone.

"What do you think?" Vince asks.

"How well do you know Cummings?"

"Very well," says Vince, a little too quickly. "Well enough. Why?"

"He was lying. The cell phone story was bullshit. I walk Tara around here all the time, and I've never had a problem with reception. And I heard Laurie clear as a bell."

"So maybe your—"

"You got one? Call your office."

Vince takes out his phone and dials his office. After a few moments he cuts off the call; it obviously worked.

"Why would he lie?" Vince asks.

"I don't know . . . maybe he wants to be a hero and catch the killer himself. But if *I* knew he was lying, then you can be sure Millen knew it even faster. And with the pressure that's about to come down, he's not a guy to jerk around."

Vince doesn't say anything for a few moments, worry etched on his face. There's something going on here, and as the lawyer, it would be nice if I knew what it was.

"Vince, are you telling me everything? Because I feel like there's a whole bunch of missing pieces here."

"I've told you everything I know. Why wouldn't I?"

I shrug, since I have no idea, and he continues. "I'll

talk to Daniel in the morning. You wanna go grab a beer at Charlie's?"

Charlie's is a combination sports bar/restaurant that is my favorite sports bar/restaurant in the entire world. Simply put, it is the Tara of sports bar/restaurants. But there is absolutely no chance that I will be going there tonight with Vince.

"Let me see . . . ," I say. "A beer with Vince, or seeing Laurie for the first time in two weeks? Mmmm . . . Vince or Laurie . . . Laurie or Vince? Gorgeous woman . . . or fat slob? A terrific evening with the woman I love . . . or a night of burping and slurping with a pain in the ass? Help me out here . . . I just can't decide."

"I'm buying," he offers.

"Even though that would be a historic event, I'm going to pass. Call me in the morning after you've spoken to our boy."

I leave Eastside Park and stop off at my house to pick up Tara before I go to Laurie's. I never leave Tara alone in the house all night, and my plan is to spend this particular night at Laurie's. Of course, it's always possible that she'll have a different plan. It's her first night home . . . she might be tired or just feel like being alone.

I ring her doorbell and she comes to the door. She's wearing one of my T-shirts and nothing else, and she kisses me in such a way as to make me confident that my plan is going to work.

And it does. Brilliantly.

• • • • •

THE FIRST THING I do in the morning is turn on
the television to see the kind of play the Linda Padilla
murder is getting. It's as big as I expected: national news
and the lead story on the *Today* show.

I'm surprised when Daniel Cummings is Katie
Couric's first interview, from his hospital room. He tells
what happened with a heavy emphasis on his heroism in
the face of danger; if Eastside Park were Iwo Jima,
Daniel would be commissioning someone to paint him
planting the flag. It's becoming increasingly clear that my
client is trying to use these murders to achieve stardom.

As an ex-cop, Laurie is anxious to hear more about the
situation, and she peppers me with questions. She can't
quite understand my role in this any better than I can,
questioning why Vince brought me into the case. And
questioning even more why I agreed to do it.

"He's my friend," I point out.

"But you don't think he's telling you everything."

I nod. "That's true."

"Why are you letting him get away with that?" she asks.

"He's my friend."

She leans over and kisses me. "I love your simplicity."

I nod. "Along with my virility, it's one of my best traits. You want to work on the case with me?"

"For free?"

"Yup. But you'll get to watch my simplicity close-up."

"I'm weakening," she says.

"And there's absolutely nothing for us to do."

"Then I'm in."

I've now accomplished my main goal, which is to have company while I'm wasting my time. Had Laurie not agreed to be my investigator, I probably would have asked Tara next.

Since I have nowhere else to go, I suggest that our first stop should be the hospital to check on Cummings's condition, though he seemed fine when he talked to Katie Couric. Laurie asks that we first stop off at the murder scene; she wants to get a feel for what happened.

I wait for Laurie to shower and dress, which is unlike waiting for any other woman. Laurie can get out of bed and be ready to leave the house in ten minutes, as fast as any guy I know. But she looks considerably better than any guy who ever lived.

We sample the radio stations on the way to the park. If the killer hoped to get maximum attention and instill maximum fear in the public, choosing Linda Padilla as a victim was a brilliant move. Her murder has ratcheted up the "state of siege" mentality in the community.

Just during our ten-minute drive, on news stations we

hear straight reporting, rehashed but unsubstantiated rumors about Linda Padilla's connections to organized crime, testimonials about the purity of her life, tip hot lines set up by the police, amateur profiles on the killer's psyche, and quotes from Captain Millen and Cummings.

Over on talk radio the callers are angry, demanding action and FBI intervention in the case. "Harry from Lyndhurst" considers the problem one of police priorities. "They got time to give me a speeding ticket, but no time to catch this killer." Harry, it turns out, is one of the more thoughtful callers.

There is still a police presence at the scene, and the public is kept away by the ten or so cops assigned to protect it. Two of them were trained by Laurie when she was on the force, and she has no trouble getting them to let us in.

Padilla's body was found in the pavilion, so that is where we go. There is a chalk outline where the body had been. I wonder whose job it is to draw that, and if they give a class in it at the Police Academy. If I were a cop, that would be the assignment I'd go after. I'd even be willing to start as an assistant chalker and work my way up.

"She was strangled?" Laurie asks.

I nod. "From behind."

"She wasn't killed here."

"How do you know that?" I ask.

She points to some scrape marks which lead to the area where the body was. "She was dragged . . . from that door . . . probably wrapped in a sack. If she was alive, he wouldn't have bothered dragging her this far . . . he would have killed her closer to the door. There's also no blood; if her hands were cut off here, even postmortem, there would be some blood."

There's something about the way she re-creates what happened here that both chills me and leaves me very sad. No one deserves to be dragged in a sack to be dumped on a cold floor. If there is a way to end a life, this sure ain't it.

We're quiet on the way to the hospital, each of us affected by what we have just seen. Laurie is frustrated; she knows this maniac has struck four times and will keep going until he's caught. She wants to be involved in tracking him down, rather than simply hanging out with the lawyer for the newspaper that is reporting the story.

"Why would he pick a guy like Cummings?" I ask.

"Certainly, he wants attention, a forum to speak to the world without exposing himself to danger. But why Cummings? It's hard to say. Isn't he a law-and-order, tough-on-crime guy? Maybe that's why the killer picked him. It's another way to thumb his nose at authority. Which also may be why he picked Linda Padilla."

"I'm not so sure," I say. "There doesn't seem to be any pattern to the victims. My guess is they were chosen at random. Padilla may just have been in the wrong place at the wrong time."

We arrive at the hospital and walk through the lobby toward the elevators. Laurie sees the cafeteria down the hall. "I just want to get a cup of coffee first," she says.

"More coffee?" I ask. "Doesn't anybody drink tea anymore? What the hell is this society coming to?"

"Investments not going well?" she asks, but since she knows the answer, she doesn't wait to hear it, and heads to the cafeteria.

When we finally get to Cummings's room, he is sitting

in a chair, fully dressed and talking to Vince. I introduce him to Laurie, and then Vince gives Laurie a big hug and wide smile. For some reason, Laurie brings out gracious behavior in human beings otherwise incapable of it.

Cummings says, with obvious frustration, "So, defense attorney, you specialize in getting clients out of confinement? How about getting me out of here?"

"What's the problem?" I ask, irritated by his tone.

"Hospital regulation bullshit," says Vince. "They have to do all kinds of paperwork before a patient can be released."

"That's nice for them, but they have five minutes. I have work to do." Cummings looks at his watch, as if that will make his threat more credible.

"Relax, Daniel," says Vince. "Your story for tomorrow is written already."

Cummings's face shows no sign of relaxing, and he opens the door, calling out to a nurse as she walks by the room. "Nurse, we need to get out of here."

The nurse answers nervously, "I'm sorry, Mr. Cummings, I'm sure they'll be here momentarily."

She closes the door and doesn't hear him ask, "Who's 'they'?"

Cummings doesn't go back to his chair and instead paces the room. He turns to Laurie and me. "Are they making any progress on the murders? I'm cut off from the damn world in here."

As I'm about to tell him that I have no idea, the door opens and Captain Millen walks in, flanked by five officers. They seem to come in a little too quickly, as if rushed, but that is not the most surprising thing about their entry. The most surprising thing is that they are holding guns.

"What the . . . ?" Cummings starts.

"Turn around! Hands against the wall!" Millen barks as his officers move toward Cummings.

Vince says something—I can't make out what—and moves toward Cummings. Vince is pushed out of the way by the officers, and Laurie grabs hold of him, keeping him out of the fray.

"Are you crazy?" asks Cummings. "What the hell . . . ?"

Millen pays no attention, screaming even louder. "Now! Against the wall!"

Cummings still doesn't react, and is roughly turned around, pushed against the wall, and his hands are cuffed behind his back.

"Daniel Cummings," Millen begins, "I am placing you under arrest. You have the right to remain silent. Anything you say can and will be used against you in a court of law . . ."

He completes the *Miranda* warning. By now Cummings has been reduced to stunned silence. "What is the charge, Captain?" I ask.

"For right now it's just the murder of Linda Padilla. But my guess is, there will be others."

He signals for his officers to take Cummings out of the room, and they do so immediately. As Cummings leaves, I say, "Do not say a word to anyone until I am in your presence." Cummings doesn't respond; the shock of all this is affecting his mind's ability to process.

"Do you understand?" I ask. "Not one word."

He finally nods slowly, then is led away.

As Millen follows them, he turns to me. "Well, lawyer, looks like you got yourself something to do."

• • • • •

I LOOK OUT THE WINDOW and see a large group of reporters and three television trucks in front of the hospital. Millen obviously leaked the word in advance so as to take full publicity advantage of the arrest.

"Let's go," I say. "They'll be taking him down to County." It's the place where the newly arrested are taken for booking and processing.

Laurie starts for the door, holding Vince by the arm and leading him along. Vince looks stricken, even more so than Cummings had, and for the first time in my memory he seems speechless.

Our car ride down to County is relatively quiet. The radio is reporting the arrest, and Millen and the DA are already planning a press conference to gloat. I attempt to question Vince, to see if he had any inkling of what could be behind this, but all he can say is, "There's no way . . . just no way."

We arrive at County and become fresh fodder for the waiting press. I am barraged with questions, but I refuse all comment, saying that I am waiting to speak with my client. I really have no idea what the facts are, and I don't want to get caught saying something that I will have to retract later. Wherever this is going, there will be a media spotlight on it the entire time, and we'll have to play the public relations game well.

Laurie, Vince, and I hang out in the waiting area while Cummings is booked, even though I'll be the only one allowed in to meet with him. I'm not sure I've ever seen Vince this upset, and I can tell Laurie is noticing this as well.

Except for the time spent waiting for a deliberating jury to return a verdict, these might be the most anxious moments a lawyer can have. The authorities feel they have the evidence to convict the accused, yet as his lawyer, I have absolutely no idea what that evidence is, or even what the facts of the case are.

This situation is even more troubling than most. With all the media attention, the district attorney and police would be particularly loath to make a mistake. They have been under tremendous pressure, but it would increase tenfold if they arrested a suspect and then released him.

They also must know that if they have the wrong man, then the world will realize it as soon as another murder is committed. They would not risk looking so foolish unless they were positive they were right.

I'm not at all sure I even want to take on this case. Cummings might well be guilty, and I don't really have any compelling need for a serial killer as a client.

Besides, I wasn't even that crazy about him when I thought he was just a law-abiding, pompous reporter.

I decide to broach this with Vince, who is the reason I'm in this mess in the first place. "You know, Cummings might want to pick his own attorney" is the wimpy way I go about it.

Vince shakes his head. "No way. You're the best. He knows that; I told him that."

"Vince, I agreed to represent you and the newspaper. I didn't know I—"

Vince interrupts me, a flash of panic in his eyes. "You've got to do it, Andy. You're the only lawyer I trust to handle this."

Just then an officer comes out and tells me that I can see Cummings. I nod, but first I want to finish this with Vince.

"Vince, it doesn't matter who *you* trust. You're not the client. And there are plenty of good lawyers. All I'm saying is—"

"No, it's got to be you." Vince doesn't seem to be willing to let me finish a sentence, so I just let the officer lead me off to see Cummings.

I've never physically been with someone when they are being processed after entering custody, but in addition to fingerprinting, photographing, emptying of pockets, and the like, the arresting authorities must go over the accused with a confidence-remover.

All but the most seasoned criminals come out of these sessions looking simultaneously depressed and distraught, and Cummings is no exception. Gone, at least for the moment, are the cockiness and air of superiority that I experienced in the past. There is not yet even room for outrage; the fear and humiliation are too dominating. It may be an indictment of myself to say so, but I like him better this way.

"Have you said anything to them since your arrest?" I ask.

He shakes his head. "You told me not to."

I nod. "Good. That becomes a rule from this day forward. Now, tell me what you know about why you were arrested."

"I don't have the slightest idea. One minute I was working with them, telling them what the killer was telling me, and the next thing I know they're saying *I'm* the killer. It's insane; they must be under so much pressure to make an arrest that they just picked the closest person."

"I'm not going to lie to you, Daniel." My mind registers that I've started thinking of him as "Daniel," rather than "Cummings," because I need to get personally close to my clients. Then my mind registers that I am thinking of him as a client, which means I must at least be considering taking on the case. Sometimes my mind has a mind of its own.

I continue. "That same pressure you're talking about would make them extra careful about charging someone unless they're sure."

His mind doesn't seem to fully register this. "So what are you saying?"

"That they must have some evidence, evidence that they consider substantial, tying you to this. You need to think about what that could be."

He nods and takes some time to think. "I guess only that I knew information . . . like where the bodies were, how they were murdered, things that only the killer could have known." He throws up his hands in a gesture of frustration. "But that's because the killer was telling me everything!"

"And why did he pick you?"

"I don't know," he says with some frustration. "I already told you that."

"It doesn't matter what you told me before. The world has changed now; you have to look at everything from an entirely different perspective. There's—"

He interrupts me. "But you don't understand—"

I return the favor, interrupting him. "It's you that has to understand . . . so listen carefully. There is a reason you're here. For us to prevail, we have to find out what the reason is, then shoot it down. And your recollections, your perceptions, can be our most valuable tools. So I know this is hard, but you don't have the luxury of worrying, or feeling sorry for yourself. You've got to help yourself, by helping me."

There is no chance that little speech will get through to him, at least not yet, since the shock of his arrest is too fresh. But if I harp on it enough, it will eventually have an effect.

For now I'll give him a specific assignment. "You know as much about these murders as the police do. So what I want you to do is piece together where you were when each one was committed. I want to know where you were, what you were doing, and if anyone saw you do it. If we can prove you didn't do any one of the four, their case falls apart."

Daniel nods, but it's not hopeful, and I've got a feeling he's going to report that he was home in bed, alone, at the time of the murders. Or that aliens abducted him and sprayed him with antimemory juice.

The door opens and Millen and another cop in plain

clothes come into the room. Millen speaks to me. "We would like to question your client, if that's okay with you."

"It's not."

"Maybe he would like to present his side of the story," he says.

"Maybe you should have given him that opportunity before you arrested him."

Millen just nods and the two of them leave. He doesn't seem terribly disappointed; he knew I'd never let Daniel speak to him. As a thorough cop, he had to go through the motions.

The guard comes to take Daniel back to his holding cell, and when I leave, there are two messages waiting for me at the desk. One is a notification from the district attorney's office that the arraignment is scheduled for tomorrow, which is Friday. They are moving quickly and don't even want to wait until Monday, another sign of confidence. They think their case is strong enough already and have no doubt the grand jury will indict based on it.

The other message is from Laurie, reporting that she and Vince will be at Charlie's, waiting for me. I head over there, though in truth I would prefer to go home and think things through.

Laurie and Vince are sitting at our regular corner table when I arrive, but it would not take Sherlock Holmes to look at this scene and know there is something amiss. First of all, there is a full plate of french fries on the table, and Vince is paying no attention to them. I can't overemphasize the inconceivability of such an event. Secondly, the television facing their table is tuned to the local news, while every other one in the entire bar has ESPN.

Vince sees me walking toward them and stands up, as if somehow that will get me there faster. "What happened?" he asks. "How did it go?"

I explain that Daniel volunteered nothing much to me and that I refused to let him volunteer anything to the police. "But they seem very confident of their case."

"What is their case? What do they have?" He's asking questions in pairs.

"I don't know, and Daniel claims not to either. I'll probably learn more when I meet with the DA, and in any event they'll have to turn over everything in discovery."

He tosses out another pair. "So this is going to trial? We can't stop it?"

"Not unless Daniel pleads guilty."

He shakes his head. "Impossible. Won't happen."

"Vince, why don't you tell me everything that you know and I don't?"

He sighs and then nods in resignation, as if this is something he dreads. "Daniel was married when he lived in Cleveland. Things didn't go well for him."

"Meaning . . . ?"

"About a year and a half ago his wife was murdered."

The thud that echoes through the bar is the sound of my stomach hitting the floor.

"Did they catch the killer?" I ask.

"Nope. It's still an open case."

"Was Daniel a suspect?"

"Of course not. I mean, you know how it is, they always check the family first. Especially since she had a lot of money; her parents left her a bundle. But there was no evidence he was involved, which he wasn't."

"And you kept all this a secret?"

He flashes some annoyance. "What secret? He didn't do anything wrong. Nobody kept it a secret. The guy's wife was murdered. Is that something you're going to go around broadcasting?"

"How was she killed?" I ask.

"She was shot." He says this with a measure of triumph, as if the difference in causes of death completely exonerates Daniel from being involved in any of this. "And both her hands were still on the body."

I look over at Laurie, who doesn't seem surprised at what Vince is saying, which means that Vince told her all of this before I arrived. She and I make eye contact, but my eye-reading skills are not quite well developed enough to know what she is thinking.

"Vince," I say, "you need to face the possibility that Daniel is guilty. There can be some civil ramifications for your newspaper, so—"

"He's not guilty. How many times do I have to tell you that?"

"You've met your quota. So why don't you tell me how you can be so sure?"

I see Laurie flinch slightly; she must know what's coming and also knows I'm not going to like it.

"I'm sure because he's my son," Vince says.

• • • • •

"I WAS IN THE RESERVES, stationed in Fort Leonard Wood, Missouri," relates Vince. "Putting in my six months so I could get out of going to Vietnam. I got a weekend pass, I met Daniel's mother, she got pregnant, end of story."

My keen intuition is telling me that her pregnancy was in fact not the end of the story, so I probe further. "So you've kept in touch with Daniel all these years?" I ask.

He shakes his head with some sadness. "No. His mother never told me about him . . . we had no contact at all. Then, when he was eighteen, he contacted me. Since then I've tried to do what I can. I mean, I'm not Ward Cleaver, but I've done okay. I've been there when he needed me. I paid for the parts of college that his scholarship didn't cover."

Vince, a responsible father. The mind boggles. I wouldn't trust him to watch my beer.

"Where is his mother now?" Laurie asks, helping me out. She knows that I have trouble speaking when I'm totally incredulous.

"She died about three years ago," Vince says.

"I don't suppose it was of natural causes?" It's an obnoxious question to ask, but Vince doesn't seem to notice.

"Yeah, some kind of cancer," he says. "I'm not sure . . . we didn't really have a relationship . . . it was just that one night."

"Why didn't you ever tell me this?" I ask. "I mean, having a son, that's the kind of thing people usually mention."

"You always tell me everything?" is his challenge back, knowing that our friendship is not nearly that intimate. "I mean, we're guys, right?"

I see Laurie roll her eyes, one of the few eye signs I can actually read.

"We sure are, and proud of it. The Two Musketeers." I'm trying to lighten things up a little.

"I guess I was ashamed," Vince says, some emotion getting through the gruff exterior. "I missed so much . . . I never saw him grow up."

"How could you know?" Laurie asks.

"I guess I couldn't. But I sure never tried to find out. Then when he wanted to go into journalism, I figured I could help him more if people didn't know he was my kid."

"Makes sense," I say, even though I'm not sure it does.

"So you'll stay on the case?" Vince asks. "You'll defend him?"

I'm in a bit of a quandary here. I've pretty much decided there is no way I'm going to take on this case, but I have no idea how to tell this to Vince. "I'll defend him" is what I say, probably not the best way to get my point across.

He smiles, and I can tell he's relieved, because he reaches out to shake with his right hand and grab a french fry with his left. "Thanks, Andy. I can't tell you how much I appreciate this. And believe me, Daniel can pay your fee, no problem."

My nod is pained; my client can pay for his defense against charges of murder with the money he inherited from his murdered wife. "Why don't you ask Laurie if she'll work on it with me?" I ask, fully subscribing to the "misery loves company" theory.

Vince's head turns toward Laurie as if it's on a swivel. "Will you?"

She reaches out and squeezes his hand. "Of course."

Vince goes at the french fries with both hands; he's feeling a hell of a lot better. "I really surprised you, didn't I?" he asks, smiling for the first time.

I nod. "You sure did. I still can't believe it. You actually had sex with someone."

We hang around for a few more minutes and then leave. Laurie and I don't go home together, since it's Thursday and we only stay together on Sundays, Mondays, Wednesdays, and Fridays. It's one of the goofy little rules we've set up to keep our relationship from moving too fast, though by now I've forgotten why fast is a bad thing.

Tara is waiting for me when I get home, and we go for a long walk. I hate walking, yet love walking with Tara. If she weren't around, I would drive to the front curb to get the mail. Fortunately, I don't have to even think about that, since she will always be around.

During the walk I make another attempt at introspection, trying to understand my feelings about friendship. A murder case is an enormous undertaking, and this one is bigger than most. It will dominate my life for months. I don't want to do it, yet I am going to because I consider Vince my friend. I only met him a year ago, I obviously know very little about him, yet that friendship is pushing me over a legal cliff.

I take Tara home and go right to sleep; this introspection stuff can get really tiring.

I wake up in the morning, not with a plan exactly, but with a desire to get things moving. I arrange for Kevin and Laurie to meet with me at the office at nine A.M. Kevin's reaction to the situation as I lay it out is fairly close to mine; he's feeling anxious to get back in the legal saddle, but not at all comfortable with the horse we are about to ride.

There is a press conference scheduled by the DA, Tucker Zachry, at ten o'clock, and we turn on the television to watch it. I'm sure that Tucker is not going to reveal key elements of their case, but I am curious to find out who in his office will be assigned to prosecute it.

Tucker Zachry was elected to his office last November with sixty-three percent of the vote, a healthy majority to be sure. Based on his looks and television presence, I'm surprised he didn't get ninety percent. He's in his late thirties, six foot two, and apparently in just as good shape as he was when he came in fourth in the Heisman balloting as a quarterback at Stanford. He has a ready smile for his constituents and was even a decent lawyer before moving into this higher office.

Obviously, I hate him.

Tucker opens the press conference with a self-promoting speech about the horror of the crimes, about his dedication to protecting the populace, and about the extraordinary police work that has resulted in Daniel Cummings being arrested. He should begin the speech with "Dear jurors," since every word he says is meant for the prospective jurors out there in television land.

There is no mention of the particulars of the prosecution and the case against Daniel. Tucker professes to wish that he could share the juicy details, but the fact that he is conducting an ongoing prosecution makes that impossible. He even waxes eloquent on the rights of the accused, rights that he wouldn't really care about unless someone mussed his hair with them.

It isn't until the question and answer session that the first piece of news comes out. "Who will be the prosecutor on this case?" a reporter asks.

Tucker permits himself a small smile. "You're looking at him."

The reporter, surprised, follows up. "You personally?"

Tucker nods. "Yes. I think it's that important. And with all the attention sure to be paid to it, I want to be the one on the firing line. If something goes wrong, I will take the heat." He pauses for effect, setting his jaw in determination. "But nothing will go wrong."

I turn the television off. "This is a disaster waiting to happen."

"That's my Mr. Positive," Laurie says.

"Have you ever seen him in court?" Kevin asks. "Is he any good?"

"Good, not great," I say. "But he's aware of his limitations, so he'll have the top people in his office backing him up. The problem is that he knows the evidence, knows the case, and if he thought there was one chance in a thousand he could lose, he wouldn't go near it."

We're all aware that there's not much we can do about refuting the evidence without knowing what it is, so I put in a call to Tucker to arrange a meeting. His secretary says he's not there, a claim that has some credibility, since I was watching him give an interview to CNN just moments before.

"I want to meet with him sometime today, after the arraignment," I say.

His secretary makes a noise that indicates she finds that timing rather unlikely. "Mr. Zachry is quite busy today."

"See if he can fit me in between Bill O'Reilly and Larry King. Or if he'd rather, I can get the judge to juggle his schedule for him."

It's a rather empty threat, since the prosecution's obligation is to turn over the evidence in discovery, not to meet with the defense attorney. But the secretary seems cowed. "I'll speak to him as soon as he gets back."

Kevin and I drive down to the hearing. Laurie really has no function there, so she heads off to wrap up some final details on her insurance case.

On the way there, Kevin says, "Listen to this." He then proceeds to flap his left arm against his body, much like a chicken. "Do you hear that?"

"What?" I ask.

"This." He flaps his arm again.

"You're flapping your arm like a chicken," I point out, trying to be helpful. "So I guess I hear a flapping noise."

"You don't hear the clicking?" he asks, renewing the demonstration.

"I don't think so. It's more of a flapping. What's wrong?"

"Rotator cuff." He flaps his arm again. "It hurts like hell when I do this."

"Is there a reason you need to do it?"

He doesn't have time to answer, as we are just arriving at the courthouse. The press is out in full force, another reminder that this case will be as high-profile as they come. Public sentiment is going to be stacked against us; there is a natural inclination by people to believe that if the police charge someone, that person is almost certainly guilty. Add to that the fact that these are murders that scared and shocked the entire metropolitan area, and we'll be lucky if a lynch mob isn't formed.

Once inside, we are brought into an anteroom to see Daniel. I want Kevin to meet him and give me his assessment, since I'm still not wholeheartedly into this representation.

Cummings has regained some of his self-confidence since the last time I saw him. He shakes Kevin's hand vigorously and welcomes him to the "team." I see Kevin wince slightly and flap his arm a few times, probably making sure the rough handshake didn't increase the clicking.

"The 'team' is what I want to talk to you about, Daniel," I say. "As I'm sure you realize, I was originally retained by Vince to represent the newspaper—and only by extension, as one of its employees, you."

He nods and waits for me to continue, so I do. "This is now an entirely different matter, and you are entitled to the counsel of your choice."

He looks puzzled, as if trying to understand what

I'm getting at. "Are you saying you don't want to represent me?"

"Not at all. I'm saying you can have whoever you want."

"Including you?"

I nod. "Including me."

He smiles, leans over, and shakes Kevin's hand again. "Then welcome to the team . . . officially."

Now that we've got a team, it's time for the coach to issue some pregame instructions. I tell Daniel that the arraignment is a formality, that the only time he will be asked to speak is to plead.

"I assume you want to plead not guilty?" I ask.

"Damn right," he says.

I go over my rather healthy fee with Daniel, which he agrees to as if it is of no consequence. He says he will ask Vince to bring him his checkbook, so he can give me a retainer of two hundred thousand dollars. I make a mental note to find out just how much money he inherited from his murdered wife.

"I want you to make a list of everybody you've ever known who might have a grudge against you. Also, everybody you've ever known that you would consider capable of these kinds of murders."

Daniel agrees to start thinking about these things, and Kevin and I go out to the courtroom. We are there before the prosecution, which is no surprise, since Tucker wouldn't have it any other way. Just as the champion comes into the ring last for a title fight, so Tucker considers himself the titleholder for this court fight.

When the Great One finally enters, he sees me and comes over, his charming smile lighting up the room. "Andrew, good to see you," Tucker says, bringing to a total of one the number of people who call me "Andrew." My guess is, he believes addressing me by a name I don't use will somehow get under my skin. It doesn't, but I'll get my revenge anyway.

"Nice to see you, Tucky my boy," I say, watching his quick, involuntary grimace. "You know Kevin Randall?" He turns and shines the charm spotlight on Kevin, which relieves me from the glare for a moment or two.

They greet each other, and then Tucker turns back to me. "I hear you were tough on my assistant."

I shrug. "All in the pursuit of justice. We need to meet."

"Isn't that what we're doing now?" he asks.

"No, right now we're exchanging insincere pleasantries and chitchat. I want to discuss the case."

His smile gets about forty degrees colder. "If you're looking for information, you'll get it in discovery. If you're looking to plead it out, you're wasting your time. This one is going all the way."

Before I have a chance to respond, Judge Lawrence Benes comes into the courtroom, and Tucker and I go back to our respective corners. Judge Benes is unlikely to be the trial judge; his role is strictly to handle the arraignment.

Daniel is brought in, and the arraignment begins uneventfully. He is held over for trial in the murder of Linda Padilla; at this point Tucker is not including the other murders. My request for bail is denied, and the setting of a trial date is postponed until a judge is assigned. Daniel's not guilty plea is spoken firmly and with conviction, which is important only because the press should report it as such.

I make a demand for immediate discovery, since there

really is nothing we can effectively do until we know what they have.

Tucker stands; he can get up and down hundreds of times without wrinkling his pants. I get up once and it looks like I hung my suit in a blender.

"Your Honor," Tucker intones, "the prosecution, in representing the people of this state, is keenly aware of our responsibilities. This case is being watched all across this great country of ours, and we will do nothing to jeopardize this defendant's rights under our Constitution. The materials to be turned over to the defense are being compiled even as we speak."

I take a moment to control my nausea and then respond. "Your Honor, if you could ask Mr. Zachry to provide transcripts of these speeches in advance, then we could stipulate to such revelations as the greatness of our country. And I should point out that it is the defense position that our country is great from the mountains to the prairies to the oceans white with foam."

Laughter erupts from the gallery, and I see a momentary flash of pain on Tucker's face. He does not like to be embarrassed, so I make a mental note to embarrass him as much as possible. If he reacts emotionally, then he might make a mistake in front of this "great country of ours."

The hearing ends, Daniel is taken back to his cell, and for the first time I notice Vince sitting near the back of the courtroom. I walk toward him, and he waits as the gallery empties out.

"Tucker doesn't look too worried," he says.

"He's not."

"I am," he says.

I can't think of anything positive to say, so I don't.

• • • • •

THERE IS A MESSAGE on my phone machine
when I get home. It's from Sam Willis, reminding me
about a commitment I had made for tomorrow night. Like
most advance commitments I make, I somehow vaguely
thought it would never arrive and had thus wiped it from
my mind. Now it's here, and I can't think of a way out
of it.

This particular event is a charity wine tasting. I don't
know exactly what that is, but there's almost no chance
I'm going to like it. I should have asked Laurie to join us;
she would have been pleased to. Laurie's social consciousness is such that she would willingly sign up for a
charity root canal.

My plan for the daytime Saturday hours is to watch
college football and indulge in some noncharity beer tasting. This is the beginning of the season, so there are
mostly mismatches between teams at the top and the bot-

tom, rather than competitive conference games. It therefore represents another day to give thanks to the inventor of the aforementioned point spread.

I watch sixteen games over nine hours. Now, this may sound like an extraordinary accomplishment, but I am a humble man, and I always share credit when it is warranted. So I want to go on record as saying that if the Academy of Televised Sports Degenerates in America presents me with its award, the coveted ATSDA, even before I thank the academy I will thank my devoted partner, the remote control.

Without it, I'd be just another commercial-watching loser, unable to control my own fate. But with the remote secure in the palm of my hand, or more often resting on my chest, I am all-powerful. I don't think I've missed an important play since the Carter administration. The remote control, to paraphrase Tom Cruise to Renee Zellweger in *Jerry Maguire*, "completes me."

As I get dressed to attend the charity wine tasting, I turn on the news to see if the world exploded while I was watching the games. I discover that while I have effectively shut out thoughts of the Cummings case during football, I'm the only one who's done so. Two of the three cable news networks are discussing Daniel's prospects, and their collective opinion seems to be that the only question is whether he will get a lethal injection or a public beheading. One of the talking heads refers to me as Daniel's "flamboyant attorney" and warns that my skills are not nearly strong enough to carry the day.

Sam pulls up outside and beeps the horn. I wave that I'll be right down, then go through my departure ritual with Tara. Just before I leave, she always jumps up on my bed and I pet her for a short while. Then I put a biscuit on the bed, but she pretends to be uninterested in it. Of course, it's always gone when I return home.

Sam Willis is my accountant and friend, not necessarily in that order. He is brilliant when the subject is money, but lacks the ambition to match. As a result, I am probably his only rich client, and when I came into my fortune, he acted like a five-year-old in a toy store.

As I approach the car, I realize with a small jolt that I have not prepared for what constitutes the competitive aspect of our friendship. We have come to call it song-talking, which basically means smoothly fitting song lyrics into what is otherwise a normal conversation. Sam is an absolute master of it, and the gap between our skills has grown steadily.

"Hey, Sam, let's get a move on it, okay?" I say as I get into the passenger seat. "We've got a ticket to ride."

It's such a weak opening that I cringe as I say it, and Sam just shakes his head sadly. He knows that true greatness is measured by the stature of one's opponents, the "Ali needed Frazier" theory. What I've just said is further proof to Sam that I'm not exactly his lyrical "Smokin' Joe."

Sam doesn't even bother to respond in kind, holding his big guns back until later. Instead, he mentions that he saw coverage of the Cummings case on television and that it was mentioned that I'm his lawyer.

"You gonna need my help?" he asks.

In addition to being a financial genius and an amazing song-talker, Sam is a computer wizard. I used him to help me on Laurie's case, and he and his assistant made such great progress that the criminals came after them. Tragically, the assistant, Barry Leiter, was killed in the process, and I will never get over the intense guilt that I feel about it.

"I don't think so, Sam."

I say this in a tentative way, and Sam immediately understands what is behind my answer. "Because of Barry?" he asks.

I might as well answer semihonestly, since he'll see through it if I don't. "Partly. I just can't take a chance."

"That wasn't your fault, Andy. We've been over this a thousand times."

He's right about that, so I avoid number one thousand and one by not bothering to answer. Instead, I change the subject. "Where is this place we're going?"

"Well, I was looking at this map," he says, holding up the map he's talking about, "and according to this, it's only just out of reach, down the block, on a beach, under a tree . . ."

My heart sinks, not because Sam has chosen *West Side Story*, but because lately he has elevated his song-talking game to a new level. He hammers me with themes, using different but related songs throughout an entire evening. Recently, we were discussing vacations, and in the course of an hour he welcomed me to the "Hotel California," promising that I would get a taste of "life in the fast lane" in a "New York Minute."

He's still looking at the map. "Wait a minute . . . on second thought it looks like it's around the corner . . . or whistling down the river."

Our destination turns out to be nowhere near the river. It's a culinary institute in lower Westchester, and we are two of about eighty people there to taste wine for charity. We're divided into groups of twenty and put into what seem like typical classrooms. The only difference is that on tables in front of each chair are five glasses of wine.

"This is gonna be great," Sam says.

"Yeah. Yippie," I say, not quite sharing his enthusiasm.

Sam lifts up one glass in a toast. "Come on, Andy, cheer up. We're gonna rock it tonight. We're gonna jazz it up and have us a ball."

"Do me one favor, will you, Sam? Just don't tell me you feel pretty, oh so pretty."

The "class" begins, and I am immediately transformed to another planet, a place where people spin wine around in their glass, analyze it as if it's a top-secret formula, and use words like "flinty," "oaky," and "brassy" to describe the taste. Not having previously chewed on flint, oak, or brass, I have no idea what those things taste like, which puts me at a considerable disadvantage. I'm not even sure what they mean when they say a wine is dry; I spilled some and had to mop it up with my napkin just like I would something wet.

My sense is that this particular charity's goal is not to educate me, but rather to get me so sloshed that I won't realize how big a check I'm writing when they make their pitch at the end. I fool them by taking little tastes, mainly because I know that I'm going to have to drive Sam home, as he is downing flinty drinks with his left hand and dry, oaky ones with his right.

I write my check and we head out toward the cars. Our walk takes a little longer than it should, since we are stopped by about a dozen reporters, as well as three or four cameramen with television lights.

"Hey, Andy," one of them calls out, "have you heard what they're saying about Cummings?"

Nothing good can come from that question, and I

cringe in anticipation. I could fake it and give a "no comment," but I want to know what has happened, and when I find out, I might well have a comment.

"No, I haven't. I've been inside, toasting to charity."

Another reporter jumps in. "They're not talking on the record, but they're saying he also murdered his wife."

"I assume the 'they' you're talking about is the prosecution. Unlike Tucker Zachry, we intend to prove our case in a courtroom. Thanks for coming, people. I recommend the wine, although it's a little oaky."

I start walking toward the car. Behind me, with the cameras off, I hear the incorrigible Sam explaining my cranky mood in terms that only Officer Krupke could understand. "He's very upset. He never had the love that every child oughta get."

I lead Sam to the car, and I get in the driver's seat. Sam looks at me with genuine concern. "Is your boy innocent?" he asks.

"That's what we're going to find out."

Sam can read me, and he knows I have some very real doubts about that innocence. "I thought you always had to believe in your clients."

"Belief is an evolving concept."

"But you're sure you want to represent him?" he asks.

"I'm sure," I say without conviction.

Sam shakes his head disapprovingly. "I don't think you should."

Just what I need, more advice. "And why is that exactly?"

"A boy like that, he'd kill your brother. Forget that boy and find another. One of your own kind. Stick to your own kind."

• • • • •

THE INITIAL EVIDENCE against Daniel Cummings arrives in three boxes at ten o'clock on Monday morning. Its promptness is a further demonstration that Tucker is going to play this strictly by the book. He has no intention of being nailed on any kind of technicality involving procedure; his case must be too good for that.

What is here represents only a small piece of what will eventually be the prosecution's case. The investigation is ongoing and in fact just beginning, but this is daunting enough.

The first set of documents is technical in nature. I am nontechnical in nature, so it takes me a while to understand them. Basically, what they say is that technology exists that can tell in fairly precise terms the location of a cell phone when it receives a call. They've employed this technology in this case, and the results run counter to

Daniel's story. According to the reports, Daniel was already in or near the park that night when he received the call, which was made from a nearby pay telephone. Daniel had said it took him fifteen minutes to get to the park after receiving the call. Even worse, Daniel's fingerprints were found on that pay phone, leaving the clear impression that he made the call to himself so as to fabricate a story.

With this information on hand, the police then executed search warrants on Daniel's house and car while he was in the hospital. Hidden in the car's trunk were Linda Padilla's clothes, including a scarf, which the police believe was used to strangle her. And wrapped in that scarf were her severed hands.

It goes downhill from there. Three other scarves, bloody but mercifully without severed hands, were found hidden in Daniel's closet at home. Tests are being done to confirm that they are from the previous three victims. I would say it's a pretty safe bet that they are.

When Kevin, Laurie, and I finish going through the documents, it's so quiet in the office you can hear a severed hand drop. It's Laurie who finally breaks the silence. "This is bad," she says, vastly understating the case.

Kevin doesn't respond, which means he agrees. It's up to me, as the lead defense attorney, to give the upbeat analysis. "This is just their side of it" is the best I can manage.

"Do we have a side?" Kevin asks.

"Not yet," I say. "But we're gonna get one."

Their faces do not show great enthusiasm, more like total dread. "Look," I say, "if you guys want to back out of this, I'll understand."

"But you're staying in?" Laurie asks.

I nod. It's not a vigorous or enthusiastic nod; it's more just having my neck go limp and letting my head roll around on top of it. But it conveys the message: I'm staying on the case, and I'm doing it for Vince.

"We've had cases that looked bad before," Kevin reasons. "I'm in."

We both look to Laurie; she is aware that hers is one of the cases that looked particularly grim before we turned it around. Countering that is what I know to be her absolute horror at the prospect of helping a serial killer. "Okay," she says. "Me too."

I'm very glad to have them aboard. "Then let's kick this around," I say.

We discuss the case for the better part of two hours, at the end of which I verbalize my evolving strategy, pitifully obvious though it might be. "Either Daniel is guilty, or someone is trying to make him look guilty. It doesn't do us any good to assume the former, so let's go with the idea of an unknown bad guy. We have to find out who it is and why he's chosen Daniel as his target."

Kevin does not seem convinced about any of this, a sign of his intelligence. "My problem," he says, "is that we seem to be talking about a killer who randomly picks and murders victims and cuts off their hands. In other words, a real weirdo."

I know where he's going; it's bothered me as well. "Yet that's not the type of person to concoct an elaborate frame-up," I say.

Laurie nods her agreement. "Unless the murders weren't random."

The problem with that is that the victims were in no way similar; there is a young nurse, a street hooker, a grandmother, and a gubernatorial candidate. It seems hard to believe there is a connection between them, but that's one of the things we have to look for.

We make the decision to look at each murder individually. If we can exonerate Daniel on any one, then he might well be off the hook on all of them. Left unsaid is the one fact that hangs over us: If there are no more murders, Daniel will look even more guilty. It's left unsaid because no one wants to talk about the obvious flip side: If someone else is brutally strangled, it makes our case. Vicious murders are a tough thing to root for.

Kevin makes the suggestion that we bring in Marcus Clark, a private investigator who helped us in Laurie's defense. His methods are unorthodox but effective, and Laurie and I both agree that we can use him. Kevin volunteers to contact him.

We also understand that publicity is going to be a key component of our efforts and that the responsibility for that will fall on me. It's not something I enjoy, but that doesn't make it any less necessary.

Two hours ago we had nothing. Now we have a plan, things to do, information to digest, a mountain to climb. Deep inside me, so deep that it could be just a gas pain, I feel a rumbling, an eagerness to get the game started.

I always approach my cases as games; it helps me kick into gear the competitiveness that I need. When I was younger, I wanted to spend my life playing baseball. I was a shortstop, and I could have made it to the majors if I could only hit the curveball or the fastball or the slider or the change-up.

So criminal law is the game I play. It's always one game, winner take all, none of this sissy four-out-of-seven stuff. And right now I'm getting ready.

Play ball.

• • • • •

I AGREE TO DO THREE interviews from the list of thirty or so requests that Edna has received. During the course of the day, each of the shows promotes my appearance as an "exclusive" interview. I assume this means that at one particular moment, I will be talking only to their interviewer. It certainly can't mean that I am going to say something unique to any one of them; what I say to one I will say to all. It would be nice if I could figure out what that will be.

I arrive at the studio in Fort Lee from which the interviews will be conducted over satellite or tape or whatever it is they use. The three cable news networks, Fox, MSNBC, and CNN, have pooled their resources, and all the interviews will be done in succession from this one place.

My interviews would be better suited to the E! Network, providing "E" stands for "evasive." Or maybe the Sleep Channel, if there is one. What I should have done was brought Tara and gone on Animal Planet.

The interviewers are moderately competent at their craft, though there is certainly not a Ted Koppel among them. They all ask the same questions, trying to gain insight as to the evidence against Daniel and the strategy we will use to combat it.

I've always been a political junkie, and the time I've spent watching politicians being interviewed has not been wasted. The trick is to decide what you want to say and then say it, without any real regard to the question asked.

Some typical examples:

Question 1: How is your client going to plead?

Answer: He is going to plead not guilty because he is not guilty. He's looking forward to a full vindication in a court of law.

Question 2: What is the evidence the prosecution has against your client?

Answer: That's not completely clear right now. But what is clear is that we will mount a vigorous defense. My client is looking forward to a full vindication in a court of law.

Question 3: What did you have for breakfast this morning?

"I'm glad you asked that, because I had eggs, pancakes, and bacon. My client wants me to be well nourished and strong for the fight ahead, since he is looking forward to a full vindication in a court of law."

On the last show, I am part of a panel of "experts," all of whom are defense attorneys and/or former prosecutors. They wax semi-eloquent about the case and have two things in common. None of them has the slightest knowledge of the facts, and all of them think Daniel will be convicted.

The host takes calls from viewers, and their comments and questions are considerably more troubling. On my previous high-profile cases, while the public naturally assumed the accused was guilty, they weren't worked up about it. In this case, passions have been stirred, and their hatred of Daniel and by extension his lawyer, me, is palpable.

I leave the studio and go home, where Laurie is waiting for me. She's gone to the trouble of making me a late dinner, which is why I neglect to mention the thirty-five thousand potato chips I had between interviews.

We stare at each other during dinner. I'm staring at her because she possesses a casual beauty that quite literally and quite frequently takes my breath away. Since she doesn't do much gasping when I enter a room, my guess is that she's staring at me for a different reason.

"I've never seen you like this, Andy."

"What does that mean?"

"When you take on a case, you jump in with both feet. Like you can't wait to attack it. And the tougher the case, the more anxious you are. But not this time. This time you're a different kind of anxious."

I nod. "I feel like Scott Norwood is lining up to kick a field goal."

"That's a little too cryptic for me," she says.

"I'm a big Giants fan, you know that, and when they were in the Super Bowl against the Bills, I was pumped. I mean, I really wanted them to win. But I also took the over, because I thought it was a very good bet."

By now Laurie must realize this is not going to be the

most intellectual of discussions, but she plows on. "What is the over?" she asks.

"You can bet on whether the two teams combined will score over or under a certain number of points. I thought the Giants would win a high-scoring game, so I took the over."

"Got it," she lies.

"So it gets to the end of the game, and the Bills kicker, Scott Norwood, lines up to try a field goal. If he misses, the Giants win, but the game would stay under the number. If he makes it, the Giants lose, but it would be over the number. So if the Giants win, I lose the bet. If the Giants lose, I win the bet."

"Andy, I think it might be time to get to the point."

"Okay. I hated that moment. I hated being torn, rooting both ways. When I win, I want to win, no reservations. I don't feel that way about Daniel yet. As his lawyer, I have to fight for his freedom, but I don't know if he should be out on the street."

"So maybe you should drop the case."

"Maybe I should. But then maybe I shouldn't be a defense attorney. Because that's what defense attorneys do: We represent people that might be guilty. And only by giving them the best defense possible do we get to find out if they really are." I'm lecturing her with condescending bullshit, and I force myself to stop.

"He's got money. He'll get a good lawyer. It doesn't have to be you."

"That's true," I say unconvincingly.

"But his father's your friend."

She is right, of course. It's all about Vince. She can see right through me. "You make me feel naked," I say.

She looks at her watch. "I was hoping by now you

would be." She comes over and kisses me, takes me by the hand, and starts leading me to the bedroom.

"Now, this I have no reservations about," I say.

"What?" she asks.

"I never think about Scott Norwood when we're making love."

"I do," she says.

MARCUS CLARK IS the most frightening human being I have ever seen. His body appears made of iron; if he should break a bone, I believe the doctor would weld it together. His bald head is so cleanly shaven I can see my cowering, wimpy, skin-and-bones, pasty-white reflection in it. But even more intimidating than his appearance is his manner, his presence. He rarely talks, and moves slowly and deliberately, yet he projects pure menace.

The notable exception to this is when he is with Laurie. When he sees her, his face lights up, or at least softens, and he sometimes even speaks in sentences upwards of three words. I have an involuntary tendency to hide behind her when he is in the room.

He's come to my office this morning to get his assignment. Marcus is a private investigator who was very helpful taking over when Laurie was under house arrest and unable to aid in her own defense. His techniques, while I don't really want to know the particulars, are extraordinarily effective in developing information.

Laurie, Kevin, and I are going to investigate the local murders, but I have a feeling that the murder of Daniel's wife could factor into this case at some point. That is what I want Marcus to look into. It will mean his spending a great deal of time in Cleveland. I could send Laurie instead, but Marcus's absence will have significantly less effect on my sex life.

"He killed his wife?" Marcus asks me.

"No, he's our client. Our clients don't kill people. They're accused of it, but we brilliantly prove that they're innocent."

"You want me to find out who killed her?"

I nod. "In a perfect world, yes. But I'll settle for whatever you can learn."

"When?"

"As soon as you can. Edna's gotten you an open plane ticket, and we'll make a hotel reservation for you."

"No spa," he says.

"Excuse me?"

"I don't stay at hotels with spas. And it's gotta be near a Taco Bell."

"Anything else?" I ask.

"Ice machine."

I look at Laurie, but she looks away. I'm going to have to deal with these travel issues on my own. "Right," I say, pretending to make notes on a legal pad. "No spa . . . Taco Bell . . . ice machine . . . you want regular cubes or the kind with those holes in them?"

I'm taking a risk poking fun at Marcus, but he lets me off the hook by ignoring me. He grunts that he can leave immediately, so I hand him over to Edna to make the travel reservations.

Kevin goes off to meet the husband of Betty Simonson, the grandmother who was the killer's second victim. I've assigned myself to check Nancy Dempsey, the first victim, but I'm at least temporarily unable to get in touch with her husband, so I decide to join Laurie in investigating the third murder, that of the street hooker. Linda Padilla, by far the most prominent of the victims, will be the last one we look into, and we'll all focus on that.

The vacant lot where the third victim's body was found is a scary place, even though it's only eight o'clock in the evening, five hours before the estimated time of death, one A.M. It's in an industrial area of Passaic, which obviously has two distinct shifts of workers. The day shifters are those who carry a lunch pail and work in the factories; the night shifters carry condoms and work on their backs.

It's the night shift that has come on when we arrive, which is just as well, since the victim was a member of that group. The police reports say that her colleagues knew her only as Rosalie, though no one knows if that's her real name. They have been unable to further identify her, but have guessed her age to be twenty.

We walk over to an area where there are three Dumpsters, behind which Rosalie's naked body was found. It is a filthy area, and I see at least three rats scurry off when we arrive. I never knew Rosalie, and never will, but I know that she died too young and with far too little dignity.

Laurie makes the same comment she made in Eastside Park, at the site Linda Padilla was found. "She wasn't murdered here."

My response is every bit as insightful as it was then.

"How can you tell?" I ask, though I know from my research that she is right. Rosalie was murdered in her own apartment; and the place was vandalized in the process.

"It wouldn't make sense; it's easy to get a hooker alone," she says. "You just have to hire her. Then she takes you to a place she has, and if you want to kill her, that's where you do it. With no one around. She would never have taken him back here; she'd have a room somewhere nearby."

We walk toward the curb, which serves as a sort of showroom for the young women. Some are just teenagers, and at least three-quarters of them are African-American, though Rosalie was white. Right now they are participating in the economic mating ritual, talking to men who pull up in cars and signal to them.

"Must be asking for directions," I say.

Laurie doesn't respond. Hooker jokes are not really her thing. Compassion and human dignity are her things.

We walk over toward two ladies, waiting by the curb for customers to pull up. One is dressed in a gaudy red dress, the other opted for gaudy green.

"Hi" is my clever opening.

They look at me blankly. If they are feeling sexual desire for me, they're concealing it well. "Cops?" Gaudy Red asks.

"Used to be," Laurie says. "Not anymore. Now I'm private."

"So what about him?" Gaudy Red asks, jerking her thumb toward me.

"He's a lawyer."

Gaudy Green snorts, and the two street hookers share a small laugh, undoubtedly mocking my profession. Then Gaudy Red asks, "So what do you want?"

"We want to know about Rosalie, the girl that was murdered," Laurie says. "We're trying to find out who killed her."

"Did you know her?" I ask.

Gaudy Red looks at Gaudy Green, who thinks for a moment and then nods her approval. Gaudy Red says, "Over there. Sondra. She was Rosalie's roommate."

We thank them and walk off in the direction that they are pointing, toward another woman, close to thirty years old, standing near a parked car, working alone. Laurie introduces us to her and tells her that we want to ask her about Rosalie.

"I don't know who killed her," Sondra says, then looks away, as if hoping we'll be satisfied with her answer and disappear.

"We understand that," says Laurie. "We're just trying to learn about her, to understand who she was. Maybe that will help us figure out why she was killed."

Sondra looks doubtful but goes on to describe the Rosalie she knew. She does so in bland generalities: Rosalie was nice, and a lot of fun and generous, and a real good friend and roommate. She could be describing a sorority sister, except if she was, we probably wouldn't be standing near garbage cans, dodging rats and watching johns drive up.

"Was Rosalie her real name?" I ask.

Sondra shrugs. "Beats me. I don't know who she was before or where she came from or why. It don't matter much, you know?"

"Can you think of any reason why she was killed?"

A flash of anger. "Yeah. Because there are weird assholes in this world, and she went off with one of them."

Sondra has very little information to provide, no matter how much we prod. She thinks Rosalie came from the Midwest, though that is just a guess, and she thinks she might have run away from a family with money, because she knew all about nice clothes, even though she didn't have any.

We show Sondra pictures of the other victims, with the faint hope she'll recognize them as somehow being connected to Rosalie. She does not, and we're about to conclude this interview when a car pulls up. A guy gets out and strides purposefully toward us. If central casting needed a pimp, this is who they would send for. He's got the car, the clothes, the attitude, the whole package.

"They bothering you, Sondra?"

Sondra's demeanor changes instantly; her fear of this man is palpable. "They ain't bothering me, Rick. We just talking."

Rick smiles briefly. "Oh, you just talking? I thought you supposed to be just working."

What happens next goes by so fast that it seems surreal. Rick slaps Sondra across the face, and she falls back. Then Laurie grabs Rick and spins him around and down face-first onto the hood of his car. He screams in pain, and I see blood spurting onto the hood from the place where his intact nose used to be.

He tries to get up, but Laurie has his arm behind him in what looks like a wrestling hold. She slams his head down again, and he moans in agony. Then she actually opens her handbag and takes out a pair of handcuffs, cuffing him behind his back.

Finally, I spring into action, albeit verbal action. "Holy shit," I say. My comment seems to have little effect on events as they are unfolding.

Sondra is crying softly, but Laurie and Rick are paying

just as little attention to her as they are to me. Laurie takes out her cell phone and calls a friend on the force, asking that officers be sent down to make an arrest. Then she takes Rick's car keys and drops them down a sewer.

Rick attempts some kind of talking noise, but his exact words are lost as they fail to navigate through the blood and smashed teeth. Laurie makes the reasonable assumption that what he was going to say was not conciliatory in nature, and smacks him hard in the back of his head.

She leans over until her mouth is maybe an inch from Rick's ear. "I'm going to have some people check on Sondra every week, and if anything bad happens to her, anything at all—if she gets hit by lightning or catches a cold—I'm going to think it's your fault. And compared to what will happen then, tonight will seem like a day at the beach. You understand?"

Rick mumbles something that sounds like "Misksh-belflk." I assume that's pimp-talk for "Yes, crazy lady, I understand real well. Please don't smash my face again."

The police show up and take Rick off to face assault and various other charges that they and Laurie will dream up. They don't seem terribly concerned by his injuries, and as an officer of the court, I assure them that Rick sustained those injuries while resisting a citizen's arrest.

After they've gone, Laurie turns to Sondra. "Do you want out of this?" she asks. "You can do better."

Sondra laughs a short laugh, as if the idea is ridiculous. "Where am I gonna go?"

"That's the easy part," says Laurie. "The hard part is wanting to."

"I'll be okay," she says.

I take out my card and hand it to her. "If you're not, call me," I say. "Next time I won't be so easy on him."

Sondra goes off, and Laurie and I head back to the car. "I didn't know you still carry handcuffs," I say, grinning like an idiot.

"I figured if I told you, you'd grin like an idiot."

"You got any more of them?" I ask, since the first pair went off with Rick.

"I do, but I only use them in the pursuit of truth and justice."

"Oh," I say. "Damn."

• • • • •

DR. JANET CARLSON must be the best-looking coroner in the United States. It's ironic, because she had to have been voted "Least Likely to Hang Out with Dead People" in high school. She's about five foot four, a hundred and ten pounds in rubber surgical gloves, and at thirty-five years old still looks like every guy's dream date for the senior prom.

But put a scalpel in her hand, and you don't want to mess with her.

I once helped Janet's sister out of a sticky legal situation with her ex-husband, so she owed me a favor. I've called in that favor about fifty times since, but she doesn't seem to mind, so I'm doing it again today.

Janet's full medical reports on the murders aren't in yet, or at least they haven't been turned over to the defense, so I go down to her office to find out what I can. As soon as I arrive she buzzes me in; she almost seems anxious for the company. Maybe because the other ten people hanging out with her are in refrigerated drawers.

"I shouldn't be talking to you," she says. "Tucker would tie me to a tree and flog me."

I close my eyes. "What a great visual . . ."

She laughs. "So what do you want?"

"Information that will clear my client."

She touches her apron pockets. "Sorry, I left that in my other apron."

We finish bantering, and she takes me through what her reports will say. "It's pretty straightforward, Andy. All four women died from manual strangulation, probably with a cloth. Cause of death in each case is asphyxiation."

"Were they sexually molested?" I ask.

"No."

I'm surprised to hear this. "Isn't that unusual, considering they were naked?"

"In my experience, very. And there was no semen found on or near the body, so it's likely he didn't masturbate, although two of the bodies were moved. But it's refreshing, don't you think, Andy? A prudish sex fiend."

"If they died from the strangulation, when did he cut off their hands?"

"Postmortem. Very neatly done . . . he took his time. Same thing with the clothes."

"They found the clothes?"

"Only Linda Padilla's," she says. "But I doubt that they were ripped off in any of the cases . . . there would have been some abrasions. I believe he cut them off after the victims were dead, most likely with the same knife he used to cut off the hands."

"Without passion?" I ask, since she's making the murders sound almost clinical.

"I would say so. If there was, it's certainly well hidden."

I thank Janet and head back to my office. What she had to say is surprising and vaguely disconcerting. I had been having trouble seeing Daniel as a psychopath and was counting on the jury feeling the same way. Janet's portrayal of the crimes is such that it may not be the work of a psychopath, at all, but rather someone making it look that way. That would make the killer smart, cold, and diabolical, a role Daniel is far more suited to.

On the more positive other hand, if the killer is more calculating than psycho, he would be quite capable of pulling off the frame we are claiming has been perpetrated on Daniel.

Vince is at the office when I arrive, and he starts in on his daily ritual of questioning me about progress in the case. I've basically been telling him what I know, for two reasons. First, I cleared it with Daniel, and second, I don't know anything.

"What do you know about Daniel's sex life?" I ask.

"What the hell is that supposed to mean?"

"It's a pretty straightforward question, Vince. Is there anything unusual that you know of?"

He's upset by the question. "Of course not. Come on, Andy, he's my son."

"Having your genes is not exactly proof of normalcy."

"The killer had weird sex stuff going on?" he asks.

"He murdered women, stripped them naked, and cut off their hands," I say. "There's a hint of the loony in that, don't you think?"

Vince believes his role in this is to convince me of Daniel's innocence. While he's babbling away about that, I glance at the call list Edna left on my desk. First on the list is Randy Clemens. He called only once, which is not a surprise, since inmates in state prison are allowed to make only one phone call a day. Next to Randy's name is Edna's note: "He needs to see you right away."

I defended Randy Clemens on a charge of armed robbery four and a half years ago. The state had a strong case, but not an airtight one. I came to like him and believe in his innocence. The fact that he's calling from prison should give you some idea of how successful I was in his defense. After he was sentenced to a minimum of fifteen years, his wife divorced him and took their daughter to California.

It is a source of ongoing pain and guilt that Randy is behind bars, and those feelings are exacerbated every few months, when he calls me with ideas he has thought of for appeal. They never have any merit or prospects for success, and it always falls to me to break that news to him. What he can't accept, what I have trouble accepting myself, is that his legal game was played out and he lost. No do-overs allowed.

I ask Edna to call the prison and arrange for me to visit Randy on Saturday. I don't want to go, I never want to go, but I can't stand the idea of him sitting in his cell, feeling that I've abandoned him.

Kevin and Laurie come back for a meeting I've called to go over what we've learned. I don't really expect anything to come from these initial efforts; I believe that if there is a motive anywhere to be found, it will be in the Padilla killing. But it's more likely that there was no motive to any of this other than lunacy, despite the curious tactics the perpetrator used.

Kevin says that he visited with Arnold Simonson, husband of Betty, the grandmother who became the second victim.

"They lived off their Social Security and his disability insurance; he hurt his back while working as a foreman in a carton factory," Kevin reports. "They were high school sweethearts, married forty-two years, hoping to move to Florida next year. Two grown kids, four grandchildren . . ." Kevin is obviously upset as he recounts this.

"So no apparent motive?" I ask.

"Zero. And I showed him the photos of the other women, but he had never seen them before."

I nod. My guess is that the only thing we're gonna find these people have in common is that they were killed by the same person.

"He showed me their family album," Kevin says. "How anybody could have hurt that woman . . ."

I discuss with Kevin and Laurie what I learned at the coroner's office, and Kevin makes the very logical suggestion that I should talk to someone with professional insight as to the killer's state of mind. I make arrangements to do that, then I leave for a meeting with my client.

Laurie heads off to talk with the husband of Nancy Dempsey, the first victim. With that out of the way, we'll be free to turn our collective focus to Linda Padilla. We need to find proof that the killer is logical, that the crimes had a motive, because only then can we make a credible case that he framed Daniel.

• • • • •

THE HORROR OF confinement is starting to take its toll on Daniel. I am told that loss of freedom is a nightmare that cannot be fully understood unless experienced. Daniel is experiencing it right now, and I can see the devastation on his face as he is led into the visitor's room. What he doesn't realize is that he hasn't yet faced the worst part. That will come if we lose the trial and the system puts him away and moves on to other things. Willie Miller once told me that the feeling of hopelessness, of being forgotten, is the toughest part of all.

Daniel sees me as his only link to the outside world, and his only hope to ever get back there. He sees me this way because it is true, and it's a pressure that makes me uncomfortable. For instance, right now, before I've said anything, Daniel is desperately hoping that I've brought some news that will end his agony.

I haven't.

My expressed purpose for being here is to bring him up-to-date on the progress of our investigation, but since there basically is none, I'm able to get that out of the way quickly. What I really want to do is probe his story about the night of the Padilla murder; I don't believe his version of events, and I'm hoping there's another explanation for his lie besides him being the killer.

"Did you know Linda Padilla?" I ask.

"Why? You think I killed her?"

I deflect this question by lecturing him on his role as the defendant. He must tell me everything there is to tell; the worst possible thing that can happen is if I am surprised in court by something the prosecution knows that I don't. Tucker will find out if Daniel had a connection to Linda Padilla, so I must know as well.

"I knew her," he says, his voice an octave lower. Actually, it could be a bunch of octaves lower, since he's barely whispering and I have no idea what an octave is.

"How well?" I ask.

"I met her a couple of times, maybe three. The last time I interviewed her."

"About what?"

"I was working on a story about organized crime in North Jersey, how it had evolved, how strong it is today . . . that was the main thrust. She kept coming up in my research, so I approached her."

I'm not surprised to hear him say this: Linda Padilla's name has often been linked to the mob, albeit always through unsubstantiated rumor and innuendo. There are those who believe organized crime supplied her with much of the information she used to rock the establishment. Of course, those believers consist mainly of those

she has attacked and/or her future opponents, but the talk
has never been completely eliminated.

"In what context did her name come up?" I ask.

"I couldn't be sure, but my sense was that she was
somehow beholden to them. I asked her about it, but she
completely froze me out. Denied it, then wouldn't talk
about it."

If Daniel is telling the truth, and if his information
tying Padilla to organized crime is correct, it could be a
link to the chalk outline of her body in a pavilion in
Eastside Park. Of course, it doesn't explain the other
murders, none of which bear the markings of mob hits,
but at least it's something.

"How are you coming on your whereabouts at the
time of the murders?"

He frowns, which is an answer as clear as any words
he can say. He says them anyway. "I was home in bed.
I'm up every morning at five-thirty, so I go to bed early.
All the murders happened after midnight, except Padilla,
and . . ."

He doesn't finish his sentence and he doesn't have to.
He wasn't home in bed the night Linda Padilla was
killed; he was in Eastside Park with her body.

I ask Daniel how his prints could have been on the
phone in the park. He doesn't know, but his theory is that
the blow he took to the head knocked him unconscious,
and the killer took advantage of that to screw off the
phone and place it in his hand. The killer then screwed it
back on, with Daniel's fingerprints on it. It is a theory
that would have little if any chance of holding up; there
is not even any conclusive evidence that Daniel lost consciousness. Yet it is a measure of our plight that I file the

idea away for further consideration and possible use later.

Daniel is sticking to his story about being miles away from the park when receiving the cell phone call from the killer. I'm going to have to get experts to question the technology, if such experts exist.

Daniel's theory about how the other scarves got into his house is less sophisticated, but he's very vocal about it. "It's a setup, Andy, don't you see? Would I leave things like that around to be found? I've covered criminal cases for ten years! I know how these things work."

While I'm at the prison, I get a message from Edna. We have been informed that the grand jury has returned an indictment, not exactly a major surprise, and that there will be a hearing on Monday in front of the trial judge. That judge has not been appointed yet, but it's expected to be announced no later than tomorrow. While judges are assigned randomly, I would suspect this will be slightly less random than most, since this trial is a political hot potato.

I leave Daniel after about a half hour, promising to keep him regularly informed of developments. I drive to the Haledon office of Dr. Carlotta Abbruzze, a shrink whom I had about five sessions with three or four years ago. It was at a time when my then wife, Nicole, and I were having some problems, and I was trying to determine if I was the cause.

Basically, I wanted to sit and talk about my marriage, but Carlotta, as she encouraged me to call her, wanted me to lie on the couch and relive my childhood. Since I can't remember a single problem in my childhood, this seemed a waste of time. Besides, I reasoned, there was always the danger that I might discover some actual childhood problems, which I had no desire to do.

Carlotta told me that I was in heavy denial, a charge I will refuse to accept until the day I die. I stopped seeing her, but we became friends, having dinner once in a while. It cost me just as much, but at least I got something to eat, and I could sit up when I talked.

Edna has made an appointment for me with Carlotta at her office. I show up ten minutes early and sit in the waiting room for her door to open. I know that it will open exactly at the scheduled time, not one minute before or one minute after.

It does open, and one of Carlotta's patients exits. We of course do not make eye contact; I don't make eye contact with anyone, and I'm not about to start with a fellow shrinkee. Carlotta follows him into the waiting area and invites me into her office.

Once we're inside and the door is closed, she says, "I assume you're not here because of a sudden craving for mental health?"

I shake my head. "Been there, done that."

I walk toward the couch to lie down, then do a brief turn and sit in the chair opposite hers. "I'm here for your professional expertise, for which I am prepared to pay handsomely."

I go on to describe the murders and what I consider the unusual actions the killer has taken. I know this isn't really Carlotta's forte, and she would never qualify as an expert in court, but I think she can give me some insight.

When I finish, she thinks for a moment, then asks, "Do you know if the victims were strangled from the front or the rear?"

I had forgotten to cover that. "From the rear. Most likely with a scarf."

She thinks quietly for a while longer. "Andy, what I know about serial killers probably couldn't fill a good-sized paragraph."

"Take your best shot."

She nods. "All right. Let's assume for the moment that the murders are a result of pathology, not motive. Because if there is revenge involved, or money, or anything like that, what I have to say is of no value whatsoever."

"Gotcha."

"The interesting factor to me," she says, "is the absence of rape, pre- or postmortem. I'm sure you know rape isn't a sexual crime; it's a crime of power or dominance. Sometimes when the rapist is intimidated by women, he will commit the rape postmortem, when the victim cannot possibly assert her will."

"But when there's no rape? No sexual assault of any kind?" I ask.

"That could suggest a fear of women so powerful that the killer can't assert dominance, at least sexual dominance, even after death. This is obviously just a guess, but the attack from behind would tend to support it."

"He doesn't even have the courage to face women head-on?"

She nods. "Right."

What she is saying seems to make sense to me. "What about cutting off the hands?"

She shakes her head. "Very hard to say. Maybe he was abused by a woman, and the method of abuse could have involved her hands. Or maybe he feels horribly manipulated by women, and this is a symbolic way to put a stop to it. There's really no way to tell with the limited information you have, Andy."

I broaden the conversation to include some nonprivileged information about Daniel, including the murder of his wife. She sees little likelihood that a murder of a spouse for money could fit with the killings we've seen these last few weeks. It's encouraging and confirms my instincts as well.

I thank Carlotta and head home, feeling a little better about things. I'm starting to open up to the remote possibility that Daniel is not guilty. The evidence says otherwise, but attacking evidence is what I do.

Laurie is waiting for me when I get home, on the front lawn throwing a ball to Tara. My two favorite women, waiting eagerly for their man to come home. Can my newspaper, pipe, and slippers be far behind?

Apparently, they can, since as soon as Laurie sees me she sends me back out to bring home some pizza. In Laurie's case, she orders so many toppings that it's more of a salad than a pizza. Since I'm a man's man, I get a man's pizza, plain cheese. That way I can eat four pieces, eat just the cheese off the other four, and give the crusts to Tara.

After dinner we have some wine. Laurie has opened a rather flinty-tasting bottle, but I decide that sitting in candlelight, minutes before bed, is not the time to lecture or educate her. Instead, she tells me of her session with Richard Dempsey, husband of murder victim Nancy Dempsey.

Laurie did not like him very much at all. On three separate occasions he let slip the fact that theirs was a troubled marriage, comments that Laurie considered inappropriate in light of the subsequent tragic events. "If

I had given him the opportunity, I think he would have tried hitting on me," she says.

"Should that ever happen, use the face-smash-into-the-car maneuver you used on the pimp," I say.

She nods. "Will do."

"Do you think he's involved in this?"

She firmly shakes her head. "I don't, Andy. The guy's a little slimy, but a serial killer? I could be wrong, but it just doesn't fit at all."

Nothing fits, and it's starting to get on my nerves. I'm also feeling tired, and what I want to do right now is get into bed with Laurie. The problem is that she seems comfortable on the couch, drinking wine and petting Tara's head.

My mind races, wondering how to lure her into the sack. I think back to the numerous techniques I tried on women during my fraternity days, but the one thing they had in common was that they never worked.

"You ready for bed?" she asks.

I fake-yawn nonchalantly. "Whenever . . ."

"Then I'll stay up for a while. You can go on to sleep. You look tired."

There's as much chance of me going to bed without Laurie as there is of me crawling into the microwave and pressing High.

"No, staying up is fine. I'm completely wide awake," I say. "I can't remember the last time I was this awake."

She smiles, a humoring-the-pathetic-idiot smile. "I think we should go to bed. You coming?" she asks.

"Damn right," I say. "I'm exhausted."

She takes my hand and we go to bed.

I am Andy the master manipulator.

• • • • •

RANDY CLEMENS HAS the same look on his face every time I visit him, and today is no exception. Once again he has a plan, an idea, and he's positive that his telling it to me will be the first step to freedom. He's hopeful and enthusiastic, and those feelings are not tempered by the fact that every time he's felt them before he's been wrong.

Unfortunately, my job is to always break the bad news. But I secretly harbor my own faint hope, the hope that one day his idea for a new appeal will be brilliant, something I completely overlooked, and will result in his being set free. In a sadistic quid pro quo, it always falls on him to demonstrate that I am wrong, simply by telling me his idea.

He enters the visiting room, and his eyes seek me out from the other visitors and prisoners, talking to each other on phones through the glass partitions. He heads toward me, though pausing to warily eye the others on his side of the glass. Seeming to decide that it is safe, he sits down.

"Andy, thanks for coming," he says. "I know it's a hassle."

"I was in the neighborhood."

He grins. "Yeah, right." Then his voice gets lower, and the wariness returns to his eyes. "Andy, I've got something. Something that could get me out of here."

I try to seem eager to hear what he has to say, but in reality I dread it. I can't stand to shoot this man down again. "What is it?"

"I know why those women were killed."

If you had given me a thousand guesses, I never could have predicted that was what he would have said. "What?"

"Andy, I can't scream it out, you know? I know about the murders, and I want you to use the information to get me released. I tell them all about it, and I get paroled. They make deals like that all the time."

"Did you know I'm representing the accused?"

The shock is evident on his face; he had no idea. "Oh, my God!" he enthuses. "This is great! This is unbelievable!"

I'm not quite ready to join in the euphoria. "What is it you know, Randy?"

Again he looks around warily, more understandable in light of what we are talking about. "It's all about the rich one. The others were window dressing."

"You mean—"

He interrupts me, shaking his head. "No, not here. But I won't let you down, Andy. Just set this up, please. Give me ten minutes in a room with the DA, and your client is in the clear."

"They're going to want a preview before they meet."

He shakes his head firmly. "Andy, I can't now. Okay? I've heard things . . . please trust me, and please get this done. I swear on my daughter's life . . . this is real."

I'm not going to get any more; he's calling the shots. And I do trust that he believes what he is saying, though I have strong doubts that he can deliver what he hopes. "Okay. I'll get right on it."

His relief is so powerful it seems to be seeping through the glass. "Thank you," he says, and walks off. He looks around, seems to pause for a moment, and then hurries out of the room.

By the time I reach my car, I've decided what to do with Randy's request. The DA's office is the obvious place to go, but I'm not about to trust Tucker with it. There is too much chance he would bury the information, even if it turns out that the information does not deserve to be buried.

Instead, I call Richard Wallace. Richard originally prosecuted Randy's case, but that is not why I choose him. Richard has always demonstrated total integrity. It's a cliché, but in his case true: He is more interested in justice than victory.

I'm lucky enough to get Richard on the phone. I tell him I need to see him about something important, but I don't overplay it. My belief is that this will turn out to be unsubstantiated jailhouse chatter and ultimately not amount to anything. He agrees to see me right away, and I ask that we meet at a nearby coffee shop. I don't want to run into Tucker.

Richard is already at a table waiting for me when I arrive. We exchange small talk, after which I lay out what Randy told me at the prison.

"This should go to Tucker," he says.

"I can't, Richard, he'd never follow up. It would be detrimental to both my clients."

Richard nods; he knows I'm right, and he's trying to find another way. "I assume everything you've just said to me is unofficial? Off the record?"

I don't know what he's getting at, but he's nodding his head, prompting me, so I nod right back. "Right," I say, going along. "Totally unofficial and way off the record."

"Suppose you officially come to me and tell me Clemens has something important to say, that it could involve the perpetrators of some serious crimes. But you don't mention which crimes, or any other clients of yours that might be involved."

I immediately see where he's going with this. "Then you would have no reason to talk to Tucker. It's the kind of thing you could and should handle on your own."

He nods. "At least until I hear what Clemens has to say."

I lean forward. "Richard, there's something I want to officially talk to you about." Feeling a little silly, I lay out the new version, and he agrees to arrange for Randy to tell his story. We schedule it for Monday morning, and Richard promises to set it up with the prison authorities.

Just before he gets up to leave, he says, "You know, the evidence was there, and I believe he was guilty, but the Clemens conviction never felt completely right. You know?"

"I know. Believe me, I know."

• • • • •

JUDGE CALVIN NEWHOUSE is assigned to preside over *New Jersey v. Daniel Cummings*. A wealthy New Englander by birth and a graduate of Harvard Law, Calvin understands the law inside and out. He's also quite sophisticated; this is a guy who knows flinty wine when he tastes it. Yet he has always tried to portray himself as a crusty, seat-of-the-pants judge with a disdain for legal procedure but a reverence for "good old country common sense." He's even incorporated a trace of a southern accent, which makes him sound like a cross between William Buckley and Willie Nelson.

Calvin's reputation is as a prosecution judge, which doesn't exactly put him in select company. I've tried one case before him, which I won when he agreed to my motion for an order to dismiss. I found him to be highly intelligent and reasonably evenhanded, so all in all I'm not unhappy with the selection. It could be better, but it could be a hell of a lot worse.

One major plus is that Calvin is unlikely to be swayed by the media coverage and public pressure surrounding the case. He's sixty-four years old, due to retire anyway, and fiercely proud of his independence. He won't fold before Tucker, but neither will he do us any great favors.

The hearing today is mostly a formality; a get-acquainted session with the judge, during which he will set the trial date and hear a few ordinary motions. Despite that fact, I don't know that I've ever seen this many members of the press in one place. Clearly, there is nothing else going on in the world.

Vince has gone to Daniel's house to get him a suit to wear, and when I see him in the suit, I'm glad there's no jury present. If Calvin were inclined to grant bail, which he won't be, the value of the suit would cover it. When there is a jury, I will not have Daniel looking so regal. He should look like a man of the people, a little tattered, with no sense of fashion. It'll be easy to pull off; I'll just send Vince to my closet instead.

Tucker has three lawyers from his office with him, all of whom I know to be quite competent. As a group they represent considerable overkill for the task at hand, unless Tucker is planning to use them to haul in the boxes of convincing evidence.

Tucker suggests a trial date in the prescribed two months and is shocked when I agree. I would much prefer a longer period of time, but Daniel has insisted we move forward quickly. He seems to have the notion that the trial will result in his being let out of prison, a concept not currently supported by any facts that I am aware of.

Calvin asks us whether discovery is proceeding

smoothly, which to a degree it is. Boxes are arriving at my office every day, and they don't even yet include the DNA tests, which will take a few more weeks. I'm not waiting for them with bated breath; I have no doubt the blood and hair on the scarves found in Daniel's house will match those of the victims. My task is to convince the jury that Daniel did not put them there.

"Your Honor," I say, "discovery has to this point been limited to the documents and reports relating to Mr. Cummings as a suspect. They indicate he wasn't viewed this way until late in the investigation. I would request that the defense be given all reports from the investigation, whether or not they relate to him as a suspect."

Tucker confers briefly with one of his colleagues, then stands. "Your Honor, the rules of discovery are very clear on this point, and they do not support the defense's request. All relevant discovery is being turned over. Defense is on a fishing expedition."

I shake my head. "Your Honor, my client was a conduit between the actual killer and the police. The police used him as such; they directed him in his dealings with the real killer. This all took place before he was a suspect. He was an integral part of their investigation, and as such we should be privy to all aspects of that investigation."

Tucker objects again; he is on fairly solid legal ground, and it would take a surprise ruling by Calvin for us to prevail. My hope is that he will bend over backward to give us every chance, knowing that if we lose this death penalty case, appeals courts will be scrutinizing his rulings for years.

"I'm inclined to grant the defense motion," Calvin says as Tucker does a double take. "If there are cases where the prosecution contends that innocent third par-

ties will be injured by these documents being turned over
to the defense, then I will review them *in camera*."

I never expected to win this motion, so I might as well
press my luck. "Thank you, Your Honor. We also request
that we be provided with any prior police investigative
reports concerning Ms. Linda Padilla, beyond those relating to her murder. We believe they may reveal others
with a possible motive to have caused her death."

This possible linkage of Linda Padilla to unsavory
characters gets the press mumbling and Tucker jumping
to his feet. His frustration is obvious. "Your Honor, there
is no foundation for this. There is nothing in those reports
relating to this case."

Calvin nails him. "You've read those reports, have
you?" He knows Tucker would have had no reason or occasion to read old, unrelated police investigative reports
on Linda Padilla, yet Tucker has just said there's nothing
relevant in them.

"I'm sorry, I misspoke, Your Honor. I actually don't
even know if such reports exist. But unless they contain
information about Mr. Cummings, they certainly could
have nothing to do with this trial and therefore are not
covered by discovery rules in this state."

Calvin gives us another win, albeit a smaller one. He will
look at those reports *in camera* but only give them to us if
there is anything that could be beneficial to our defense.

I once again bring up the question of bail, though I'm
aware it's always a nonstarter in a capital case. "Are
you trying to waste the court's time, Mr. Carpenter?"
Calvin asks.

"No, Your Honor, I am trying to prevent a man who
has never previously been charged with a crime, who is
not a flight risk, and who has always been a distinguished

member of the community from sitting in a jail cell while we get around to finding him not guilty."

Tucker stands. "Your Honor, the state—"

Calvin cuts him off. "Request for bail is denied. What's next?"

I stand. "Your Honor, we have filed a motion for change of venue with the court. We feel strongly that the already strong public awareness and reaction, which has been further inflamed by Mr. Zachry's self-serving press conferences, has made it impossible to empanel an impartial jury. We—"

He cuts me off. "I read the motion, as well as the prosecution's response. It may take a little longer than usual, but we'll get our jury. Motion denied. We finished here, gentlemen?"

We're not quite finished, though my last issue is sure to be a loser. "Your Honor, Mr. Zachry has been telling the press that his case is airtight on all four murders, yet he's held back charging my client for the first three. He's obviously concerned that his airtight case might spring a leak, and he might need a second chance if he loses this one. I would therefore request that he not be allowed to use evidence from those other murders unless he includes them in the charges for this trial."

Tucker states his position directly from the statute, which is that the other evidence is "proof of motive, opportunity, intent and preparation." I know I'm not going to win; I'm simply creating an issue for appeal.

Calvin rules against us, and I head back to the office to brief Kevin and Laurie on my conversation with Randy Clemens. They're more hopeful about it than I am, probably because they don't understand Randy's desperation to find something that will free him.

"So he said it was all about Linda Padilla?" Laurie asks.

"He didn't mention her name; I think he was afraid we'd be overheard. But he referred to the 'rich' victim, and I don't see how the others qualify."

Marcus calls from Cleveland to fill us in on his progress, and we put him on the speakerphone. Talking to most people on the phone is not quite the same as talking in person; there are facial expressions and body language that can be almost as important as the spoken words. Marcus is a notable exception. The inanimate phone captures his expression and mannerisms quite well, is just as bald, and contains the same percentage of body fat.

Marcus has talked to the detective that was assigned to the murder of Margaret Cummings, Daniel's wife. He tells us that the detective is shedding no tears for Daniel's current plight, since he has always had a hunch that Daniel was behind Margaret's death.

Daniel was widely considered a solid citizen in Cleveland, and support for him through his ordeal was almost unanimous, the detective being the notable exception.

"Does he think Daniel pulled the trigger?" Laurie asks.

"Unh-unh . . . farmed." That is Marcus-speak for "No, the detective is of the opinion that our client employed a subcontractor to do the actual deed on his behalf."

Marcus goes on to grunt that a young man had been arrested for the murder but that the case against him fell apart, and he was no longer a suspect.

Marcus has certainly not found any real evidence implicating Daniel, which is no surprise, since apparently the Cleveland police didn't either. I ask him to stay in

Cleveland and keep digging, though it makes me slightly uncomfortable to do so. The truth is that there is little chance he can uncover anything to help Daniel's defense against the multiple-murder charges. If I were to be honest with myself, which I try to do as rarely as possible, I would admit that I'm hoping Marcus can help me learn more about who it really is we are defending.

The weekend starts tonight, and I am very much looking forward to it. Laurie is going to spend the entire time at my house, which at first glance seems like an increase in our normal scheduled time, but really isn't. That's because it's a college and pro football weekend, which means that even though we'll be in the same house, we'll have almost no daytime interaction.

As we get close to the trial date, we'll all be working seven-day weeks, but we're still far enough away that we can have some relaxation. Tonight's relaxation consists of sitting in my living room and watching *Godfather* I and II on DVD on my big-screen TV. It's the one large purchase I've made since coming into my money, and it has been worth every penny.

Laurie and I sit on my couch and watch the movies, a bowl of popcorn and Tara between us. Tara positions herself there so she can be petted from both sides, and neither of us minds. It is literally stunning how right these times with Laurie feel, and for the first time it flashes through my mind that maybe we should get married.

The next flash is the realization that Laurie has never brought the subject up, not even once, not even in passing. I've always been pleased by that, relieved actually, but now I'm starting to wonder. Shouldn't she be plotting to win me? Pressuring me to make an honest woman out of her? Telling me her goddamn clock is ticking?

I decide not to bring the subject up, but the next thing I know it's dribbling out of my mouth. "You never bring up marriage," I say.

My timing is not great, since just as I'm saying it Jack Woltz is discovering the bloody horse head in bed with him. Laurie screams, as she does every time we watch that scene. Moments later, when she calms down, she asks, "What did you say, Andy?"

"I said, 'Watch out, I've got a feeling there's a severed horse's head in that bed with him.'"

We go back to watching the movie, and I successfully keep my mouth shut until just about the time that Michael goes to visit the don in the hospital. He discovers that the guards have been sent away, though I've always wondered why they never bothered to inform Sonny about that little fact. Michael goes to the phone and dials, at the exact moment the phone in my house rings.

"I'll get it," I say. "It's probably Michael telling me to get some men down to the hospital to guard the don. Can we spare anybody?"

"No," she says. "All our button men are out on the street looking for Solozzo."

I nod and pick up the phone. "Hello?"

"Mr. Carpenter, this is County General Hospital calling."

For an instant it registers as comical that it actually is the hospital, but I just as quickly realize that getting nighttime calls from hospitals is never a good thing.

"What's the matter?" I ask.

"We have a woman here . . . she's been shot."

"Who is she?" I ask worriedly, but glad that Laurie is sitting next to me.

"She hasn't been able to give us her name; she's in surgery. But she was carrying your card in her purse."

I'm not sure how to ask this. "Does she appear to be . . . a lady of the evening?"

"Yes, I believe she does."

"I'll be right there." I hang up and turn to Laurie, who has heard my end of the conversation and is worried herself. "There's a woman in the hospital . . . a gunshot victim. I think it's Sondra."

"Damn," she says, and without another word walks with me out the door and to the car.

• • • • •

LAURIE IS SILENT during the ride to the hospital. I don't know what she's thinking, and I don't feel like I should ask. It's only when we pull into the parking lot that she breaks the silence.

"I shouldn't have left her there," she says. "I should have dragged her out."

"You did all you could."

She shakes her head. "No. I could have pulled her away and shown her something better. Made it easier for her. Instead, I asked her if she wanted to leave. She said no, and I said fine."

"Rick is the villain of this piece. Not you."

Sondra is out of surgery by the time we arrive. We stop in the recovery room to see how she is and to confirm that it is really her. She's still out of it from the anesthesia. The doctor says she took the bullet in the shoulder and has lost a lot of blood, but that eventually she should be okay. A half inch to the left, and she'd be dead.

Drive-by shooting, not baseball, is a game of inches.

A hospital official brings us into his office, then asks us if Sondra has any insurance. Somehow I don't think Rick provides major medical for his employees, so I sign a form taking financial responsibility for the costs. I wonder if they would otherwise throw her out into the street and if they would first disconnect the tubes helping her breathe.

The officers that answered the initial call have since left, but Detective Steve Singer of the Passaic police arrives to talk to us. He and Laurie know and like each other, which is the good news. The bad news is that I once took him apart in a cross-examination, and my guess is every time he shows up at a murder scene he hopes that I'm the victim.

Singer tells us Sondra was shot in a drive-by, but there are no witnesses so far willing to come forward. He asks how we came to know Sondra and how she came to have my card. I tell the story, after which he looks at Laurie, hoping she'll refute what I have to say.

"You know anything about this?" he asks.

Laurie nods. "I was there, Steve."

I see a quick flash of disappointment on his face, then a nod of resignation. He was hoping to at least arrest me for solicitation of prostitution, but he now knows that's not going to happen.

"Okay," he says. "What else can you tell me?"

"She had a pimp, a guy named Rick. He hit her while we were there," I say.

Suddenly, Singer's face brightens. "Wait a minute, I

heard about this," he says to Laurie. "You kicked his ass, right? The guys were talking about it."

"He slipped and fell," she says. "I just neglected to catch him."

He turns to me. "What were you doing while the lady was punching him out? Holding her purse?"

His question confirms my low opinion of his intelligence. He knows nothing; the fact is that Laurie wasn't even carrying a purse that night. It was more of a handbag.

I fire back. "Maybe if you geniuses hadn't let the pimp walk so fast, a woman wouldn't have been shot tonight."

Singer grunts, goes to the phone, and calls in to the precinct. He talks softly for a few moments, holds on for a short while, and then hangs up, a self-satisfied look on his face.

"Rick is still in custody, genius."

This is a little embarrassing, but I recover quickly. "Then he had it done."

Since nothing I say has any credibility with Singer, Laurie jumps in for support. "It's too big of a coincidence to be otherwise, Steve. Rick was humiliated, and he didn't want to come straight at me, so he went after Sondra, knowing I'd blame myself."

Singer seems to think this is sound reasoning, and he leaves to talk to Rick at the jail. "I'm gonna miss his wit," I say to Laurie after he's left. A few moments later the doctor informs us that Sondra is conscious and we can see her.

She's very much weakened; a .38-caliber bullet in the shoulder has a tendency to do that. She also has no idea who shot her. "A car just pulled up real slow, and I saw the window open, and I don't remember anything after that."

"But you think they were aiming for you? Was there anyone else around that could have been the target?" I ask.

She shakes her head sadly. "No. It was just me. Just me."

She is unable to provide any helpful information, and she's soon going to have to answer the same questions from the police, so we let her doze off.

In the car going home, Laurie says, "We have to help her, Andy."

"She's got to want that help," I point out.

She shakes her head. "No. That's what we said the other day. She didn't want it, so we backed off. Like we did our good deed and that's enough. Well, it wasn't enough."

"And a better plan would be . . . ?"

"To help her whether she wants it or not, and let her see if we're right. Then if she feels the same way, we can back off. But we cannot send her back on those streets without trying a hell of a lot harder."

"What does that mean in the real world?"

"It means finding her a job and a place to stay. It means putting her into a position where she can develop some self-respect and dignity."

"Sounds good to me," I say.

• • • • •

I RUSH THROUGH my Monday morning walk with Tara so I can meet Richard Wallace at the prison. He's scheduled to interview Randy Clemens at nine-thirty, and there's no way I'm going to be late.

I arrive early enough to eat breakfast at a nearby restaurant called Donnie's House of Pancakes. I order banana walnut pancakes, which when they are served turn out to be regular, heavy pancakes with bananas and walnuts on top. It makes me feel old, but I can remember a time when the bananas and walnuts would have been *inside* the pancakes.

I decide to share this piece of nostalgia with the waitress, since there are only three other people in the restaurant and she's not busy. "It makes me feel old," I say, "but I can remember a time when the bananas and walnuts would have been *inside* the pancakes."

"Whatever," she says, demonstrating a disregard for cultural history. "You want coffee?"

"Not until after the Olympics," I say.

"Whatever."

I head over to the prison at nine-twenty, carrying the pancakes around like a beach ball in my stomach. I've got a feeling I'm going to be taking them with me wherever I go for a while.

Waiting for me at the gate are Richard Wallace and Pete Stanton. I'm a little surprised to see Pete, since Richard hadn't mentioned bringing him, but I suppose a police presence is called for, especially if Randy is going to implicate someone in the murders.

"Good morning, guys," I say.

They don't return the greeting. "Andy, I tried to reach you, but you had already left."

There is probably a scheduling foul-up; such things are very common in the prison bureaucracy. "Scheduling change?" I ask.

"Andy, Clemens is dead."

It is as if he hit me in the face with a four-thousand-pound medicine ball. "What happened?"

"Somebody slit his throat this morning, outside the mess hall. I'm sorry, Andy."

All I can think of is Randy's daughter, who will never get to know what a great guy he was and how much he loved her. When she's old enough to understand, I'm going to look her up and tell her.

Pete puts his arm on my shoulder and speaks for the first time. "Come on, Andy, the warden is waiting to see us."

They lead me inside, and by the time we get to the warden's office, my sadness is beginning to share space with my certainty that this cannot be a coincidence. Randy has been in this prison for four years, never once having a problem or altercation of any kind, and the day he is going to talk to us about the murders, he is himself killed.

"There was a commotion in the hallway," says the warden. "A fight, some yelling, everybody milling around. Clemens wasn't involved, but it was probably staged so that he could be killed without anyone seeing it happen."

"So more than one person was involved?" I ask.

"Definitely. It was an organized effort."

"Suspects?" Richard asks.

"Plenty of suspects, but no evidence. But I can tell you, if something like this happens in here, it's very likely that Dominic Petrone wanted it to happen."

Dominic Petrone is the head of what passes for the North Jersey mob, an organization that is still functioning quite effectively. He and Randy Clemens are from different worlds. There is no way Dominic had ever heard of Randy, nor had any kind of grudge against him. If he ordered Randy's death, it is because he was told that Randy was about to say something that could hurt him.

It has to come back to Linda Padilla and her alleged mob ties. And if it does, and if the mob is somehow involved in these murders, then my client is actually innocent. Too bad my other client had to die for me to realize it.

I drive back to the office, replaying in my mind the last visit I had with Randy. I remember the wariness in his eyes as he looked around the room, the way something caused him to briefly stop as he was leaving. He knew that what he had to say was dangerous, but he was so anxious to find a way out of the prison that he was taking that chance.

I also think back to the words he used, trying to remember them exactly. He referred to the victims besides "the rich one" as "window dressing." Among the many things I don't know are how Randy came to know this and why the killer needed "window dressing" at all.

Marcus is waiting for me at the office when I get back, sitting stoically as Edna regales him with stories of her latest triumph. She's managed to combine and satisfy her two interests in life, crossword puzzles and finance, by discovering various business publications with financially themed puzzles. Marcus isn't saying anything, which could mean he's interested or not interested or asleep.

In any event, his characteristic muteness is doing nothing to dampen the conversation. Edna peppers her sentences with phrases like "Right?" and "You understand?" and "You know?" and seems to pretend that Marcus is answering, as she nods and continues.

He has returned from Cleveland, having gathered as much information as he could. There wasn't much to learn: Daniel was a widely respected member of the press who had no criminal record whatsoever and no known tendency toward violence. The community, from politicians and business leaders on down, supported him through the ordeal. Counterbalancing that, in addition to the detective's hunch, are some of Margaret's acquaintances, who say that their marriage was troubled and that she was considering leaving him.

Marcus's hunch is the same as that of the Cleveland police: He thinks Daniel may have either killed her or had it done. Like the detective, he can't come close to proving it. It's just that the inheritance, the troubled marriage . . . these are things that arouse Marcus's detective instincts. The presumption of innocence is not a concept that Marcus holds dear.

Laurie and Kevin arrive for a meeting on how we will approach the investigation of Linda Padilla. They are stunned to hear about Randy. Neither knew him, so while they are sympathetic, it's natural that they focus on the impact this might have on our case.

Randy's death enhances the credibility of the information he was going to provide. Kevin and Laurie share my view that there is almost no chance that his murder was a coincidence. He was going to name names, and we can only assume that the owners of those names, be it Petrone or anyone else, took steps to make sure that didn't happen.

I call in Edna to ask her to report on the results of an assignment I had given her, which was to watch as much televised coverage of the Padilla killing as she could find.

There has been a recent tendency, probably since Princess Diana died, for television networks to cover funerals in their entirety. I'm at a loss to know what news value there is in showing people grieving and singing upbeat, gooey songs, but it must generate good ratings. I want to go on record and say that if anyone sings "You Light Up My Life" at my funeral, I will die of embarrassment. Actually, Sam Willis will probably song-talk it.

The plus side of the coverage, at least from our point of view, is that it is easy to get a handle on who were the important people in Padilla's life. These are the people we will talk to, and Edna does a very good job of filling us in.

I give out assignments for each of us to cover. There is simply never enough time to prepare for a trial, and I want us moving quickly and efficiently. The meeting then breaks up, and Laurie stays behind.

"Sondra is doing okay," she says. "But her recovery will take a while."

"How long will she be in the hospital?"

"She can leave in a few days," she says, "but she needs to rest for at least six weeks."

"Where will she do that?"

"My house."

I'm not surprised, but not happy to hear this for selfish reasons. Will Laurie be willing to leave her alone and spend nights at my house? Will she still feel comfortable having me stay over at hers? Is she starting down a path that is going to be filled with frustration?

"Are you sure that's a good idea?" I ask. It's a wimpy, completely ineffective question, unlikely to make her snap her fingers and say, "You know, I don't think it is. Let me tell her to go back on the streets."

She nods. "I do. But this is my thing, Andy. You don't have to be part of it."

I'm glad to hear this, because I don't want to be involved in any way; I've got enough on my plate. "Are you going to get her a real job?" I ask.

"I'm going to try."

"Let me see what I can do," I say, thereby involving myself and crowding my plate a little more.

I catch a break when Vince calls, and I mention I want to see Michael Spinelli, Linda Padilla's campaign manager. It turns out that Vince knows him very well, which is true of pretty much everyone in the Western Hemisphere. It also turns out that Vince doesn't like him, which is true of pretty much everyone, period. But he owes Vince a couple of favors for past press coverage, so Vince offers to set up a meeting ASAP.

In the meantime, I take a ride down to the Tara Foundation to see how things are going and to apologize for not spending more time there helping out. I want to refine the apology, making it short but meaningful, because it's one I'm going to have to deliver many times during the course of the trial.

Willie greets me enthusiastically and updates me on the foundation's progress. "So far this week we placed Joey, Rocky, Ripley, Sugar, Homer, Hank, Carrie, Ivy, Sophie, and Chuck," he says.

We have a veterinarian come in twice a day, and we let her name the dogs for us. She initially got carried away by the chance to display her creativity and named the first three dogs Popcorn, Kernel, and Butter. We've toned her down considerably, and the names are more normal now.

I'm pleased that the dogs Willie mentioned are now safe in their new homes, but guilty that I never even got to meet Homer, Sugar, and Chuck. The only end of this partnership I am holding up is the financial, and that is the least significant.

Willie shows me pictures of the dogs with their new owners. "Man, I am good at this," he says, an assessment with which I agree.

"Yes, you are. You send out the records?" I ask. We give the dogs all their shots and make sure they're spayed or neutered. After someone adopts a dog, we mail them all of those records, since they need them to get a license.

"Not yet."

I look over at Willie's desk, or at least where his desk would be if it weren't completely engulfed in sheets of paper. "Let me take a shot at it," I say, and go over to try to restore order.

It is while I'm trying to find Ripley's rabies certificate that the stroke of genius hits me. "You really can use somebody to come in and help you out," I say, hoping that Sondra isn't afraid of dogs.

"You mean somebody to work with me?" He shakes his head vigorously. "No way. I work alone."

"I'm not talking about working *with* you. I mean working *for* you. You would be the boss."

"I'd be the boss?" Clearly, I've piqued his interest.

I nod. "The total boss. The ruler. The kingpin. The Grand Kahuna. You could tell her what to do and when you want her to do it. Within reason."

"You said 'her,'" he notices. "You got someone in mind?"

"Could be. I know someone who might be perfect. But she won't be available for about six or eight weeks."

"Where'd she work before?" he asks.

"I think she was in the motel field. She's also been in and out of the automotive industry."

It doesn't take much more to sell Willie on the idea, and I leave the foundation looking forward to receiving plaudits from Laurie for dealing so quickly and successfully with her problem.

Sometimes I even amaze myself.

• • • • •

NO MATTER WHO killed Linda Padilla, one of the many secondary effects of the crime was to take away Michael Spinelli's meal ticket. It's a safe bet that Spinelli, as Padilla's campaign manager, was planning to follow her to the governor's mansion and beyond. Her death means it's time for him to come up with a new plan.

Vince has set up my meeting with Spinelli at Padilla campaign headquarters. I'm sure a couple of weeks ago this place was bustling with activity, but as I enter no one asks me or cares who I am. It has become an organization without a reason for being, and dejection surrounds the place like faded wallpaper. The few remaining staffers are quietly packing their things, and I ask one of them where Spinelli might be. He points to an office and returns to what he is doing.

I enter Spinelli's office and introduce myself, which prompts an immediate and unsolicited soliloquy. "I damn well shouldn't be talking to you," he says. "I mean, I know everybody's entitled to a defense, but nobody forced you to represent the son of a bitch. If it was up to me, I wouldn't talk to you. But you know what a pain in the ass Vince can be."

"That's something we can agree on."

"So what do you want?"

"I want to know about Linda Padilla."

"You mean, like, what did she eat for breakfast? Or how fast she could run a mile? You think you could be a little more specific? Because I don't feel like chatting about this forever."

"Okay," I say, "here's how it works. At the end of the day I want to find out who killed Linda Padilla. So I ask questions about her. I can't only ask what's important, because I won't know what's important until after I've asked a hell of a lot more questions. Of course, if you know who killed her, and why, you can blurt it out and save us both a lot of time."

"The police think your client killed her," he says.

I nod. "Yes, they do. I'm working on a different theory. My theory is that he's innocent."

He sighs and sits at his desk. "So where should I start?"

"With your relationship to her," I say.

"I'm a political consultant; I find politicians and try to move them up the ladder. I teach them what to say, how to say it, and who to say it to. But they need to have something special going in, something that's there before I get to them, or they can only go so far. Linda had it, and there was no ceiling for her. None at all."

"Why did she want to go up that ladder? What was in it for her?" I ask.

"The real reason, or the one she would give if your client hadn't killed her and you could ask her yourself?"

The question isn't worthy of a reply, so I don't give him one.

"She would tell you she wanted to help the people on the bottom," he continues. "So that everybody could have a shot at the American dream like she did. She would even have believed it while she was saying it."

"So what was it really? The power? The celebrity?"

"Duhhh . . ." is his mocking reply, letting me know that of course it was the power and celebrity, that it's always the power and celebrity.

"Was she wealthy?" I ask.

He nods. "Loaded. Linda had the first nickel she ever made, and the last couple of years she was making a shit-load of nickels."

I continue asking questions, but he answers mostly in generalities, not providing much insight into who Linda Padilla was. There's a good chance he has no idea, that she never let him get close.

I finally ask about the rumored connections to Dominic Petrone and organized crime, and he's careful and measured in his response. "I never saw them together. Nothing was ever said in front of me."

"But you have reason to believe she knew him?" I ask.

"I don't have reason to do anything."

Finally, probably to get me out of there, he suggests I talk to Padilla's boyfriend, one Alan Corbin. Corbin is a high-powered businessman and had only recently been seen with Padilla in public. According to Spinelli, they were considerably closer than they let on to the press.

"Just don't tell him that I sent you to him," he says.

"Why not?" I ask. The fact is, Corbin was next on my

list to talk to anyway, so Spinelli's naming him is not in any sense a big deal.

"He's not a guy I want pissed at me."

My next stop is Sam Willis's office, to ask him to use his computer expertise to help us on the case. It's a move I make reluctantly because of the death of his assistant. But we need someone, and Sam has often expressed a desire to contribute, so I convince myself it's okay.

I spend about ten minutes repeatedly and obnoxiously telling him to be careful, that if he senses anything unusual or dangerous, he is to stop and call me. There's no reason to think he's in any danger, but I want to make totally sure he's safe. He promises he'll call, more as a way to shut me up than anything else.

"I want you to find out as much information as you can about these people," I say, referring to the victims. I give him the documentation we've accumulated from the police reports and other sources. "I especially want you to look for any connection at all between them. If they ate at the same restaurant, sat in the same section at Mets games, whatever, I want to know about it."

He glances through the documents. "Not much here," he says. "Is there a last name on this one?"

He's talking about Rosalie, whom we and the police know almost nothing about. "She was a street hooker. I'll get her roommate to try and come up with any information she can, but there won't be much. Hold her off for last."

He nods. "Okay. This could take a while."

Sam's ability to hack into computers and come up with information is legendary. It also was once criminal, and I represented him when charges were brought against him for hacking into a large corporation's computer system. He had done it in retaliation for the corporation's mistreatment of one of his clients. I got him acquitted on a technicality and in the process developed a healthy respect for his unique talents.

"If you can't come up with anything, don't worry about it," I say, knowing he will take it as a challenge.

He motions me closer. "Listen, do you want to know a secret? Do you promise not to tell?"

He's doing the Beatles, but I pretend not to notice. "I promise," I say, though he knows I noticed.

"If it's in the computer, and it always is, I can find out anything about anyone."

It's a process that truly amazes me. "How does it all get in there?"

He shrugs. "Companies that people deal with share the information with other companies—that's part of it. But you wouldn't believe how many people sit in their rooms and type their life into their computers." He shakes his head sadly. "All the lonely people . . . where do they all come from?"

My mind, already cluttered, races to find a Beatles reference that I can counter with. Alas, I cannot, so I decide to leave and let Sam get started. "Call me if you come up with anything good. Okay?"

Sam nods. "Okay. And take it easy, Andy. You look tired. Something wrong? Did you have a hard day's night? Been working like a dog?"

Got it. "I don't know," I say, "it must be this case, but suddenly, I'm not half the man I used to be. There's a shadow hanging over me."

He nods. "Let it be. I'm speaking words of wisdom. Let it be."

● ● ● ● ●

ALAN CORBIN DOESN'T want to talk to me.
I suspect this because I've been trying to reach him for a
week with no luck. And that suspicion was strengthened
somewhat yesterday when he accidentally picked up my
call and said, "I ain't fucking talking to you, you little
roach."

Vince knows Corbin, of course, since Corbin is an in-
habitant of this planet, but even he has been unable to
arrange a meeting. I've used Vince to get messages to
him, and one of them was a threat to subpoena him for a
deposition. It was an empty threat, since I'm not legally
empowered to do so, and Corbin's lawyer called me and
told me to back off.

Since backing off is not my forte, I sent another message, again through courier Vince, in an attempt to be
more persuasive. I warned that I was going to go on
Larry King and tell the nation—actually the world, since

CNN is seen everywhere—that Alan Corbin has very strong underworld connections and was in fact Linda Padilla's link to Dominic Petrone.

Vince further conveyed to Alan, although he said Alan was by this time screaming so loud he might not have heard, that the only way I would cancel the *King* interview is if there was a scheduling conflict. For instance, if I were talking to Corbin instead.

After threats of lawsuits for slander and libel, and so much wrangling and negotiating that Vince likened it to the U.N. Security Council, Corbin agreed to see me in his office for fifteen minutes. That is why I am right now in his reception area, with his secretary glaring at me as if I were Andy bin Laden.

I'm finally let in to the great one's office. It's immediately evident that there is a difference between "high-powered businessman" and "tall-powered businessman." Corbin can't be more than five foot five; one of his reasons for dating the much taller Linda Padilla must have been to secure her help in reaching things on high shelves.

"Thanks for seeing me," I say cheerfully.

He looks at his watch. "You're on the clock, asshole. You've got fifteen minutes." He's referring to the agreed-upon length of our interview, and I'm somewhat put off by his attitude.

I look at my own watch. "You're short," I say.

"I told Vince fifteen minutes," he insists.

"I wasn't talking about the time, I was talking about your height," I say. "You're short. I would say . . . five two-ish? Asshole?" It's a tough call whether or not I should be coming back at him like this, but there's no chance I'll get something out of him if he thinks I'm just going to accept his bullshit.

He seems ready to go back at me but then thinks better of it. We're even with the insults, and he wants to get this over with.

"Ask your questions," he says.

"Who might have had reason to kill Linda Padilla?" is my first softball.

"No one that I know. But then again, I never met your client."

"She made a career out of blowing the whistle on people, every one of whom would have a grudge against her. What I want to know are the special ones, the ones who really hated her, who she might have been afraid of."

"Linda wasn't afraid of anything or anybody."

"Tell me about her connections to Dominic Petrone."

He laughs a mocking laugh. "You can't be serious."

"I'm not asking you if they were connected. I already know that from five different sources. What I want to know is the extent of the relationship."

He hesitates, unsure of what I know or how to respond.

"I will ask you these same questions on the stand if I have to," I say.

"Don't threaten me."

"Look," I say, softening my voice and acting conciliatory, "my only interest in this is proving my client is innocent. To do that, I just may have to find out who is guilty, or at least provide the jury with a reasonable alternative. I only care about Petrone if I think there's a chance he had Padilla killed. If there's nothing there, I don't bring in Petrone and I don't bring in you."

He thinks for a moment; the idea of avoiding future involvement appeals to him. "She knew Petrone," he says.

"She met him at business dinners, political gatherings, that kind of thing."

Those kinds of meetings are quite conceivable. Petrone has the appearance and manner of a sophisticated businessman, and he has relationships with important people from the legitimate side of the tracks.

Nevertheless, I'm skeptical. "You make them sound like casual acquaintances. I know it was much more than that."

He nods. "He liked her, thought she was smart and had guts. He sort of took her under his wing. And she liked him, but she knew it would look bad for her politically. So she kept him at arm's length."

"Did that piss him off?"

He stares hard at me. "Dominic Petrone would never have done anything to hurt Linda Padilla. No way. No how."

"Is that right?" I ask skeptically.

He nods. "That's very right. He wouldn't harm a hair on her head. But you? He'd break you like a twig and bury the pieces under Giants Stadium."

Oh.

• • • • •

TRIALS DO NOT creep up on a lawyer. Birthdays and holidays creep up. The start of the baseball season creeps up. Trials steamroll; one minute it seems like you have plenty of time to prepare, and the next the bailiff is asking you to rise.

The bailiff will be asking us to rise in the case of *New Jersey v. Cummings* the day after tomorrow. We're not ready, not even close. But it's not the timing. Our real problem is, we haven't made progress refuting the evidence, evidence that seems to increase daily.

Vince has asked me to meet him at Charlie's tonight for a final pretrial discussion. It's one I'm dreading, almost as much as I'm dreading the trial itself.

I'd feel better if Laurie were able to join us, but she's with Sondra tonight. They're out to dinner, a sort of celebration that Sondra has finally recovered from her injuries. Tomorrow I'm bringing her down to the foundation to meet Willie, who has been asking me every day for weeks when his devoted underling is arriving.

Vince has grown increasingly subdued and depressed over the last few weeks and appears the same when he arrives tonight. We order beers, and I wait for the questions that I know are coming.

He throws me a curve. "I want to announce that Daniel is my son," he says. "I don't want it to be a secret anymore."

Vince has to this point not come forward with his relationship to Daniel. It would be a brave thing to do, since it would expose Vince to the same kind of public scorn and hatred as the rest of us in Daniel's camp. It is also a piece of news that can only impact Vince's career and reputation negatively.

"That's your call, Vince."

He nods. "But I want to make sure it doesn't hurt his chances in any way."

"In the trial? I don't see why it would. It might even be a slight positive, maybe make him a little more human and worthy of support. But the impact on the trial wouldn't be big enough either way for you to factor it in."

"Then I'm going to do it," he says.

His decision made, I change the subject. "Vince, how well did you know Daniel's wife?"

"Margaret? I knew her . . . we weren't close or anything. We went out to dinner a bunch of times."

"When you visited, did you stay at their house?"

"Nah, I stayed at a hotel. It was easier that way."

"Did you like her? How were they together?"

I expect a quick "Yes" and "Great," but that's not what I get. Vince takes a while to think about it, measuring his answer. "She was always nice to me," he says, "and I never saw them arguing or anything . . ."

His answer invites a "but . . . ," so that's what I give him. "But . . ."

"There is a poem," he says, "by Edwin Robinson. It's called 'Richard Corey.'"

I nod. I'm vaguely familiar with the poem, mainly because Simon and Garfunkel had a song that ripped it off. The fact that Vince is talking about it is rather stunning. Until now I thought his intellectual awareness extended about as far as "knock, knock" jokes.

He continues. "It's about this really wealthy guy, who everybody in the town thinks has the greatest life in the world. At the end of the poem, they're all shocked 'cause the guy goes home one night and puts a bullet in his head."

"So Daniel and Margaret seemed to have a great life, but you didn't think it was real?"

He nods. "Something like that. She had all this money, and they lived in a great house and had fancy cars and stuff, but there was something missing . . . something a little off. I couldn't place it then . . . I can't even place it now . . . but I felt it."

Vince seems like he's getting upset, so I try to lighten the moment. "So now I've learned that not only did you once have sex, but you've also read a poem. What a life you've lived."

My effort at lightening lands with a heavy thud. "Andy, you've been on this for a while now. You think Daniel could have done this? Killed those people? Killed Margaret?"

It's the first time I've seen him exhibit any doubt, though I've always suspected it had to be there. It's ironic because I've become more and more willing to believe that Daniel is innocent. "I don't know anything about Margaret, Vince. I can't really give an opinion on that. These killings here, though, they don't fit with Daniel. But I'm not going to lie to you . . . I'm not sure, and I definitely could be wrong."

"Thanks," he says, and then without another word just gets up and walks out of the place.

This is not at all the Vince I know. Except for the part where he didn't pay the check.

I pick Sondra up first thing in the morning for the drive over to the foundation. The transformation in her has been remarkable. It's not just the conservative clothing Laurie has gotten for her; it's also a change in attitude. Her reluctance to go after this new life has gradually faded, if not to eagerness, then a willingness to give it a shot. Laurie has performed miracles with her.

I'm a little nervous about Sondra and Willie meeting. He could come on with a heavy-handed "me boss, you slave" routine, which might cause her to bail out. On her part, she could decide that, even though she claims to like dogs, feeding them, cleaning their cages, and doing menial paperwork don't constitute an upward career move.

There is also the potential for a natural clash of personalities. Both are strong-willed and independent, used to taking care of themselves and only themselves. The idea of a close working relationship might be culturally repugnant to either or both of them.

Sondra and I enter the foundation building. Willie is nowhere to be seen, so I tell Sondra to wait as I look for him. He turns out to be in the back, playing with one of the dogs that has kennel cough, a minor ailment but one that is contagious. Dogs that have it must be quarantined for seven days.

"Your assistant is here, Willie."

He jumps up enthusiastically. "All right! There's a lot to be done around here, man. Let me get my list."

He hasn't met Sondra yet, but he's actually written down a list of tasks for her to do. "Hold off on the list, Willie. And go easy on her at the beginning, okay? Your personality can take a few decades to get used to."

He doesn't respond; I don't think he's heard me. He's too busy rushing to meet his devoted servant.

Willie gets out there before I do, preventing me from making the formal introduction. The first thing I hear is Willie's voice. "Sondra!"

"Willie! I can't believe it!" she yells, not concealing her delight.

By the time I get in the room, they are hugging each other and laughing, and Willie is whirling her around. This introduction has gone somewhat better than I expected.

"Let me guess," I say. "You two know each other." My hope is that their relationship did not begin with Willie as a customer of hers.

"For a long damn time, man," Willie says. Then, to Sondra, "How long has it been?"

"Too damn long," she says.

I'm finally able to ascertain that "damn long" takes them back to high school. They actually dated in their junior year and shared many of the same friends.

"What you been doing?" Willie asks as I cringe.

"Hooking," says Sondra, and Willie nods, as if she had just said, "Marketing."

"And writin' letters," says Willie. "I really appreciated that. I should have called you when I got out."

"That's okay," Sondra says. "You were busy."

Willie, seeing I'm puzzled by the conversation, explains that Sondra wrote to him in prison, among other things telling him to hang in there, and that she knew he could never have committed such a crime.

I can't remember when anything I've planned has gone as smoothly as this meeting. Willie starts showing Sondra around the place, so I leave, but there is no way they notice.

On the way out, I hear Willie ask Sondra, "You want a cup of coffee? We got every kind there is."

• • • • •

"ROT IN HELL, you son of a bitch." That's the spray-painted message on my front curb as I take Tara out for her morning walk. It was done sometime during the night, no doubt timed to provide an inauspicious start for me on this, the first day of the trial.

It's strangely unintimidating, maybe because the perpetrator felt he needed the cover of darkness, but more likely because of what has gone on these last few weeks. I have received over twenty death threats and at least a hundred hate messages, and their impact has lessened even as their anger and level of threat seemed to increase. Kevin and Laurie have both suggested my using Marcus as a bodyguard, but I've resisted doing so. Why, I'm not sure. It must be a guy thing.

The morning paper contains a piece written by Vince revealing that Daniel is his son. It is thoughtful, intelligent, and poignant and therefore will certainly not make a dent in the public consciousness. The angry voices out there are simply too loud for anything to be heard over them.

The trip to the courthouse is a further unnecessary tip-off on what is to come. It seems as if every person in New Jersey has shown up to either demonstrate or watch the others do so. The demonstrators seem to be peaceful, probably because they do not represent opposing points of view. Everybody has branded Daniel a killer, and his death will be the only acceptable outcome.

I'm able to reach the courtroom only because I have a special pass that lets my car through the barricades. Our defense team was provided with only two such passes, and Kevin is picking Laurie up on the way in.

Today is jury selection, and when I arrive, I see that enough prospective jurors have put down their anti-Daniel protest signs to fill the courtroom. Within a few minutes, everybody is present and in their seats. Daniel is brought in, and voir dire begins.

Every single one of the one hundred and eight prospective jurors admits to knowing about this case, but ninety-nine of them claim they can be open-minded in deciding it. It is my task to determine, through gentle probing of their attitudes and experience, the few of them that might be telling the truth.

Tucker, for his part, has a different challenge. Since this is a death penalty case, he wants to make absolutely sure there are no jurors who are opposed to capital punishment. Tucker would view life imprisonment for Daniel as a defeat; lethal injection as a modest victory; torture and public beheading as a triumph. I don't think the chance of acquittal has even entered his mind.

Considering the circumstances, the jury that we come

up with isn't half-bad. Kevin thinks we did great, and Daniel shares his enthusiasm. Even though Daniel reads the newspapers each day, and even though I've always been straight with him about our chances, I don't think he has a clue as to how dim those chances are.

The preparation necessary in the days just before trial is incredibly intense, and we've been working fourteen-hour days. But with opening statements tomorrow, I observe my superstitious ritual of taking the night off from work.

I usually spend the pretrial evening quietly, with Tara, but this time I've amended it to include Laurie. I ask that we not talk about the trial, and she happily agrees. It helps me clear my mind and ready myself for the job ahead.

Laurie makes dinner, and afterward she suggests that we go to the den to play some gin. I think she does so as a way to boost my self-confidence, since she is the worst gin player that has ever lived. She speculates to the point that she takes cards with no regard to whether or not she needs them; I think she just goes by whether she likes the color or the pictures. I have always been an outstanding gin player, memorizing every card played and never taking an unnecessary chance.

We play five racks, and she wins only four.

With that confidence boost behind me, I take Tara for our walk. It is a time when I can think of the job ahead of me, especially the points I want to make in my opening argument. Most important, I must make myself remember to have fun.

There is a scene in the movie *Dave* where Kevin Kline, impersonating the president, is about to confront Congress at a personally perilous time. He sees that his adviser looks stricken with worry, and he stops to tell the man to "enjoy the moment." That's what I must do to be effective in trial. It is a game to me, and I am at my best when I am enjoying that game and playing it loosely and confidently.

As Tara and I are heading back, a car drives down the street toward us. Suddenly, there is a crashing noise, and I see that a liquor bottle, obviously thrown from the car, has landed less than a foot from Tara's head. "You're going down, asshole!" is the yell that comes from the idiot in the passenger seat as the car roars away.

I reach down and pet Tara everywhere, making sure she hasn't been cut by the shattered glass. She seems okay, but shaken by the scare, as I am.

So far I'm not having much fun.

• • • • •

"NOT TOO MANY weeks ago, we were all afraid" is the way Tucker begins his opening argument. "People were dying, our neighbors were being mutilated and murdered. We worried for our wives, for our mothers and grandmothers, for our daughters. Because there was a monster out there targeting women, unsuspecting women who were going about their lives, until one day they didn't have those lives anymore."

Tucker is very well aware of the public sentiment regarding this case, since to be unaware would have required spending the last few months on the planet Comatose. He wants to put the jury in the frame of mind where not convicting Daniel would be threatening the safety of their friends and relatives.

"The police have done an extraordinary job investigating this case. They have gathered facts, not theories or suppositions. They have discovered items in Daniel

Cummings's possession that absolutely prove he murdered these people. As a prosecutor, I am grateful for that. As a member of this community, I am very grateful for that. They've done the hard work; my job is the easy one. I merely have to lay out those facts for you, so you can make your own decision.

"This defendant taunted you, and taunted the police, even as he killed. Mr. Cummings pretended to be the one person that the murderer contacted, the one person that he trusted to speak to the world on his behalf. That is how he stayed in the spotlight, even as he lurked and slaughtered in the shadows.

"The judge will guide you throughout this trial. One of the things he will tell you, which I will also tell you now, is that the state does not have to prove motive. I can only guess as to why Daniel Cummings went on this murdering spree. The true answer lies somewhere in the dark recesses of his mind.

"But not only don't I have to prove what his motive was, I don't really care. Because it simply doesn't matter; what's done is done, and it can never be set right. It may sound harsh, but this trial is not about compassion, it's not about understanding, and it's not about rehabilitation. This trial is about protection. It's about you, as representatives of this community, saying something very simple."

He turns and points at Daniel. "It's about saying that you, Daniel Cummings, are finished murdering. Now it's your turn to be afraid."

He turns back to the jury. "Thank you for listening."

Tucker has done a masterful job; even I gagged only once or twice. There is no way I can effectively counter it, not at this stage. All I can do is make our presence felt, by making it clear to the jury that we are not going to roll over and die.

I stand. "Ladies and gentlemen of the jury, that was a beautiful speech, wasn't it? I don't know about you, but I was hanging on Mr. Zachry's every word. Of course, my reason for listening so intently was a bit different than yours. I was waiting to hear something that was true. I'm still waiting.

"Mr. Zachry did not offer you the specific facts of the case, so I won't respond to them. He'll have plenty of time to present his side, and so will I. Of course, he said that Daniel Cummings was a murderer, and he is simply wrong about that. But that argument also is for a later date.

"One thing Mr. Zachry did say was that certain incriminating items were found, not on Mr. Cummings personally, but in his car and apartment. This he says constitutes possession, and possession he considers evidence of guilt."

I reach back with my hands and place them behind my hips, then look puzzled. Not feeling my wallet, I start to pat my right back pocket. "Excuse me . . . I seem to have misplaced my wallet."

I go back to the defense table, quickly looking through my personal papers and briefcase. I glance at Kevin, who holds up his hands in a gesture indicating that he has no idea where the wallet could be.

I then walk over behind the prosecution table, look around for a moment, and reach under Tucker's chair. There, where I taped it to the leg, is my wallet. I rip it off the leg of the chair, hold it aloft, and feign astonishment. "Mr. Zachry, how could you?" Then, "Bailiff, arrest this man!"

The jury, not exactly the best and brightest, finally understands and roars with laughter. Tucker goes ballistic, screaming his objections. Calvin, though I think he's secretly amused, comes down hard on me, telling me in no uncertain terms that I am not going to turn his courtroom into a circus. Business as usual.

I resume my opening as if nothing happened. "What disturbed me the most about what Mr. Zachry had to say was his characterization of you as society's protectors. You could read every lawbook ever written, and sometimes I feel like I have, and never find that. Not anywhere. Not once. You are the trier of fact. You decide who is guilty and who isn't. That's all. If the result of that decision is that society is protected, that's great. But your role is simply to make the correct decision about guilt or innocence. Believe me, that's enough to have on your plate.

"Wherever we go, whatever we do, we bring the person that we are with us. None of us has been dropped from another planet, with no life history and all empty pages. We act reasonably consistent with our past actions.

"Yet Mr. Zachry would have you believe that Mr. Cummings, with no criminal history, acted horribly criminal. With no violent history, acted horribly violent. With obvious intelligence, acted horribly stupid." I shake my head. "I'm sorry, but it doesn't fly. He's asking you to make sense out of something that makes no sense at all.

"Lastly, I want to talk to you about something that must be on your minds. Since Mr. Cummings's arrest, these horrible murders have stopped. You may be thinking that this fact in and of itself is evidence of his guilt. It is not.

"Daniel Cummings is not here today by chance. His

presence as the defendant was planned and perfectly orchestrated by the actual killer. For that person to have committed additional crimes while Mr. Cummings was in custody would have been to defeat his own plan. It would have been foolish for the killer to elaborately frame Mr. Cummings and then commit an act that would prove his innocence.

"Daniel Cummings has hurt no one. And you protect no one by taking his life away.

"Thank you."

I go back to the defense table, satisfied that I made the points I wanted to make. Kevin nods his approval and Daniel looks pleased, while trying to maintain the impassive exterior that I instructed him to maintain. I notice him making eye contact with a group of seven people, all from Cleveland, who have made the trek here to show support. Two of them are giving him the thumbs-up, which I will instruct them never to do again.

What they and Daniel don't seem to realize is that this was easy, and these were just words. Starting tomorrow, we have to deal with the evidence and the facts.

There is no such thing as a normal workday during a murder trial. You work as hard as you can until the hours run out, and then you start again the next day. Court lets out at four, and my standard procedure is to convene a meeting of the team at my house at five-thirty. We order in dinner and spend the night preparing for the next day's witnesses, as well as looking at the "big picture."

I get home and walk Tara, then rush back to order dinner. I want to make sure I do the ordering rather than Laurie, since if left in her hands, Kevin and I will be stuck eating healthful food all night.

Preparation for tomorrow's court day goes relatively

quickly, as Tucker will be putting on mostly foundation witnesses, slowly building his case. It gives us time to think about our own defense, pathetic though it currently is.

We have been totally unable to make any connection between the victims, and I think it's safe to say that there is none. Linda Padilla remains our focus; Sam has not found any significant information, financial or otherwise, on the other victims. We have two possible theories, equally unlikely and difficult to prove. One is that Padilla was the main target and the others were killed to obscure that fact. The other is that all the victims were chosen randomly, by a killer whose only goal was to frame Daniel.

Kevin goes over the list of people and companies that Padilla caused varying degrees of trouble for with her whistle-blowing. Unfortunately for us, the very prominence of her "victims" works against us. Corporate criminals can be as low as their less upscale brethren, but it's hard to picture most of them strangling women and cutting off their hands.

Nevertheless, our situation is bleak enough that we have to pursue everything. Laurie and Kevin divvy up the list to check them out, putting some aside for Marcus as well. Complicating matters is that many of them are spread out around the country; Padilla by no means limited herself to local wrongdoers.

Particularly annoying, and reflective of our lack of cohesion, is the fact that one of the companies is in Cleveland. Had I known, I could have had Marcus check it out while he was there. The subject is an enormous corporation called Castle Industries, named after its founder, Walter Castle. It was found polluting the water in a Cleveland suburb, and a leukemia cluster emerged.

Padilla's actions cost the company a hundred million dollars, more than my fortune but probably not that big a deal to Walter Castle. And somehow I don't see a sixty-year-old billionaire running around cutting off naked women's hands in protest.

There are a few other entities that seem slightly more credible as potential revenge-seekers. I'm just guessing, of course, but my first choice would be a clothing company called Lancer. Padilla revealed them operating sweatshops, which is a major public relations negative if you do it in a place like Thailand. The problem is that they did it in Alabama, and Padilla caught them in the act. It devastated them; they were a quarter-of-a-billion-dollar company one day, bankrupt the next. The owner of the company, one Rudolph Faulk, was particularly embittered, claiming that Padilla set him up.

Kevin and Laurie have their own personal favorites. We discuss them for a while, but I can't say that I'm remotely optimistic we're going to turn up a serial killer in their midst. If one of these people wanted Padilla dead, they might kill her, but would likely not preface their actions with murders of random, innocent women.

What we have in our favor is that we don't have to prove anyone's guilt. What we have to do is come up with a credible alternative killer for the jury to consider, a daunting enough task in itself.

Kevin is about to leave when the phone rings. I answer it, an act I regret immediately, since it's Marcus calling. It's impossible for me to understand a word that he says over the phone; I find myself yearning for subtitles on the bottom of the screen.

I put Laurie on the phone, and she seems to have no

problem deciphering his words. She even takes notes, and after a minute or so hangs up.

"Marcus wants you to meet him at this address," she says.

I look at what she's written; the location is a particularly run-down industrial area just north of Paterson. "Did he say why?" I ask.

"No, but if Marcus made the call, you can be sure he thinks it's important."

"I'll go with you," Kevin says.

I offer a simultaneous sigh and nod; I'm not pleased to be spending the next hour or so with Marcus when I could have been in bed with Laurie. "Are you going?" I ask her.

"No, he said I couldn't. Said it was okay if Kevin went, but that I definitely should stay here."

"That make any sense to anybody on this planet?" I ask.

Kevin shrugs. "Probably to Marcus."

●　●　●　●　●

KEVIN IS EVEN LESS pleased than I am when we arrive at the location Marcus has given us. It's on Bergen Street near the river, an old abandoned junkyard that the faded sign indicates was once aptly called "Paterson Waste Material." Two rats scurry away as we open the door; they're probably ashamed to be caught living here.

"This place is awful," understates Kevin.

Through the darkness I see a faint light coming from under a door, so I point it out to Kevin, and we walk toward it. I call out, "Marcus?"

"Yunh," is the return grunt that I get, and since it seems to be coming from behind the same door, I open it.

The room is surprisingly bright, causing me to adjust my eyes so that I can see. Once I'm able to see, I regret making the adjustment.

Except for some strewn garbage, some of which seems

to be smoldering in the far corner, the only objects in the room are a wooden table and chair. On the otherwise empty tabletop is a knife, about the size you would expect Crocodile Dundee to carry. Its point is sticking into the table, and the handle of the knife is pointing straight upward.

Marcus stands near the table, and another man, whom I don't recognize, sits in the chair. The man is maybe forty-five years old, five ten, a hundred sixty pounds, balding slightly, and naked.

"He's naked," says Kevin.

"You don't miss a thing," I say. The situation is surreal, and made more so by my realization that Marcus was demonstrating a prudish streak by telling Laurie not to come down here. He didn't want to embarrass her or himself by having her see this naked guy. The naked guy, for his part, doesn't seem embarrassed at all. His dominant facial expression is fear, with perhaps a little anger thrown in.

"Uhhh . . . Marcus. Who is this guy and why is he naked?"

"Jimmy," Marcus says, then points to the corner. "I burned his clothes."

The mystery of the smoldering garbage has been solved; now we're getting somewhere. "Why exactly are we here to meet Jimmy?" I ask.

Marcus doesn't answer me directly, instead issuing instructions to Jimmy. "Tell him."

"Come on, man," moans Jimmy. "I told you what can happen if I . . ."

Marcus just looks at him, then looks at the knife. Jimmy looks at Marcus, then at the knife. Kevin and I look at each other, then at the floor. I'm sure I've had more uncomfortable moments, but it would take a while to think of one.

"I was in the prison when they killed your friend," Jimmy says, no doubt referring to Randy Clemens and completely getting my attention. "I was one of the guys arguing in the hall, to get the guards looking at us. But I didn't kill him; I didn't even know what they were doing until after it was over."

"Why did they do it?"

He summons up the dignity to laugh a short, derisive laugh at my expense. "What do you think? He stole their crayons?" He shakes his head at the stupidity of my question.

Marcus takes a step toward Jimmy, which serves as a dignity-remover. Jimmy continues. "To shut him up. He overheard some things, and he wasn't smart enough to keep quiet about it. When he called you, they put him away."

"What did he overhear?"

Jimmy shakes his head. "I don't know, but it had something to do with those murders."

"Was Dominic Petrone involved?"

Jimmy flinches noticeably, then seems to pause, as if considering his position. The survival rate for people who squeal on Dominic Petrone isn't too high. On the other hand, Jimmy is naked in a room with Marcus and a knife. Talk about your "six of one, half a dozen of the other."

He probably makes the decision that Marcus and the knife represent a more immediate threat, so he starts talking again. "I don't know for sure, but it's a pretty good bet. The guy who arranged the prison hit was Tommy Lassiter, but I doubt he'd be doing it without Petrone setting it up."

"Who is Tommy Lassiter?"

Jimmy almost does a double take at my question, then looks over at Marcus. "Come on, man . . ." is his way of telling Marcus he shouldn't have to explain this to me, an obvious idiot.

"Tell him," Marcus says.

Jimmy does as he is told. "Lassiter is a button man, the best there is. He's a psycho, but if Lassiter wants you dead, you are dead. That's it."

"Does he work for Petrone?" I ask.

"Among others. He works for money. Sometimes it's Petrone puttin' up the money, sometimes it's someone else. This time, I don't know for sure . . . I swear. But Petrone is the best bet."

There isn't much more for us to get out of Jimmy, and the rest of the conversation centers around him getting us to collectively swear that we won't reveal he talked to us. I agree and ask him to keep the secret as well, but even Marcus moans at the request. If Jimmy were to tell anyone he was here, he would effectively be committing suicide.

I take Kevin back to my house so he can get his car. On the way there, he says, "What do you think Marcus would have done?"

"You mean if Jimmy didn't talk?" I ask.

"Yes."

"I think he would have done whatever he had to. I think if they played a game of chicken a thousand times, Marcus would win every time."

This answer doesn't please Kevin very much. Kevin would prefer that trials and investigations play out the way they were drawn up in law school. The problem is, I don't believe Marcus went to law school.

"But Marcus is on our side? He's one of the good guys?" Kevin asks.

I shake my head. "We don't find out who the good guys are until the jury tells us."

"I think by then it's too late," he says. "Way too late."

• • • • •

THE FIRST WITNESS Tucker calls is Officer Gary Hobart, the first policeman to arrive at the site of the Padilla murder. Usually, the initial patrolman is not a significant witness, as his function is mainly to secure the scene and wait for the detectives. In this case, Hobart is far more important because Daniel was on the scene when he got there.

"What was the defendant doing when you arrived?" Tucker asks.

"He was lying down on the stairs leading up to the pavilion. About two steps from the top."

"Was he conscious?"

"Yes," says Hobart. "He spoke to me."

"What did he say?"

"That the killer called him . . . told him to come to the park."

"Did he say anything about a murder that might have taken place there?" Tucker asks.

"No. He said he did not know what might be in the pavilion, that he was attacked on the steps. He thought he had lost consciousness."

Hobart goes on to testify how he entered the pavilion, saw Linda Padilla's body, and immediately secured the scene. He questioned Daniel briefly, before the detectives arrived and took over.

Tucker turns the witness over to me. There's not much for me to go after, but I want to at least make our presence felt to the jury.

"Officer Hobart, how did you come to be in the park that night?" I ask.

"The dispatcher sent me there. They received a 911 call."

"Who made that call? If you know."

"I don't believe the caller gave his name."

"Was the caller there when you arrived?" I ask.

"No."

"But this anonymous caller was on the scene that night? And saw what happened?"

He shrugs. "I really don't know what they saw, or if they even saw anything."

I nod. "Right. Maybe they didn't see anything. Maybe they called 911 to report that nothing was happening at the pavilion in the park at one o'clock in the morning. And maybe your dispatcher sent you out to confirm that nothing was happening. Is that how you figure it?"

Tucker objects that I'm being argumentative, and Calvin sustains. Hobart switches tactics and talks about the vagrants in the park and how they would not want to give their names, for fear of getting involved. I've made my point, that there was someone else on the scene, so I move on. I bring out the fact that Hobart saw the wound on Daniel's head and that there was significant bleeding.

"What is your responsibility once the detectives arrive?" I ask.

"To make sure the area remains secure," he says.

"Do you brief the detectives on what you've learned at the scene?"

He nods. "Yes. Absolutely."

"And you offer your impressions as well? If you think they are significant?"

"Yes."

"You're trained in these types of things?"

"Well . . . sure."

"And whatever you tell them, you later put in a report?" I ask.

"Yes."

I get a copy from Kevin, then hand it to Hobart and get him to confirm that it is in fact the report he submitted. "Please show me where in the report you voiced suspicions about Mr. Cummings."

"There's nothing like that in there."

"So everything seemed normal to you? You didn't suspect Mr. Cummings hit himself in the head?" I ask.

"No . . . not really. But I had other things to pay attention to."

"And you left Mr. Cummings alone while you looked around?" I ask, the clear implication being that if he suspected Daniel of anything, he wouldn't have left him unguarded.

"Yes."

"No further questions." I haven't done that much with Hobart, but that's okay, since there was little damage to repair. That will come later, when Tucker trots out his big guns. We had better be ready.

I head back to the office after the court day ends. Our team meeting isn't until six at my house, and I've agreed to meet with some of Daniel's supporters from Cleveland. They asked for twenty minutes of my time, but I'm hoping to wrap it up in ten.

When I arrive at the office, three of the seven people in the courtroom today are already there waiting for me. Edna has one of them engaged in a conversation about investments and finance. She introduces him as Eliot Kendall, who I know from reputation is the son of Byron Kendall, founder and chairman of Kendall Industries, an enormous trucking company headquartered in Cleveland. As the president of the company and future heir, Eliot must be worth hundreds of millions of dollars, yet he patiently listens as Edna tries to get him to transfer his investments to her cousin Fred.

The other two visitors are Lenny Morris, a fellow reporter of Daniel's at the Cleveland newspaper, and Janice Margolin, the director of a local Cleveland charity which Daniel actively supported.

Eliot Kendall is no more than thirty, and though Lenny and Janice are at least twenty-five years his senior, Eliot seems the natural spokesman for the trio. He explains that the others in court today had to go back to Cleveland, but that the three of them "are here for the duration."

"So how can I help you?" I ask, trying to move this along.

Eliot smiles. "That's what we're here to ask you. We're here to support Daniel, which means we will support you in any way we can."

"Thank you," I say. "But I think we're covered."

"I'm sure you are. But if at any point you need some extra pairs of hands, no job is too small." The others nod enthusiastically in agreement. "And while I doubt money is an issue for Daniel, if it becomes one, I'm available to help. You tell us your problems, we'll help solve them."

This is an impressive display of support from some pretty substantial people. It pleases me that my client is so well liked and respected by them. "Thank you, I'll keep that in mind," I say, keeping things as bland as I can. Despite their offer to hear our "problems," I'm not going to get into any specifics of the case with these people.

"There's also something you should know," Eliot says. "We've hired a private investigator to look into things. Not to get in your way . . . just a fresh pair of professional eyes. If we uncover anything helpful, it's yours to use as you see fit."

My initial reaction to this news is negative; it feels like an invasion of my turf and a potential annoyance. On the other hand, maybe it will turn up something. Besides, they aren't asking for my approval.

"As long as your investigators do not claim to be representing the defense."

Eliot nods agreeably. "Absolutely. No problem."

"Daniel is lucky to have such good friends," I say.

Eliot smiles a slightly condescending smile. "Let me tell you a brief story, Mr. Carpenter. My younger sister ran away from home when she was fourteen . . . left a note saying she couldn't deal with her problems anymore. My family kept things very quiet, foolishly not wanting to confront the embarrassment. Finally, my father decided that the media could help spread the word, perhaps help find her. We didn't know Daniel, but we knew of his reputation, so we gave him the story."

I search my mind for a memory of this story but can't come up with one. "Did you find her?"

His shake of the head is a sad one, as the remembered pain seems to hit him head-on. "No, but not for lack of effort on Daniel's part. He made finding her his personal crusade, but that's not why I remain grateful to this day. He treated the story, my sister, and our family with incredible compassion and sensitivity. No sensationalism, no grandstanding . . . just outstanding reporting by an outstanding human being. He's been my friend ever since."

It seems a sincere tribute and is echoed by less dramatic stories from Janice and Lenny. I finally extricate myself from the meeting by promising to keep in touch should I need their help in any way. What I don't tell them is that their stories would qualify them as excellent character witnesses for the penalty phase of the trial. That will only come if we lose the case and are trying to avoid a death sentence.

I'm finally able to get them out the door, and I head for the meeting at my house. Laurie and Kevin are there when I arrive, and I can tell from the pained expression on Kevin's face that Laurie's already ordered dinner. Since we are real men who cannot survive on tofu and veggie burgers, I break out the potato chips and pretzels, and Kevin dives for them like they are life preservers floating in the ocean.

My overriding concern with this case is that it is going along too predictably, too comfortably, and that we are gliding down the path to defeat. "I've got to shake things up," I say.

Kevin nods; he knows what I'm getting at and agrees. Kevin is much more conservative than I am, so if he believes that I need to shake things up, I probably should have done so already.

"What do you mean?" Laurie asks.

"It's like when you blitz in football," I say, and Laurie moans. "Sometimes a defense is overmatched, and it's not the best strategy, but a blitz rattles the offense's cage and puts a lot of pressure on. Hopefully, something good will come from that pressure. Either way, it's better than just sitting back and letting Tucker drive down the field."

"Exactly," Kevin says.

"I've got an idea," Laurie says. "Can we try and get through one five-minute period without you making a football reference? Can we try and intellectually elevate things a bit?"

I look at Kevin, who seems agreeable. "Sure," I say. "Think of it in ballet terms. If everybody comes out in tutus, the audience just sits there. It's no big deal, 'cause that's what they expect. But dress the dancers in leather garter belts and Mickey Mouse ears, and the audience is on their toes, wondering what the hell is going on. It shakes them up."

Kevin nods. "Or in opera, if you start off with the fat lady singing, the audience doesn't know what to think. Is it over? The fat lady has already sung, right?"

Laurie smiles. "See? Isn't that better? We're on a much higher plane now."

We adjourn early, partly because I have to think things through on my own and partly so Kevin and I can avoid whatever it is Laurie has planned for dessert. I'm not sure my stomach could handle tofu jubilee or broccoli brûlée.

Willie comes over, bringing with him some paperwork that we have received from the city Animal Services department. He also brings along Sondra—in fact, they are holding hands. Since there is no automobile traffic in my living room, I have to assume he's not helping her cross the street and that their relationship has quickly graduated from employer-employee.

Further circumstantial evidence of their romantic involvement is the fact that she is wearing an expensive watch and very expensive locket, with a large blue stone that I believe is alexandrite. I'm far from an expert on jewelry, but I once represented a client accused of stealing some uncut alexandrites, and I know how valuable they are.

Sondra has never worn the watch or locket the other times I've seen her. Since we're not paying that much in salary for her work at the foundation, Willie has apparently taken some of his coffee earnings and bought her the jewelry.

"How's the trial going?" Sondra asks.

I shrug. "Okay. Could be better."

"You gonna win?"

Willie interrupts. "Of course, he's gonna win. I'm standing here, aren't I? This guy doesn't lose."

Sondra doesn't look that pleased with Willie's assessment. She and I have talked about this; she wishes me the best, but if Daniel is responsible for killing Rosalie, she wants him strapped to a table with a needle in his arm.

Willie and Sondra invite Laurie and me out with them; they're going dancing at a club. The idea has absolutely no appeal to me, but I appreciate the invitation, so I look at my watch for an excuse. "It's almost nine-thirty," I say. "I need to get some sleep."

Willie nods. "So grab a couple of hours. We're not going out until midnight."

I express my amazement at this, and Willie and Sondra

proceed to tell me about this other world that exists out there, a world where people go out and have what they consider fun while I am in bed doing what I consider sleeping. These people seem to exist on another plane, using the resources of our planet while "normal" people like Laurie and me are tucked away with no need for them. Willie and Sondra are in the unique position of straddling both worlds, and I'm sure there is much to learn from them. Just not tonight, because I'm tired.

• • • • •

D<small>ONALD</small> P<small>RESCOTT</small> SPENDS all day, every day, looking at fibers. He does this for the New Jersey State Police, and if you possess both a desire to be a cop and a self-preservation instinct, it's a good job to have. There is even less chance that Prescott will get shot at than the guy who draws the chalk outlines around bodies.

Tucker has called Prescott to testify to his analysis of the fibers on the scarf used to strangle Linda Padilla, which was found with her severed hands in the trunk of Daniel's car. The police have even located a sales receipt from a store which shows that Daniel bought that exact scarf, or one just like it.

Tucker holds up the scarf, which has been submitted into evidence. "Are these fibers distinctive?" Tucker asks.

"I'm not sure how you define 'distinctive,'" Prescott answers. "But they're not very common. The scarf is expensive, and as you can see, the color is rather unique."

Tucker looks really interested, as if he's hanging on every word Prescott says. The uninformed, a group that no doubt includes the jury, might not realize that they've rehearsed this testimony at least three times.

"Did you have occasion to examine any clothing belonging to the defendant?" Tucker asks.

"Yes. I was sent the clothing he was wearing the night of the murder."

"Did it contain any fibers?" Tucker asks.

Prescott smiles slightly at the imprecise question. "Many. Fibers are everywhere, on virtually everything. If you're asking if fibers consistent with the scarf were on his clothing, the answer is yes."

Tucker smiles. "Thank you, that's exactly what I was asking. Were there many such fibers consistent with the scarf or just a few?"

"Many," Prescott says. "He had recently handled that scarf, or a garment just like it. But most likely that one."

"Why do you say that?" Tucker asks.

"Because the fibers on his clothing had blood on them. Linda Padilla's blood."

Tucker turns the witness over to me, and every head in the courtroom swivels toward me, challenging me to deal with this disaster.

"Detective Prescott, was my client standing, sitting, or lying down when he touched this scarf?"

"I have no way of knowing that," he answers truthfully.

"Was he conscious or unconscious?"

"Again, I can't really answer that."

I nod. "Could Ms. Padilla have already been dead when he touched it?"

"I suppose it's possible. It's not within the scope of my examination," he concedes.

"Does the scope of your examination allow you to tell whether anyone else besides my client and the victim touched the scarf on the day of the murder?"

"No, it does not," he answers.

"So if I can present a hypothetical, based on the scope of your examination and your testimony here today, it's possible that Mr. Cummings was lying down, unconscious, with Ms. Padilla already dead, when a third party rubbed the scarf on him?"

Prescott's expression is pained; he knows that Tucker will have him for lunch if he agrees to this. "I have seen nothing to substantiate that. Absolutely nothing."

"Do you have anything that would eliminate it as a possibility?"

"Logic," he says, a comeback so good I would like to wrap the scarf around his neck.

"Detective Prescott, I based the hypothetical on your testimony. Would you like to go back over that testimony so you can adjust your answers? Or were you testifying accurately and truthfully the first time?"

He looks at me with undisguised disdain, but when he speaks, his voice is quiet and controlled. "Scientifically, the hypothetical you present is possible. Not in any way likely, but possible."

"Thank you," I say with a small sigh, conveying to the jury that it took a lot of effort, but the truth finally came out. "Detective Prescott," I say, "are you familiar with the name Dominic Petrone?"

The mere mention of Petrone's name sends a shock wave through the gallery, and that jolt sends Tucker leaping out of his chair. "Objection, Your Honor! This is cross-examination, and the subject of Mr. Petrone never came up in direct."

Tucker is right, of course, and Calvin sustains the objection. It's just as well, since I really didn't have a question to ask about Petrone. I simply wanted to introduce his name as a way to shake things up. Judging by the buzz in the gallery and the suddenly alert faces on the jury, I seem to have accomplished that quite well.

I let Prescott off the stand, and Calvin adjourns court for the day in deference to a juror's doctor appointment. I briefly have a flash of hope that the doctor will determine the juror cannot continue in his role, thereby forcing a mistrial. Unfortunately, there are six alternate jurors waiting to take his place. If I'm going to get help from the world of medicine, it's going to take something on the order of bubonic plague.

Because of the early adjournment, we're able to move our team evening meeting to late afternoon. It's short and uneventful, and the progress report is especially brief, mainly because we're not making any. We're taking Tucker's roundhouse punches and responding with light jabs, not a recipe for judicial success.

Kevin leaves at about seven o'clock, and Laurie and I decide to go to Charlie's for dinner. Before we leave, I take Tara for a walk, since she hasn't been out for quite a while.

We're about a block from the house when Tara pulls me over toward the grass next to the curb, where a car is parked. It's dark out, so I can't see what it is she's moving toward.

I lean down to get a closer look when suddenly the rear passenger door to the car opens. Something gets out of the car, either an enormous man or an average-sized gorilla, and grabs my arm. Almost simultaneous with that, Tara snarls and lunges for the gorilla's leg.

Gorilla yells in pain and pulls his leg away from Tara. As he does so, a blur flashes across my eyes, and the next thing I know Gorilla is thrown—actually, it's more like launched—over the car, bouncing off the trunk and landing with a thud on the ground.

I'm still frozen in the same spot, displaying my characteristic inability to react physically to an emergency. My eyes are functioning, though, and in another brief instant they are watching Marcus as he holds a gun on Gorilla, who is trying to shake the cobwebs from his head. The gun is dark, shiny, and rock-hard, just like Marcus, and it looks as if he has merely grown an extension on his hand, in the shape of a gun.

The driver of the car gets out, also holding a gun, which he points in the direction of Marcus, Tara, and me. Gorilla, less groggy now, takes out his own gun and joins the pointing club. Tara and I are the only ones without guns, though her teeth are bared and seem just as threatening as their weapons.

The driver speaks first, in a surprisingly calm voice. "There's two of us, friend." He's talking to Marcus, and the implication is that there are two of them in the fight, but only Marcus on the other side. It's demeaning to me, though true enough.

"Yuh," says Marcus, seemingly unperturbed by the imbalance.

"So drop the gun, friend," says Driver.

"Nuh," says Marcus.

"He bit my fucking leg," says Gorilla, misstating Tara's gender but making his point.

"Nobody has to get hurt," Driver says. "Mr. Petrone just wants to talk to the lawyer."

He means me, so I force my mouth to speak. "In my country, we have friendlier ways to arrange conversations."

Driver smiles. "He thought you might not respond to an invitation. Hey, if he wanted you dead, you'd be dead. We would have driven by, and you'd be lying on the cement, with your brains all over the grass."

I look at Marcus and he nods slightly, which I take as a sign that he agrees with Driver. "Where is he?" I ask.

"Get in and find out."

Marcus nods again. "Okay," I say. "But Marcus and his gun go with us." I turn to Marcus. "If you're willing." He grunts, but his head moves slightly up and down in midgrunt, so I take that as a yes.

I tell them to wait for me, and I walk Tara home. When I enter the house, Laurie sees the look on my face. "What's the matter?" she asks.

I quickly relate what's happened, and she asks a bunch of questions. I notice that the one question she doesn't ask is the one I've had in my mind all along, which is, "What the hell was Marcus doing there?"

"You don't seem surprised that Marcus was there," I say.

She doesn't hesitate. "I've had him watching out for you. You've been annoying some dangerous people."

"You should have told me," I say.

"Then you would have stopped it, and Marcus wouldn't have been there to save your ass tonight," she responds.

Laurie isn't happy that I'm going to meet Petrone, and less happy when I refuse her request to go along. "This is real man's work," I joke as I walk out the door. She doesn't think it's that funny, and neither do I.

The truth is, I'm scared shitless.

• • • • •

THERE'S NOT TOO MUCH chitchat in the car on the way to Dominic Petrone's. In fact, the only thing that is said is when I apologize for being late. I explain without much subtlety that, while I was at home, "I called my friend Pete Stanton of the Paterson police and told him where I was going. Just in case we have an accident."

No one seems impressed by this maneuver, or if they are, they neglect to mention it. Marcus and Gorilla share the backseat, and I'm in the front with Driver. All the guns have been put away, which has a calming effect on everybody but me. I'm a nervous wreck.

Intellectually, I know there's not much to worry about, at least for tonight, but the prospect of being summoned by Petrone is more than a little intimidating. My fear is that he's going to make me an offer I can't refuse, and I'm going to refuse it.

Driver drives us to a quiet West Paterson neighborhood, known by everyone, even me, to be the area in which the biggies in the mob reside. Rumor has it that there hasn't been a robbery in this neighborhood since Calvin Coolidge was president.

Petrone's house, at least from the outside, is modest. It's a traditional colonial, two stories, and the property is both well kept and well defended. An ornate but imposing iron fence surrounds the grounds, and we drive up to a gate with three security men, all about the size of Gorilla.

They wave us in, not taking their eyes off Marcus as we go by. We enter the house through the front door, and I am immediately struck by the fact that the inside seems like a normal home. Two teenagers are playing video games in the den as we pass by, I can hear the Knicks game on a television coming from the upstairs, and the kitchen has some dirty plates in the sink. Maybe Clemenza has made some pasta sauce.

We are brought to an office in the back of the house and led in to see Dominic Petrone. I've met him at a couple of local charity dinners; Petrone is very willing to be seen in public. He's like any other successful businessman, except for the part where he has button men on the street.

Petrone is sitting behind his desk watching the Knicks. He smiles when we come in and then makes brief eye contact with Driver, who picks up the remote control and shuts off the game. It's impressive, but although I could afford it, I wouldn't want someone to operate my remote control for me. A real man does his own clicking.

Gorilla takes a seat on one side of the room, and Marcus sits on the other. Petrone stands up and greets me with a smile. "Andy, good to see you," he says. "Thanks for coming by."

"Thanks, Dominic," I say. "I was in the neighborhood, so I figured maybe I'll stop in and see my friend Dominic Petrone."

He nods. "Glad you did. Glad you did. Have a seat."

He motions me to a chair in front of his desk and walks back behind that desk and sits back down. "So I was watching the news, and all they're talking about is how you mentioned my name in court today."

"Think of it as free publicity."

"Or I can think of it as very annoying."

"Or here's a third possibility," I offer. "You can think of it as me defending my client."

He considers this for a while, and the silence in the room is stifling. Finally, he says, "I don't like too many people in this world. Maybe ten, outside of my family. Most people, I don't care about them one way or the other."

He pauses, and I can't think of anything to say, so I don't.

He continues. "But on that short list of people that I like, right near the top, was Linda Padilla. I would never have hurt her, ever. And I don't want it suggested in public that I would."

The arrogance of the man is mind-boggling. He actually seems to think that I will stop mentioning him in court simply because he's announced that he finds it annoying. It is the insufferable attitude of a man who considers himself all-powerful. On the other hand, he could have me killed simply by making some more eye contact with Driver.

I decide to surprise him with my vast knowledge. "Are you saying you didn't hire Tommy Lassiter?"

A flicker of surprise flashes across Petrone's face, and I sense a slight reaction from Driver behind me. "Impressive," says Dominic.

"Stop. You'll make me blush. Did you hire him?"

"No."

"Do you know where he is?" I ask.

"You become less impressive as you go along. If I knew where he was, we would be speaking of him in the past tense."

"Do you know why he would have killed Linda Padilla?"

Dominic nods. "For money. Or to get back at me. Or both."

"Why would Lassiter want to get back at you?"

"Suffice it to say we are not the best of friends. The 'why' is none of your business. And I am getting tired of your questions."

"One more. Why would he kill the others as well?"

"Mr. Carpenter, I brought you here to tell you that I had nothing to do with these murders and that I insist you stop implying that I did. Once you do, I will help you in your efforts."

This is a surprise, and too tempting to let go unexplained. "How will you do that?"

"That remains to be seen. I have the ability to influence events, which is all I will say about it."

If he's not going to be specific, I won't either. "I can't promise anything. My client's life is at stake."

He nods. "As is your own." And just in case that was too subtle, he points to Marcus. "Even a man as imposing as this cannot protect you forever."

Dominic leaves the room, effectively ending the meeting. Driver and Gorilla drive Marcus and me back to my house, leaving us without so much as a word about what a fun evening they had.

I see Laurie looking out at us through the front window. I immediately decide I would rather be in there with her than out here on the street with Marcus. But this guy may have saved my life, so I feel like I owe him something.

"Thanks," I say to Marcus. "I really appreciate what you did tonight."

He shrugs. "Yunh."

"You want to come in? Have a drink or something?"

"Nunh," he says, and walks away. I walk toward my house and Laurie, thinking that "nunh" is the most beautiful word in the English language.

● ● ● ● ●

LAURIE AND I STAY UP most of the night talking about my meeting with Petrone and whether it should
or will have any impact on the trial. I ask her what she
thinks he will actually do if I continue to point the finger
at him.

"If he's smart, he'll wait a year or two and make your
death look like an accident," she says.

"And if he's not smart?"

"He'll have your brains blown out a few weeks after
the trial."

"He seems pretty smart," I offer hopefully.

She nods. "Good. It gives you time to get your affairs
in order."

She's kidding—at least I hope she is—and I move the
conversation toward Petrone's impact on the trial. I have
a very real dilemma in that at the end of the day I believe
Petrone. His fond feelings for Linda Padilla seem gen-

uine and tie in directly with what her boyfriend, Alan Corbin, told me. I've never had any strong reasons to believe Petrone is involved in this, so I have some ethical problems with continuing to insist that he is, misleading the jury in the process.

I could switch my focus to Tommy Lassiter, but his name is not publicly known, and it will have far less psychological impact than Petrone's. It would also have the secondary result of pissing off a crazed hit man, something my parents specifically warned me against as a youth. While the other kids were always being admonished to "be careful crossing the street" and "be home early," my mom and dad would throw in, "and don't go pissing off any crazed hit men."

The real question is how much I should let my personal physical jeopardy get in the way of my client's representation. Should I report what has gone on to Calvin? I don't think so; I'm not sure that there's anything he could do, and his knowledge would possibly inhibit my actions.

Our staying up so late talking leaves me a little bleary-eyed when I get to court in the morning. Tucker looks typically fresh and confident, easy to accomplish in light of his having an entire state full of lawyers to do his leg-work, and a powerful case to present to the jury.

"Rough night, Andy?" he asks with a smile before Calvin enters the courtroom. For a moment I consider the possibility that Tucker knows about my session with Petrone, that perhaps he is having me followed. It's unlikely; the more plausible explanation for his comment is that I look like shit.

I look around the courtroom and notice that Vince is in his place, as is the Cleveland contingent, minus Eliot

Kendall. It's the first day that Kendall has missed, though I doubt that it represents a crack in his support for Daniel.

Tucker's first witness is Neal Winslow, the chief engineer for the cell phone company that Daniel uses. His appearance is to demonstrate that Daniel was lying when he said he was fifteen minutes away from Eastside Park when he received what he claimed was the phone call from the killer.

Tucker and Winslow have rehearsed this testimony well, and Winslow describes the process by which towers cover certain areas, and that a cell phone's general location can be determined by the tower that "handled" the call. His presentation is clear and concise, and such that even a technological moron can understand it. I know this because I happen to be one.

Daniel's apparent lie has two negative consequences, one of which has already taken place. It served as the impetus for the police to get a search warrant, which led to all the real evidence subsequently discovered.

The other consequence, almost as serious, will set in if I can't shake Winslow's testimony. The jury will ask themselves why Daniel would have lied about something like this, and their answer will be that it was to cover his guilt. It is something that I have grappled with since that night, and Daniel has never come up with a satisfactory explanation.

"Mr. Winslow," I begin, "why is it that sometimes I can receive a clear cell phone call, but at other times I have no service in the same location?"

"There could be a number of factors. Weather . . . heavy usage periods . . . they would be the most likely reasons."

"So weather and heavy usage can impact service?"

He nods. "Definitely."

That gives me a little progress in casting doubt on the science, but it's a small victory.

"Now, you told Mr. Zachry that the cell tower has a radius of about four miles."

"Right," he says in answer to a question I didn't ask.

"So if the tower were in the middle of Times Square, it would route calls to my cell phone if I were on the corner of Madison and Eighty-fifth, three miles away?"

He shakes his head. "No, in Manhattan the towers would have a much smaller radius."

I look surprised, though I'm not. "Really? Is it a different type of tower?"

"No, but—"

I interrupt. "Then why is the range different?"

"Because of the many tall buildings. We refer to it as the terrain."

"So terrain can make a difference also? Just like weather and heavy usage and who knows what else?"

Tucker objects to my characterization, and Calvin sustains. I withdraw the question and move on. "Mr. Winslow, assuming perfect weather, normal usage, and average terrain, the radius is four miles. Correct?"

"Approximately."

I smile at the increasing inexactness of this science. "Yes, *approximately* four miles. Right?"

"Yes."

"So it covers a total diameter of eight miles? In such a perfect world?"

"Yes."

"Now, Mr. Zachry read Mr. Cummings's statement from that night into the record, where he said he drove fifteen minutes after getting the call. Did you hear that?"

"Yes."

"Did he say anywhere in that statement that he drove fast, or even in a straight line?"

Tucker objects. "Your Honor, this is not within the witness's area of expertise."

I shake my head. "I am simply asking his recollections based on what he heard Mr. Zachry read. I can give him a copy of the statement, and then his recollections will be perfect."

Calvin overrules Tucker, and Winslow answers. "I didn't hear him read that he drove fast or in a straight line, no."

"Do you ever drive in North Jersey, Mr. Winslow?"

"Yes. Every day."

"Do you find that the speed with which you drive depends on things like weather and heavy usage and terrain?"

The jury and gallery laugh and Winslow can't suppress a smile. "I do," he says.

"Traffic is an inexact science, isn't it, Mr. Winslow?"

Tucker objects and I withdraw the question. I let Winslow off the stand and sit down next to Daniel, who, despite my admonitions, looks positively euphoric.

● ● ● ● ●

LESS THAN THREE HOURS after court is adjourned, my shuttle flight is landing at Logan Airport in Boston. I haven't been here in almost twenty years, but the drive into the city brings home the memories as if they were yesterday.

As a teenager, I was a huge Larry Bird fan, which caused me some uncomfortable moments living in the New York area. But I took the abuse from my friends, and while Bird was in the league I was a traitor to my beloved Knicks. I was, heaven help me, a Celtics fan.

My father handled the situation well, and didn't do what other Knicks-loving fathers would do. He didn't beat, starve, or humiliate me, though in retrospect I deserved it all. Instead, he tolerated my treasonous impulses, in fact did more than that. He would take me up to Boston to watch play-off games in Boston Garden.

Fortunately for me, the Knicks were terrible in those years and never made it to the play-offs themselves.

Boston Garden was an amazing place, a true shrine to basketball as it should be played, and attending a game there was unlike attending a sports event any place else in the world. The Celtics were blessed with talent, smarts, and a relentless will to win, a team worthy of their home, and I'm glad to have witnessed them in action. But today Larry Bird is retired, the old Boston Garden is no more, and I am securely back in the Knicks fold.

I arrive at Carmine's, a small downtown restaurant, at seven-thirty, and Cindy is already there, waiting for me at the bar. She is a very attractive brunet, looking even better than the last time I saw her, which was almost six months ago. The guy on the next stool over is futilely attempting to hit on her, and if you gave him three hundred guesses, he couldn't come up with her occupation. She is Cindy Spodek, FBI special agent, Organized Crime Division.

I met Cindy last year when she testified at Laurie's trial. Cindy had become aware that her boss at the Bureau, until then considered an American hero, had in fact been running massive, illegal operations that extended to murder. Her turning on him was an act of real courage, and she did so at great jeopardy to her career.

In the months that have passed, she's been reassigned to the Bureau's Boston office, but has survived the expected backlash from her colleagues. I last spoke to her a couple of months ago, and she seemed fairly happy. Her career was back on a decent track, and she had met a guy that she felt just might be the one.

Cindy brightens when she sees me, and gives me a warm hug and kiss. It's enough to send Mr. Barstool on to more receptive pastures, and he makes his way down the bar. Cindy and I head to our table in a quiet corner of the restaurant.

We exchange pleasantries, including pictures of our dogs. Cindy has a two-year-old golden named Sierra that I rescued and gave to her. She thinks Sierra is the best dog in North America, an impossibility unless Tara and New Jersey have relocated below the equator without my knowing it. But I tolerate this nonsense because I'm here on a mission.

"Thanks for seeing me on such short notice," I say.

She frowns. "Yeah, right. You reeled me in like a fish."

I called Cindy yesterday and left message saying that I needed to talk to her about Tommy Lassiter. I knew she wouldn't be able to resist that, and I further knew that she'd learn everything about Lassiter that she could before we met.

"So what do you know about Lassiter?" I ask.

She smiles the smile of someone barely tolerating an idiot. "To save time, I decided on the rules for this conversation on the way over here," she says. "Here's how it's going to work. You tell me why you're asking and what you already know, and then I'll decide if I'll say anything or just leave you with the check."

I grin. "Sounds fair to me," I say, and lay out the particulars of Daniel's case and what I know about Lassiter's involvement in it. She listens intently and doesn't ask any questions until I've finished.

"How do you know Lassiter is involved?"

"Marcus got one of the prisoners involved in Randy's murder to talk."

She frowns, mainly because she knows Marcus. "Marcus reasoned with him?" she asks.

"Yes. He can be very reasonable when he wants to be. I believe it's your turn to speak."

She considers this for a moment, then nods. "Tommy Lassiter is an extraordinarily talented and cold-blooded murderer. He is also a maniac. The Bureau wants him very badly."

"Does the Bureau have any information connecting him to my case?"

She shakes her head. "Not that I'm aware of."

"There are a lot of murderers in this country; what makes him special enough to be on your radar?"

She hesitates before answering, as if deciding whether or not she should confide in me. I'm sure she thought this out before coming here, so it must be significant enough that she's having second thoughts. "Because he's added a new wrinkle to the process. His fee is twice as high as anyone else's because he does more than just murder."

"How's that?" I ask.

She looks at me intently. "This is just between you and me. That's it. Agreed?"

I nod. "I'll tell only Laurie and Kevin."

She continues, since she knows they can be trusted. "He also provides a guilty party, to throw suspicion away from himself and the people who hire him. He frames someone; it's part of his full-service operation. And he's good at it."

This piece of news hits me right between the eyes. For the first time I truly believe, I truly know, that Daniel is innocent of these murders. It is simultaneously a huge weight lifted from my shoulders and an incredible pressure added to those same shoulders. It is now far more important that I get him off.

"Will you testify to this?" I ask.

She laughs a short laugh. "Are you out of your mind? Of course not."

"An innocent man is on trial for his life."

"Maybe, or maybe Lassiter had nothing to do with it. And with no other evidence, you couldn't even get my testimony admitted if I were willing to give it, which I'm not."

"Let me worry about getting it admitted," I say.

"Andy, think this through. If word of this got out, every murderer in every prison in the country would be filing appeals saying that Lassiter was the real murderer and that he planted all the conclusive evidence their prosecutors used."

I understand her point, and I don't try to refute it, at least for now. The fact is that her testimony would not be admissible at this stage anyhow. I would first need to independently tie Lassiter into Daniel's case, and neither Marcus's informant nor Dominic Petrone is about to raise his right hand and tell it to the jury.

She adds, "Be careful with this, Andy. Lassiter is more than a tad insane."

I nod, change the subject, and we have a thoroughly pleasant dinner, absent talk of serial killers and severed hands. She waits until we're having coffee to smile and make her announcement. "Todd and I are getting married."

"Congratulations. Who the hell is Todd?"

"I told you about him. He's a Boston cop. A captain."

"How long have you known him?"

"Three months," she says. "But I would have said yes after three weeks. When you know, you know."

I nod, silently wondering why, if Todd and Cindy and I all seem to "know," Laurie remains in the dark.

"Things still well with you and Laurie?" Cindy asks.

She seems to have read my mind, so I get a little defensive. "Yes, well . . . very well . . . totally well . . ."

She smiles. "Sounds like you've reached new levels of wellness."

"We have."

"So when are you getting married?" she asks.

"Married? Me? No, thank you. I'm a free spirit . . . an eagle. No woman can clip my wings. I've got women all over the world. Paterson, Passaic, Trenton . . . you name it."

"So Laurie doesn't want to get married?"

I shrug. "Not so far."

On the flight home I try to figure out what I've learned and what I still have to learn. I now completely believe that Tommy Lassiter killed Linda Padilla, though demonstrating that to a jury is very much another matter. What I don't know is who, if anyone, hired him, or why he needed to kill three other women in the process.

Also puzzling to me is why he chose Daniel to frame. There are much less visible people, with far fewer resources, that he could have more easily pinned it on. He chose Daniel in such a way that the entire series of murders played out as a public spectacle, yet Lassiter's previous history was always to lurk in the shadows.

He could have planted the incriminating evidence on virtually anyone, yet he chose Daniel. Daniel must have made himself an inviting target, or perhaps he had a previous connection to Lassiter that he hasn't shared with me.

It's time to talk to my client.

• • • • •

"HE TOLD ME HE KILLED my wife." Daniel says this after considerable prodding, actually berating, on my part. He says it after I told him that he was going to lose this case unless I knew all the facts, every single one of them. And he says it with a shaky voice, the emotion of that night and the night his wife died coming back to him in torrents.

He seems so upset that I restrain my very real desire to strangle him with his handcuffs. This represents something that was critical for me to have known at the very beginning, not now, at the beginning of the end.

"When did he tell you that?" I ask, maintaining a calm demeanor.

"The night he killed Linda Padilla. That's what he said when he first called me."

"What else did he say?"

"That he would meet me in the park. That he would

tell me who paid him to kill my wife . . . to kill Margaret."

"And you believed that he killed her?"

He nods. "He was telling the truth. Absolutely."

"How do you know that?"

"He knew what she was wearing . . . a bracelet I had given her for her anniversary. He said he took it . . . he described it." He nods vigorously to punctuate his point. "There's no doubt, Andy. He killed her."

"Okay. So you got to the park . . . and then what?"

"I went to the place we were supposed to meet, the steps near the pavilion. He must have come up on me from behind, because the next thing I remember I was lying on the steps and talking to the cop."

"Why didn't you call the police in the first place?"

"He said if I did, or said anything to them, I'd never find out who ordered Margaret's death. I needed to know that . . . I still do."

"Is that all?"

He shakes his head but is silent for a few moments, apparently weighing his words. "No . . . he said he had the power to frame anybody he wanted for Margaret's death," he says, then more quietly, "He said he could make me appear guilty."

"So that's why you never told this to the police?"

"Partly, I guess. But mainly, it was because I didn't want to lose contact with this guy. You've got to understand, I never dreamed they would charge me with Padilla's murder. Hell, when I first spoke to the cop, I didn't even know she *was* murdered. When they arrested me, I felt like I couldn't change my story."

I'm trying to process all this new information but having a difficult time. Right now all I can think about is what a selfdestructive asshole my client has been. It would make me feel better to tell him so, but I'm not sure his psyche could handle it.

"You've been a self-destructive asshole," I blurt out, choosing my feelings over his psyche.

"I know," he moans, making me sorry I said it. "Is all this too late to help?"

"I don't know," is my honest reply. "What else haven't you told me?"

"That's it. I swear."

"Do you believe that someone paid to have your wife killed?"

He thinks this through for a few moments. "I know he killed her, and I doubt very much that Margaret knew him. So I have no reason to doubt that he was paid for it."

I head back to the office to brief Laurie and Kevin on what I've just learned. We talk about the possible ways we can get this information to the jury, but it's a short conversation because at this point there is just one possible way, and that is to have Daniel testify. It is not something I'm inclined to do, but fortunately, it's not a decision I have to make right now.

I call Pete Stanton at the precinct, but I'm told that he has the day off. I try his cell phone number, and he answers on the first ring. I tell him that I need to discuss something with him, and I can actually hear his ears perk up through the phone, as his mind races to figure out how he can cost me money. Pete has never really handled my wealth very well, so he tries to reduce that wealth in any way that he can.

"Maybe we can talk after the Knicks game," he says.

The Knicks are playing the Lakers tonight, and I was thinking of going over to Charlie's to watch it, so Pete's request is surprisingly painless. "You want to meet at Charlie's?" I ask.

"I don't think so. I'm getting tired of that place."

"So where do you want to watch the game?"

"Courtside."

The game is starting in four hours, is completely sold out, and Pete is expecting me to get tickets. He knows that the only possible way I could do that would be to call a scalper and pay a small fortune.

"You know," I say, "you're a greedy lowlife who has no understanding of the meaning of friendship." I didn't want to have to come down on him so hard, but he needs to understand that I feel strongly about this.

"Blah, blah, blah, blah, blah," he counters. "Pick me up at the airfield at six."

"You're still doing that?" I ask.

"It's more fun than sex," he answers.

There's no logical response for that, so I don't offer one. Pete earns extra money at Teterboro Airport by taking pictures of people while they are skydiving and selling them the pictures if they make it to the ground alive. They are mostly beginners, out for a fun time, and Pete has been skydiving for many years.

I understand skydiving about as well as I understand Swahili and women, which is to say not at all. People jump out of planes so that they can get to the same ground they were safely on before they boarded the plane in the first place. Why is that exactly?

Of course, they are given equipment that guarantees their safety. Specifically, that equipment consists of a pack of nylon that they open up while hurtling toward the ground at about twelve million miles an hour. Now, I had never realized what an incredibly powerful substance nylon is. For instance, I've never heard of prisoners in maximum security prisons trying to cut through their nylon bars in a futile attempt at escape. Nor have I overheard a father at the lions' exhibit at the zoo telling his frightened son not to worry because the nylon cage provides all the protection they could ever need.

Of course, the nylon is not the last resort. Sky divers also wear a little helmet for protection. Since they don't wear body armor, if the nylon doesn't open or hold up, are they supposed to try to land on their heads?

Death-defying acts like this are to me nonsensical. Why would I do them? What is the upside if everything goes perfectly? That I live? I can do that at home on the couch.

I arrive at the airfield just as Pete floats down. He sells his pictures and is in my car by six-fifteen. We're at Madison Square Garden in less than an hour, first stopping at the will-call window so I can pick up the eight-hundred-dollar courtside tickets left by the good people at Irwin's Ticket World. We then head for the seats, stopping only so that I can buy Pete a pair of thirty-six-ounce beers, one for each hand.

The first half is a disaster. The Knicks commit fourteen turnovers, are outrebounded on both ends of the floor, and head to the locker room down by sixteen, which represents one point for every hundred dollars I spent on the tickets.

The arena is understandably quiet during halftime, so I try to address the reason I'm here in the first place. "So let's talk," I say.

"Now? In the middle of Madison Square Garden? Come on, man, let me enjoy the game. We can go to Charlie's afterwards and talk all you want."

"I thought you were tired of Charlie's."

He nods. "I was, but I'm over that now."

The Knicks are down by twenty-seven at the end of the third quarter, which is also when they stop selling beer, so I'm able to get Pete to leave. I start our talk on the way, since I'd just as soon this date not turn into an all-nighter.

"Do you know anything about Tommy Lassiter?" I ask.

He becomes instantly alert, no small feat considering he's carrying around a bathtub full of beer in his gut. "What have you got to do with him?"

"He murdered Linda Padilla."

He shakes his head. "He's a contract killer; the best there is. But he's not a serial killer."

"I'm not speculating, Pete. I'm positive."

"So take the proof that makes you so positive, show it to the judge, and get your case dismissed."

"I have nothing to show the judge. But there's no doubt in my mind."

"Tell me how you know," he says.

"We got one of the prisoners at County to talk. He said Lassiter arranged Randy Clemens's murder."

"You got someone to turn on Lassiter?" he asks, not concealing his incredulity.

I nod. "Marcus was persuasive with someone."

He knows Marcus, so no further explanation is necessary. "So what are you asking me?"

"To help me catch him."

Pete laughs, not the reaction I was hoping for. "Okay," he says, "park over there and wait, and I'll chase him toward you."

"I'm serious, Pete. This guy keeps killing people; now might be a good time to get him off the streets."

He's now controlled himself to just a few chuckles. "Is he currently in the area?" he asks.

"I don't know. I've got a feeling he might be. I know he was here the nights those people died."

"Andy, you don't know if he's within a thousand miles of here. You have no evidence that he killed those people. What the hell do you want me to do, close the state borders?"

"Isn't Lassiter already wanted for murder?" I ask.

"Of course. He was born wanted for murder."

"So I'm a credible source telling you that I have information that he was recently in this area. Isn't that enough for you to put out an APB or whatever the hell you guys put out?"

"You want me to go to my captain with this?"

I nod. "And tell him that somebody you trust, a god-damned officer of the court, came to you with this. Get him to send his picture out to every cop in the state. And get me a copy of his picture as well."

"Come on, Andy . . ."

"What's the downside, Pete? That he's gone and we don't find him?"

He nods. "Okay."

Satisfied with this concession, I bail out of the trip to Charlie's and drop him off at his house. When I get to my house, it's almost midnight and Laurie is already in bed.

"Hi," she says sleepily. "How did it go?"

"He said he'll do the best he can."

She smiles. "Good. Come to bed."

I start to get undressed. "I forgot to tell you. Cindy's getting married."

"That's nice," she says, though I think she's more intent on falling back to sleep than hearing what I'm saying.

"She says that when you know, you know."

"Mmmm" is all she can muster, now almost completely out of it.

"I think she's right about that. Don't you?"

"Mmmm."

I'll take that as a yes.

• • • • •

CAPTAIN TERRY MILLEN is Tucker's final witness and the one that ties his case up quite nicely. Millen was in charge of the murder investigation from the early point in which the state police were called in, and he had the most connection to Daniel of anyone in law enforcement.

The physical evidence has already been powerfully introduced, so Tucker will undoubtedly let Millen's testimony focus on Daniel's unique knowledge of the murders. His contention is that Daniel knew these things only because he was the killer, while our defense is that the killer was simply communicating the information to Daniel.

Before Millen takes the stand, I lose a heated argument during which I again oppose the introduction of testimony concerning the three other victims and especially photographs of them. This defeat makes it official: We have received no benefit at all from Tucker's decision to limit the charges to the Padilla murder.

Tucker starts off Millen's testimony by showing all of those photographs and letting the full impact of their gruesomeness inflame the jury. Daniel tries to obey my instructions to remain as impassive as possible, but I can tell from the look on his face that he is having an emotional reaction to them. I'm sure part of that reaction must be that he is aware the world thinks he is responsible for this carnage.

During a break, Daniel leans over to me. "Can I have copies of your files on the other victims besides Padilla?"

Until now, Daniel has been studying up on the Padilla murder but hasn't come up with any helpful insights. He hasn't looked at the other files because he hasn't been charged with those murders. "Why?" I ask.

"I don't know, maybe it will jog something in my mind. Some way to prove I couldn't have been at one of the murders." He shakes his head. "It's not like I've got a lot of other things to do, you know?"

I agree to get him the copies, though I have little hope he'll come up with anything at this late date.

The break ends, and Tucker again starts to question Millen. "When did you become involved in this case, Captain?"

"After the second murder, Mrs. Simonson. We were called in to consult. It was after the third murder—all we have for her name is Rosalie—that we took over, and I was officially placed in charge."

"What did the defendant tell you about that murder?"

"He told us that she was murdered in her own apartment, that her hands were cut off, and that her body was left behind a particular Dumpster," Millen says.

"Did the defendant say how he knew all of this?"

Millen nods. "Yes, he said that the killer phoned him and bragged about it."

"Did the information turn out to be correct?"

Again Millen nods. "Every word of it."

"By the way," Tucker asks, "have there been any more murders of this exact type since the defendant's arrest?"

"No."

Tucker takes the next three hours getting Millen to recount every communication he had with Daniel, emphasizing the many facts that Daniel knew about the murders that turned out to be true. By the time he turns Millen over to me, the words "the defendant" and "the killer" seem to be interchangeable.

"Captain Millen," I begin, "during all these conversations with Mr. Cummings, when he was giving you all this information, did you believe he was communicating with the killer?"

"I wasn't sure," he says. "I had my doubts."

"When you say you had your doubts, do you mean you thought he might have been lying?"

"It certainly crossed my mind."

"And if you thought he might be lying, but he had all this accurate information, then you must have thought he might have been the killer?"

"That's correct."

"Maybe you can help me, Captain. The prosecution turned over copies of their evidence in discovery, but they seem to have left out the surveillance report. Do you have a copy?"

He looks puzzled. "What surveillance is that?"

"The surveillance on Mr. Cummings."

"To my knowledge, he was not placed under surveillance."

"I see. So you believed Mr. Cummings was very possibly lying, which means you believed he was very possibly the killer, but you did not have him watched? You had no fear he would murder again?"

Millen is in a box. My guess is, he did not suspect Daniel until the cell phone story proved a lie, and therefore had no reason to have him followed. Claiming now that he doubted Daniel's story all along makes him look partly responsible for Linda Padilla's death.

"He was not followed," Millen says, tight-lipped.

"Why not?" I ask. "You didn't consider him a potential danger to the public?"

"It's very easy to look back and judge decisions; hindsight is twenty-twenty. But we were in the middle of an intense investigation . . ."

"So you thought he might be the murderer, but you didn't have him followed because the investigation was too intense? You operate more efficiently in mellow investigations?"

He doesn't have a good answer for this, so I ask basically the same question another half dozen times until Tucker objects and Calvin orders me to move on.

"In your dealings with Mr. Cummings, did he seem like an intelligent man?"

"I suppose so," he says grudgingly.

"Were you familiar with his work as a crime reporter?"

"Somewhat."

"When you searched his car and apartment, were you surprised that the evidence was right there for you to find it?"

"Nothing surprises me anymore. If the world operated

solely by logic, these people wouldn't have been killed in the first place."

"So you admit it would be illogical for Mr. Cummings, or any guilty person, to keep the evidence in his apartment like that?"

"Serial killers are not logical people."

"Are they self-destructive?"

"Sometimes."

"Do they want to be caught?"

"Often they do."

"Captain, do you believe my client hit himself in the head in Eastside Park that night?"

"I do."

"With what?"

Millen reacts, though he certainly had to know this was coming. The police never found anything that could be shown to have hit Daniel's head.

"I don't know. He must have gotten rid of it."

"Where?"

"I can't be sure," he says. "We couldn't test every piece of wood in the entire park."

"But you tested everything within five hundred yards of the pavilion?"

"We tried to."

"You *tried* to?" I say with mocking disbelief. "Any chance you succeeded?"

He stares a dagger at me, but his voice is controlled. "I believe we did."

"No DNA evidence tying anything to Mr. Cummings?"

"No."

"So you believe that Mr. Cummings was self-protective enough to hide the incriminating weapon he used to hit himself, but self-destructive enough to leave the severed hands in his car?"

I've trapped him in a small corner, and he looks worried. He finally comes up with, "As I said, serial killers are rarely logical. It would be nice if what they did made sense, but it often doesn't."

"It would also be nice if your testimony made sense. No further questions."

My eye contact with Kevin as I head back to the defense table confirms my fears. I made headway, but not nearly enough.

Since this is Tucker's last witness, Calvin adjourns for the day, giving me until Monday morning to come up with some kind of defense case. As I leave the courtroom, I find myself alongside Eliot Kendall. It's the first time I've seen him in almost a week; I had assumed that his business interests had called him back to Cleveland.

"Mind if I walk with you?" he asks.

"Not at all," I lie. I'd rather be alone to rehash today's testimony in my mind, but he asked nicely and I don't feel like insulting him.

We go down the courtroom steps and start heading toward the parking lot. "I haven't seen you around for a while," I say.

He nods. "I was back home. My father died."

"I'm sorry. I didn't know." Eliot's father was Byron Kendall, an enormously powerful trucking magnate, possibly a billionaire. If I weren't so consumed with the trial and oblivious to the world, I probably would have learned about his death from the media.

He nods sadly. "Thank you. He was eighty-four and very sick for years, but it still comes as a shock."

"Is your mother alive?" I ask.

Another sad shake. "No, she died almost fifteen years ago. What about you? Parents alive?"

"No. My mother died four years ago, my father last year," I say. "Being an orphan, even a middle-aged one, takes some getting used to."

He nods, and we don't say anything for a while, each reflecting on what we have lost. He breaks the silence. "How's the case going?"

I want to tell him the truth, that his friend is in deep, deep shit, but I don't. "We're plugging along," I say. "It's a struggle."

"My investigators have drawn a blank," he says. "I probably should have hired local rather than bringing guys in from Cleveland." He grins a wry grin. "We don't have the home-field advantage here."

A good idea hits me, a rarity these days. Eliot has been offering his help all along, and I've been fending him off, but that's about to change. "Can you come back to my office?" I ask. "There might be a way you can help after all."

He practically salivates at the opportunity, and ten minutes later we're back at my office. I get right to the point. "Have you ever heard the name Tommy Lassiter?"

His expression is blank. "No. Who is he?"

"He's a professional murderer, a hit man. I have reason to believe that he murdered Linda Padilla and the other women."

"You know that for sure?"

I nod. "Pretty much."

"This is great. You want me to have my investigators look for him?"

"No, I'm about to let the media do that. Did you know Daniel's wife?"

"Margaret? I knew her . . . I mean, not very

well . . . but I went out to dinner with her and Daniel a few times." He looks confused. "Why? What does she have to do with this?"

"It's important that you keep this in confidence," I say.

"Of course. Sure."

"I also have reason to believe that Lassiter murdered Margaret."

"Why? Why would he do that?"

"That's where you come in. Lassiter works for money; if he killed Margaret, he was hired to do it. What I need to know is who might have done the hiring. Who would have wanted her dead and had the money to make it happen."

Eliot sits down, lost in thought. "I don't know . . . I can't think of anybody that might have done that. I've always assumed it was a random murder . . . some psychopath."

"It's something you could look into, if you're so inclined. Since it's on your turf, you'd have home-field advantage."

He promises to do so and expresses his appreciation for the opportunity. I lead him into the outer office, where Willie and Sondra are waiting for me. Sondra looks gorgeous and is decked out in even more jewelry than the last time I saw her, having added a ruby bracelet to the gold watch and alexandrite locket. I make a mental note to gently suggest to Willie that he slow down on the expensive gifts, though it is certainly none of my business.

I introduce Willie and Sondra to Eliot, who seems to be more interested in staring at Sondra than Willie. I briefly wonder if Eliot would be more or less interested in Sondra if he knew her employment history, then I wonder if Willie is noticing Eliot staring at her. Because if he is, Eliot could soon be skydiving out the window without a helmet or Pete to take his picture.

Just in case, I rush Eliot out the door, then return to them.

"You see that guy staring at Sondra?" Willie asks me.

"Come on, Willie," Sondra says. "You think everybody is staring at me."

"Damn right," he says.

Willie goes on to say that they stopped by to tell me the foundation was going to be closed on Monday and Tuesday, that they were going to head down to Atlantic City for a couple of days of gambling and relaxation.

I'm hit with a sudden wave of envy. I would like to forget Daniel and Tucker and Calvin and Dominic Petrone and especially Lassiter by planting myself at a blackjack table. Nobody's life would be at stake, and my toughest decision would be whether to stand, draw, or double down.

But I'm not going to go. I'm going to stay here and be miserable. It's what I do for a living.

But first I'm going to go on television.

● ● ● ● ●

THE MEDIA HAVE CALMED down lately, which has resulted in my receiving fewer death threats and crank calls. Unfortunately, the reason that the furor around the case has lessened is that things have been going so well for the prosecution. The public feels secure that Daniel is going to be convicted and put to death, so there's much less for them to be upset about.

My plan this evening is to shake things up in media land, and I've scheduled an interview on CNN. To do so, I simply had to tell them that I was going to be making news, not simply rehashing my view that my client is innocent.

Laurie accompanies me into the city, and we park at a lot near Penn Plaza. The attendant comes over and says, "Forty-one dollars." I assume he's making me an offer for the car, but it turns out that's the flat rate to park for the evening. New York parking lots are a better investment than coffee.

We leave the lot and start walking toward the CNN offices. It's a typical early evening in Manhattan, with wall-to-wall people on the streets. I'm about half a block from the building when I look slightly toward the right and see something that jolts me.

Tommy Lassiter.

He's staring at me, smiling, and then suddenly he's not there, having melted into the crowds.

"Jesus . . . ," I say, and take a few steps toward where he was standing. A few steps is all I can take because of the masses of people.

"What's the matter?" Laurie asks.

"I'd swear I just saw Tommy Lassiter."

"Where?"

I point in the direction, but of course he's nowhere to be seen. "He just looked at me and smiled and then disappeared."

"Are you sure it was him?" she asks.

I was sure in the moment, but I've never been one to recognize faces, and I've never seen Lassiter in person. "I think so. Especially because of the way he looked at me. Like he was taunting me."

"You're under a lot of stress, Andy. It may not have been him. What would he have to gain from following you?"

"Maybe to stop my going public with his name. To scare me off. Which would not be that tough to do."

She shakes her head. "He's got more effective ways to scare you than smiling."

She's right about that, so I try to forget the encounter and we go into the building. About an hour goes by before they are ready for me, and I'm brought into the studio, hooked up with a microphone through my shirt, and we're ready to go.

The interviewer is Aaron Brown, an intelligent, soft-spoken man who seems to have thrived in cable news despite those qualities. I've chosen him because I want my news to be taken seriously, not dismissed as the sensational ramblings of a desperate defense attorney. Even though that's what it is.

Two minutes into the interview, he comes straight to the point. "I understand that you have something new to reveal tonight."

I nod. "Yes. I know the identity of the real killer of Linda Padilla, as well as the others."

He takes this revelation in stride. "And who might that be?"

I reach under the table and get the picture of Lassiter that Pete provided me. I hold it up for the camera. "His name is Tommy Lassiter. He's a contract killer, a hit man. A very successful one."

"What do you base this accusation on?"

"A number of sources, some of whom I cannot mention tonight. But one of those sources was Randy Clemens, a former client of mine who was recently killed in prison." I go on to detail the conversation I had with Randy prior to his death, and the details of that death.

Brown asks me why I am going public with this news, rather than bringing it before the judge and jury.

"Because the people that have confirmed this information to me are afraid to testify. Without any direct evidence, none of this would be admissible. But that is why I am here, to reveal Lassiter's identity and show his photograph, in the hope that others with information will come forward."

The interview continues for another ten minutes, and by the time I get outside, other members of the media have created a mob scene in front of the studio. I hold an impromptu press conference, during which I make my pitch again. In answer to a question, I deny that one of my reasons for going public is to have the accusation reach the unsequestered jury. I deny this even though it's true.

As Laurie and I leave the studio, I'm feeling pretty good about the session and what it accomplished. We walk down Seventh Avenue and then turn onto Thirty-fourth Street toward the parking lot. The streets are far less crowded than they were before, since rush hour is essentially over, but I find myself still looking around warily for another sighting of Tommy Lassiter.

A few steps after making the turn, I hear a slight popping sound and feel an impact in my chest. I hear Laurie give out a short scream, and as I reach for the point of impact, I feel a sticky liquid on my hand. I look down and see that my shirt and hand are a bright red.

I'm not in pain, but rather stunned, and it is this plus dawning fear that sends me to my knees. I can hear the crowd around me on the street yelling, and some people are running for cover. Laurie comes to me to hold me on the ground, and I am literally shaking in fear.

I let her lower me farther to the ground, but I am slowly realizing that I am not hurt. "Oh, my God, Andy. It's paint," she says. "It's paint." She's half laughing, half crying. "It's paint."

It takes me a moment to realize that my lifeblood is not literally draining from me onto the street. Once I do, I instantly know what has happened. Lassiter has given me a demonstration of his power; obviously, this could have been a bullet, and I would be dead.

"Where is he?" I say, but I know that he is nowhere to be found.

Laurie, no longer worried about me, jumps up and scours the crowd, but Lassiter has melted away. I stand up, feeling some embarrassment, and we don't wait for the police. We rush to the parking lot, get our car, and head home.

Laurie drives, and I spend the ride trying to reduce my anxiety level. Lassiter was trying to scare me, and on that he more than succeeded. But he was not trying to kill me, merely to demonstrate that he could do so. And his primary goal, I believe, was to have fun, to receive a bizarre diabolical pleasure. Cindy Spodek was right when she said he was insane.

When I get home, I get in the shower and scrub off the paint that has penetrated to my skin. Once I've done so, Laurie, Tara, and I watch the reaction to my interview on television. It is all that anyone is talking about, and Lassiter's picture is everywhere. To my surprise, most of the pundits are not dismissing this as a desperation ploy, but rather taking it seriously. The scene on the street goes unmentioned, as if it never happened.

I slowly start to feel like myself again. I have to admit that I'm enjoying the coverage and feeling pleased at my ability to dominate the news. Laurie seems to tire of it more quickly than I do. "Feel like watching a movie?" she asks at about ten o'clock.

"A movie? You want to watch a movie? We're watching real life, and you're sitting here with a real star!"

She nods. "And it's thrilling, just thrilling. But just for a brief break from all this exciting reality, let's watch some fake life, with a fake star. Shall we?"

Not waiting for an answer, she searches through the movie channels and settles on *Witness*, with Harrison Ford. "This should do it," she says. Tara barks her agreement, and I am officially no longer a part of the evening's entertainment. And though it's a great movie, and I watch it with them until the end, Ford cannot begin to match my screen presence.

I wake up at seven in the morning to take Tara for a walk. Laurie stays in bed, and my plan is to join her again when we get back. I negotiate with Tara, and she agrees to cut the walk down to a half hour, providing I buy her a bagel. Little does she know that I was going to buy her one anyway. Chalk one up for human shrewdness.

I try to accomplish all this without fully waking up, and I'm doing pretty well until we approach the house. I am horrified to see Vince Sanders pulling up in front. I briefly consider sneaking in the back and then not answering the doorbell, but if Vince is up this early in the morning, he's not going to give up that easily.

"Vince, what a pleasant surprise," I lie.

"You got coffee?"

I nod. "In the house. But I'm not drinking it until after the Olympics."

He holds up a bag. "Good. I got donuts. And wait'll you see what else I got."

I let him in the house. "Laurie here?" he asks.

"Upstairs," I say. "In bed. Which is exactly where I was going to go."

"You trying to make me feel bad?"

"Yes."

He considers this for a moment. "It ain't working. You know I've been doing a lot of research on this. Well, guess what? Walter Castle hated Margaret Cummings."

It could be because I'm still half-asleep, but it takes me a while to mentally process this information and identify Walter Castle. He is the Cleveland billionaire whose company lost over a hundred million dollars when Linda Padilla identified it as having caused a leukemia cluster. It is the connection I wished I would have had Marcus check out while he was in Cleveland. We have since gone over all of Padilla's possible enemies, but none, including Castle, jumped out at us.

The fact that he even knew, no less hated, Daniel's wife is a significant piece of news. "Why did he hate her?" I ask.

Now Vince gets smug, knowing his statement has jolted me from wanting him out of my house to anxiously waiting to hear more. "What happened to that coffee?"

I get Vince the coffee and wait while he downs a donut, not too long a wait, since he does so in one bite. "Margaret had a lot of time on her hands, and she tried to put it to good use. So she was active in a lot of causes, the environment, public health, that kind of thing."

He inhales another donut, taking his time and relishing the fact that he has the floor. "She was the first one to raise the possibility of a leukemia cluster, and she wouldn't let go of it. Padilla didn't get in until much later, which made the story go national. And get this: Daniel wrote a story about it."

He hands me the story and I skim through it. It's really just a few paragraphs, obviously early on in the health controversy, recommending that it be thoroughly looked into.

"There's not that much here," I say.

"Right. But it was Margaret he hated. Daniel was just backing her up. The whole episode destroyed Walter

Castle's reputation . . . his legacy. So he has Margaret killed and then ruins Daniel. The perfect revenge."

I'm not nearly as confident as Vince that this is the break we need, but it's certainly an interesting development requiring and deserving much more investigation.

Laurie comes into the room, still in a bathrobe. "Good morning, Vince, want some granola?"

"Are you crazy? That stuff'll burn a hole in your stomach."

She goes into the kitchen and comes out a few moments later with a tasty bowl of granola and skim milk. Vince tells her about the Walter Castle connection, and she thinks it's worth Marcus going back there to check. I agree, and also think I will put Eliot Kendall's people on it, since it's on their turf. I call Eliot on his cell phone, and he is excited about the news. He's on the way to visit Daniel in the jail, and I give him permission to update Daniel on the developments.

For the next hour and a half, Vince peppers me with questions about Lassiter and whether I'll be able to get my suspicions about him before a jury. He's pleased, as I am, about the press coverage my interview has gotten. "You were the only thing on television last night," he says.

"Not in this house. Laurie and Tara watched Harrison Ford."

Vince puts his finger down his throat in a gagging gesture, which sends Laurie upstairs to put on a sweat suit for her morning jog. I use this opportunity to get Vince out of the house so I can spend the rest of the day preparing for court on Monday. I have a tradition, which is even more important during football season, to rest the day before I open my case, which is why I want to be free to spend Sunday in front of the television.

• • • • •

IF GOD HAD WANTED humans to communicate, he wouldn't have invented caller ID. But I'm glad that somebody did, because I love it. It's not the greatest invention of all time, which is to say it's not quite up there with the point spread and the remote control, but it's in that still-wonderful second tier, right alongside the cash machine, satellite TV, and light beer.

Combined with the answering machine, caller ID enables me to permanently avoid anyone I don't want to talk to on the phone, which is most of the world's population.

The Giants are playing the Dallas Cowboys today, and nothing short of an earthquake above 7.0 is going to get me off the couch. Certainly, a ringing phone won't do it, though the phone rings repeatedly during the game. One of those times is when I'm making a hurried trip to the bathroom, and I glance at the caller ID. It's my office number—no doubt Kevin is spending Sunday working—but I don't pick it up. If it were President Heather Locklear calling from the White House, I wouldn't pick it up.

The game is a magnificent rarity: an offensive explosion by the Giants that results in a thirty-point victory. As the fourth quarter begins, the camera starts focusing on an obviously upset Jerry Jones, the Cowboys' owner, fuming on the sidelines. It's poetry; I've hated Jerry Jones ever since he bought the team and fired longtime coach Tom Landry, though I hated Landry as well. I especially hated Jerry because he brought in Jimmy Johnson and immediately started beating the Giants and winning Super Bowls. Today is sweet revenge, and it tastes best hot.

There are two minutes left in the game, and the Giants are running out the clock, despite my screaming admonitions for them to run up the score even more.

The door opens and Laurie comes in. She doesn't say anything, simply walks to the TV and turns it off.

I'm stunned. "Correct me if I'm wrong, because I must be wrong. But did you just turn off a Giants-Cowboys game?"

"We've got a witness," she says. "Let's go."

"A witness to what?" I ask, but she's already on the way to the car. I stifle the instinct to turn the game back on, and I follow her out the door.

Laurie tells me that Kevin has been trying to reach me all afternoon but that I haven't been answering my phone. "I didn't hear it ringing," I lie. "Tara must have been barking."

"Right. That Tara can really bark."

Kevin is waiting for us in my office with a man, probably in his early forties, wearing sneakers, jeans, and a pullover shirt. The man is drinking a beer, interesting only because I don't keep any in my office. Either he brought his own, or he sent Kevin out to get him one.

Kevin introduces him as Eddie Gardner, a truck driver who travels the country but whose home base is North Jersey. He turns the floor over to Eddie, so that he can repeat for me what he saw.

"It was September fourteenth," Eddie begins. "I saw a guy pick up a hooker on Market Street in Passaic."

I look up at Kevin, who nods at my unspoken question, indicating that September 14 was in fact the night Rosalie was killed.

"What were you doing there?"

He smiles with some embarrassment. "Hey, come on, man. What do you think? I had just come back from a two-week haul—that's how I remember the date—and I had some extra money . . ."

"So you were there as a customer," I say, stating the obvious.

He shoots a quick glance at Laurie, then nods. "Right. A customer."

"Who was the guy you saw?" I ask.

He points to the newspaper on the desk, with Lassiter's picture on the front page. "Him."

"What time was it?" I ask.

"About one o'clock in the morning."

"So you were there to pick up a hooker, but you were looking at the other customers?"

"I notice things," he says.

"And how is it you noticed *him*?"

"He pulled up in his car, and usually the girl comes

over and gets in the car. That's how it's done. But this guy leaves his car running and gets out. Then he walks around, trying to figure out who to take, like he's out shopping, you know? He picks one, and they go back to his car and pull away. It just seemed weird, so I remembered him."

"Why didn't you come forward earlier?" Laurie asks.

"I didn't see the picture until today," he says. "And I'm on the road a lot, so I hadn't known there was a murder that night."

We question Eddie for a while longer, and when we're finished, he gives us a number at which he can be reached. He's willing to testify, even though it will cause him some personal embarrassment.

After he leaves, Laurie speaks first. "I don't believe him."

"Why?" says Kevin, his surprised tone revealing that he disagrees.

Laurie shakes her head. "I'm not sure. It just seems too easy, too pat." She turns to me. "What about you?"

"I've got some doubts myself," I say. "But I can't be any more specific as to why."

We talk about it some more, and Laurie takes on the responsibility of checking into Eddie's background. Absent any significant negative discoveries, we agree that his story is credible enough that we have to put him on the stand.

In terms of the impact on our case, it can be enormous. Eddie provides a way to introduce Lassiter into the courtroom. Our alternate theory will be before the jury and might well create the reasonable doubt necessary to get Daniel off.

I have my doubts about Eddie's veracity, but on its

face his story stands up. As a lawyer, I cannot introduce testimony I know to be false, but I do not have to have an affirmative belief in its truth. That is for the jury to decide after they hear our side of the story.

And starting tomorrow they will.

• • • • •

TUCKER GOES MORE than a little nuts when we meet in Calvin's chambers before the start of the court day. I can't blame him: I've just announced that we intend to call Eddie Gardner as a surprise witness.

"Your Honor," says Tucker, "we've had the defense witness list for weeks, and the day they are to begin their case we have this bomb dropped on us? It's outrageous."

Calvin turns to me, but I put up my hands as if it's not my fault, which in fact it isn't. "Your Honor, the witness came to us yesterday, as a result of the publicity from my television appearance Friday night."

He interrupts me. "An appearance which I am not at all happy about."

That's too bad, Calvin, is what I'm thinking. What I say is, "In the last two months Mr. Zachry has been on television more than Oprah Winfrey, and far more than

I have. Perhaps Your Honor would like to issue a gag order; the defense would certainly have no objections." Especially since we've already got Lassiter's picture out to the public.

He lets it drop and gets me to agree that I won't put Eddie on the stand before tomorrow, an easy concession, since that was my plan anyway. I want to give Laurie a chance to dig further into his background.

I make time to talk with Daniel before court, and he's more optimistic and excited than he's been since this started. Eliot told him about the Walter Castle connection, and he's embarrassed that he hadn't seen it, but he didn't know Castle had been a target of Linda Padilla. He considers it very promising, but not nearly as large a cause for celebration as Eddie's appearance on the scene.

My first witness is Cheryl Kelly, a reporter for Vince's newspaper who happened to be in Daniel's office when he got the first call from the killer.

I get her to recount the events, then ask her about Daniel's reaction. "What did he say when he got off the phone?"

"That somebody just confessed to a murder," she says. "Told him how it was done and where the body was."

"Did he seem surprised?"

Tucker objects, but I counter that I am merely asking for the witness's impressions. Calvin lets her answer. "Yes. But he wasn't sure he believed it. He said it was probably a crank."

"Did you at any time think Mr. Cummings was putting on an act, that the call wasn't real?" I ask.

She shakes her head firmly. "Absolutely not."

I turn her over to Tucker. "Did you hear a voice on the other end of the phone?" he asks.

"No."

"Are you and Mr. Cummings very close friends?"

"No, not really. We just work together."

"Has he ever lied to you?" Tucker asks.

"No. I mean, I don't think so," she says. "Not that I'm aware of."

"So he could be lying and you might not be aware of it?"

Backed into a corner, Cheryl has to admit that she might not be able to tell if Daniel is lying. It's a nice move by Tucker and partially negates a witness of already modest significance.

The rest of the day is taken up by similar witnesses who spent time with Daniel during the period when he was in contact with the killer. All of them completely believed, and still believe, Daniel's story.

Tucker takes the same approach with each, which is to demonstrate that they have no certain knowledge that Daniel was telling the truth. He does not spend much time on each, signifying to the jury that he doesn't consider their testimony very important.

He's right about that.

Our nightly meeting is devoted to how we will handle Eddie on the witness stand tomorrow. Laurie has checked him out as best she can, though she warns that she had little to go on and little time to dig.

Kevin's view is that we just let him tell his story, quickly and concisely. I agree, but I'm more concerned with the argument that Tucker will present to Calvin afterward. Our defense view is that Eddie's testimony opens the door to other testimony about Lassiter, possibly from law enforcement officials. Tucker will say that those witnesses have no specific knowledge of Lassiter's involvement in this case and therefore should not be permitted to testify. It will be a struggle; Calvin could come down either way. But it's a fight we have to win.

Eddie seems a little nervous and tentative when he arrives at court in the morning. It's understandable: He's about to enter the glare of the national spotlight and talk about the night he went to pick up a hooker. It's a sign of how little I know about my own witness that I don't even know if he's married.

He proves to be a decent witness on direct examination. My questions are straightforward, as are his answers, and he lays out what he saw that night, much as he did in my office. He speaks softly and without much emotion, but his words cause obvious excitement in the jury and gallery.

The defense has thrown its best punch. The battle has been joined.

I turn Eddie over to Tucker, who is trying to look confident despite what he has to consider a major blow to his case.

"Mr. Gardner, you testified that you are a truck driver and that you often drive cross-country. Is that correct?"

Eddie nods. "Yes."

"How is it you know you were in this area on that particular night?"

"I keep a log for my employer of where I am at all times. It's how I get paid."

Tucker nods; this seems reasonable. "And your previous trip ended two days before the night of the murder?"

Eddie nods again. "Right. I got home on the twelfth; the murder was on the fourteenth."

"At about one A.M.?"

"Right," agrees Eddie.

Tucker makes some notes, then turns a page on his legal pad. "Are you familiar with the number 201-453-6745?"

"Yes. It's my cell phone."

Uh-oh. I don't like where this is going.

Tucker takes a sheet of paper and gets permission from Calvin to approach the witness. He hands it to Eddie, who looks intently at it, still seeming unworried.

Tucker directs him to two calls made that night, at 12:45 and 12:51. Based on the area codes of the numbers called, they were both in this area.

"Did you make those calls?" Tucker asks.

"I don't remember," Eddie says. "I guess so."

"Does anyone else use your cell phone?"

"No."

"And it wasn't stolen?" Tucker asks. "You still have it?"

"Yes."

Tucker introduces another document into evidence, which he asks Eddie to read. It is an affidavit, signed by a vice president at Eddie's cell phone company.

Eddie's voice grows softer as he reads one particular sentence. "The two calls in question were made from within four miles of Camden, New Jersey, more than ninety miles from the city of Passaic."

A bomb has been dropped in the courtroom, yet when I look around, I don't see any charred wreckage. All I see are jurors and press and citizens and a judge staring right back at me. Kevin looks like he may throw up on the defense table, and Daniel is somehow able to obey my edict to look impassive. He may just be in a state of shock.

If it weren't so sad, it would be laughable: Dominic Petrone had promised to help me if I kept his name out of the trial. I did keep his name out, but only because Lassiter's name was a ready and preferable substitute. Now it seems obvious that Petrone has delivered on his promise by providing me with a witness to support my case. The problem is that the witness is lying, and my case has blown up in my face.

Thanks, Dominic.

Eddie finally gets off the stand, but not before Calvin publicly directs Tucker to pursue perjury charges against him. Calvin then tells Tucker and me to come back for a meeting in his chambers.

Tucker is surprisingly subdued in chambers, though I wouldn't blame him if he were turning cartwheels. Calvin asks me how this disaster happened, and I tell him the truth, minus my previous conversation with Petrone. Both Calvin and Tucker seem to accept my denial that I knew Eddie was lying when I put him on the stand, and Calvin doesn't seem inclined to sanction me further.

"I think you've probably suffered enough," he says.

There's no doubt that I have suffered, but not as much as my client, who I happen to be sure is innocent. There is virtually no chance that the jury will agree with that assessment, not now that his defense has been shown to be lying in front of them.

I make it through the afternoon court session in a semifog. I can only liken it to a team in the last game of the World Series, when the other team scores ten runs in the seventh inning to take a fifteen to nothing lead. The trailing team goes through the motions in the eighth and ninth, but they know the boat has sailed.

Ironically and pathetically, my next witness is a cell phone technology expert, whom I've brought in to show that the science is inexact as it relates to the night Linda Padilla died. I make some decent points, but Tucker blows me out of the water with his cross-examination.

"If your technology shows a call was made from Camden, could it actually have been made in North Jersey?"

"No," says my expert.

Game, set, and match.

Our team meeting tonight is more like a wake, with my body the one on display. It is incredibly frustrating: We know who the guilty party is, but we can't take advantage of that fact. Worse, we've been shown to be liars, which is to say that the jury will not believe anything we tell them for the rest of the trial.

Laurie and I take turns beating ourselves up. She feels she should have done more to check out Eddie, though there really is no way she could have in the time allotted. She would not have access to cell phone records, nor did she have the manpower at Tucker's disposal.

For my part, I put someone on the stand that I was unsure of. In doing so, I staked the reputation of the defense on his testimony, and it took Tucker less than five minutes to leave that defense in shreds. I blew it, plain and simple.

Kevin tries to make both of us feel better, an impossible task if ever there was one. After a half hour or so he gives up, and turns his efforts toward motivating me to prepare for court tomorrow. It's not an easy job; I would rather spend tomorrow having my eyeballs plucked.

The phone rings and I jump to get it, anything to not have to think about the mess we are in. I don't even bother to look at caller ID; which is okay, because Willie's voice is on the other end.

"Andy? It's me."

"What's going on?" I ask, hoping to be drawn into a long conversation about dog adoptions or coffee futures or anything else not having to do with our case.

"Sondra was attacked," he says, and I now realize his voice is shaky.

"Is she all right?"

"Yeah, I think so. She says she is. It happened in front of my house."

"I'll be right over," I say, and he doesn't try to talk me out of it.

I tell Laurie and Kevin what has happened, and Laurie comes with me to Willie's. Kevin stays behind to go over tomorrow's witnesses, pathetic though they may be.

Willie still lives in a very run-down area of Paterson. He bought a small house and has done a lot to fix it up. He is wealthy enough to live pretty much anywhere he wants, but feels like he would be a traitor if he left his old neighborhood. I wonder if what has just happened will change his mind, but I doubt it.

Sondra is lying on the couch when we arrive. She seems shaken but not badly hurt. Willie is more upset than I have ever seen him, even when he was on death row.

"Tell me what happened," I say.

"We got home from Atlantic City about an hour ago. I dropped Sondra off in the front and went to park the

car because our garage is filled with stuff. I came back
and saw her on the steps, with this guy grabbing her
from behind."

I turn to Sondra, who picks up the story. "I couldn't
find my key, so I was waiting for Willie. The guy
grabbed me around my neck; I didn't see him coming."

Willie takes over, describing how he ran toward the
house screaming and the guy took off. Willie hesitated
to make sure Sondra was okay before picking up the
chase, which allowed the attacker to get away.

"If I had caught him, I'da killed him."

I have no doubt Willie would have done just that.
"Did he take anything?" I ask. I look at the alexandrite
locket still around her neck. "Any jewelry or anything?"

Sondra shakes her head. "No. I don't think so."

Willie asks if he needs to call the police, and I say
that it would be a good idea. Sondra hadn't seen her attacker, but at least calling would alert the police to be on
the lookout for him in the area.

Willie, mostly because of his past experiences, has a
healthy distrust of the police, but he makes the call. He
reports that they don't seem too distressed, but promise
to send an officer over to take a statement.

Laurie and I stay around awhile, mainly because I
don't want to go back and deal with the grim realities of
court preparation. The doorbell rings and I answer it,
fully expecting it to be the police. I am very surprised to
see Kevin standing there.

"I didn't know Willie's phone number, but I knew
where he lived," Kevin says.

"Sorry," I say, "I should have called you. Sondra's
fine; just a little shaken up."

"That's not why I'm here," Kevin says, and for the first time, I notice he has a weird expression on his face.

"What is it?" I ask.

"There's been another murder," he says. "A woman's been strangled and her hands were cut off."

● ● ● ● ●

DENISE BANKS HAD been out dancing with friends at the Belmont Club in downtown Paterson, approximately six blocks from Willie's house. Friends say that she complained of a headache and left the club alone at eleven P.M. Her body was discovered an hour later in an alley fifty feet from her car.

We get this information from television, along with an unconfirmed report that Ms. Banks was strangled and her hands were cut off. If the reports are correct, either the same killer has struck again, or a copycat killer has taken over.

We are all stunned, both because of the murder itself and also because of the strong likelihood that Sondra was almost the victim. It's certainly possible that there were two attackers in the area around that time, but I don't believe in coincidences, and I'm not going to start with this one.

We head over to the murder scene, and Willie and Sondra come along. Their report to the police is even more significant now, but in all the turmoil it may take the cops a while to get around to them.

Vince is already on the periphery of the scene when we arrive, though he has no more information than we do. I'm sure he's upset that a woman has been murdered, but his focus is elsewhere. "You think this will get Daniel off?" he asks, and I deflect the question, mumbling that we'll have to wait and see exactly what happened.

Laurie says, "I'll take Willie and Sondra inside."

I nod. "We'll be right here."

She then leads them into the area where the police are concentrated, able to make her way in because she knows most of the officers guarding the periphery.

Vince, Kevin, and I spend the next hour and a half standing in the same spot, waiting for their return. I see a number of people that I know leave the scene, including the coroner, Janet Carlson. She sees me and just shakes her head sadly; it's another night of exposure to the inhumanity of humans. I wouldn't do her job for all the money in the world.

Finally, Laurie, Willie, and Sondra come out, and I'm very pleased to see that Pete Stanton is with them.

"Let's find someplace to talk," Pete says.

"I know a coffee shop three blocks from here," says Vince.

Pete shakes his head. "Let's go somewhere private."

I'm sure Pete doesn't want to be seen talking with the enemy, and I don't blame him. I also don't want a big crowd for this conversation, but there's no way we're going to get rid of Vince. "I think we should help Willie get Sondra back," I say. "She's been through enough tonight."

Willie shakes his head. "I don't need no help. There ain't nothing going to hurt her."

I believe him totally and they head home. The rest of us go back to my house, with Pete taking his own car. I ask Laurie what she has learned, but she explains that everybody was tight-lipped, and she was going to give up when she saw Pete. He was heading out, and he agreed to fill us in.

Pete asks us not to reveal that he spoke with us, since he knows Captain Millen would have a stroke if he found out. Pete also knows that all this information is due to us in discovery anyway, so he is merely giving us a couple hours head start.

"It's the same killer," Pete says.

"No chance it's a copycat?" I ask.

He shakes his head. "Not according to Janet. She said the angle of the strangulation and the way he cut are identical. She said it's the same guy; she told Millen while I was there."

"What did he say?"

"That she shouldn't jump to conclusions, and should go back and examine the body more carefully."

"Which she's doing now?" Laurie asks.

"Yeah. But she told me her opinion won't change, that there's no doubt."

"Anything else we need to know?" I ask.

He nods. "The killer left a note. I think I remember the exact words . . . 'Only fools kill the messenger.'"

This is another bombshell in a night full of them. "He's talking about Daniel," I say. "He had said that Daniel would reveal him to the world. Daniel was his messenger, and he's telling the cops they are killing the wrong guy."

Pete leaves, and Kevin and I immediately start to focus on the most effective way to use this information in court. We are both confident that it will be admissible, and we discuss strategy in case Tucker resists. More likely, he'll see it as a futile effort; he knows as well as I do that every juror must already know about tonight's events by now.

Laurie and I aren't in bed until almost three A.M., and we spend some more time reflecting on the amazing turn of events. Today was a true disaster in court, but now I don't see how we can lose.

"Too bad Denise Banks had to lose," she says.

This comment jolts me; it's pathetic how little attention I've paid to Denise Banks. I've been so caught up in my own situation that a victim of a vicious murder became a piece of a strategic struggle.

Also absent from my thinking has been the fact that the killer is still out there, probably preparing to strike again. Once again his actions defy understanding: Why go to all the trouble of framing Daniel only to commit an act that could get him off the hook days before his certain conviction?

I fully believe that Lassiter is the murderer, but these are not the actions of a dispassionate contract killer. It seems like more of a game, or an ego trip, a taunting way to embarrass the police. A more deadly version of his paint-ball game with me on the Manhattan street.

I'm up at six, refreshed despite getting less than three hours' sleep. I watch the news as I prepare to go to court, but though it's far and away the dominant story, there is less-current information than I got from Pete.

At seven I get a call from the court clerk: Calvin is

summoning us to his chambers for an early meeting. Laurie takes Tara for her walk, and I pick up Kevin so that we can strategize before our meeting. The way Calvin handles this will decide Daniel's fate.

"Well, gentlemen, we've got some issues to deal with" is how Calvin begins. He invites Tucker to update all of us on the events of last night, and Tucker quickly does so. His version has Janet Carlson less confident that the killer is the same, and neglects to mention the note.

"Did the killer contact anyone?" I ask innocently. "Or maybe leave any kind of message?"

Tucker nods and grudgingly tells us about the note. "You leave anything else out, Mr. Zachry?" Calvin asks with obvious annoyance.

Tucker says that he has not, and goes on to argue that this latest murder should not be presented to the jury, that it could be a copycat and does not change the facts concerning the previous murders.

We are prepared for this argument, but any first-year law student could win it. Kevin gives me a copy of the transcript of Tucker's direct examination of Captain Millen. I read back to Calvin the exchange during which Tucker asked if any further murders have been committed since Daniel's arrest.

When I'm finished reading, I drive the point home, though it's already been made. "Clearly, if the question was proper when the prosecution asked it, it will be proper when I call Millen back to the stand and ask it again."

Tucker has no answer for this, at least none that Calvin finds remotely persuasive. He asks me whom I plan to call, and I tell him just Millen and Janet Carlson. He decides to delay the start of court until after lunch, to give both of them time to get here.

I use the additional time to talk to Kevin about our final strategy for these witnesses, though it will be a cakewalk. When we're finished, I realize I haven't talked to Daniel since all this went down, and I arrange to meet with him in a court anteroom.

The first thing Daniel says when he's brought in is, "Is it all true? Did he really kill someone else?"

I confirm that it is in fact true and bring him up-to-date on where we stand. He takes it all in, a look of some wonderment on his face. When I finish, he says, "It's weird: An innocent person dies and it makes our case." My opinion of him instantly goes up a very large notch; his reaction is exactly what mine should have been.

Understandably, he soon focuses on the trial. "Is there any way we can lose? I mean, there has to be at least reasonable doubt now, doesn't there?"

I always try to be honest with my clients when I have bad news, so I might as well continue with that approach when the news is good. "Unless we get another surprise, I think Tucker will have to move for a dismissal."

I call Captain Millen to the stand, and before I start my questioning I have to make sure I'm not salivating. He doesn't put up any real resistance, answering my questions honestly and dispassionately. He admits his belief that Denise Banks's killer is the same person who killed Linda Padilla and the other women, though he says he cannot be sure.

Janet Carlson is next, and she puts the finishing touch on a perfect afternoon. She says there is no doubt that one man has done all the killings.

"So if we assume that Mr. Cummings has been in custody for the past three months, would you say there is reasonable doubt that he killed Linda Padilla?"

She looks at the jury as she answers. "I would say there is no doubt whatsoever. Mr. Cummings did not kill Linda Padilla."

Tucker does not cross-examine and asks for a brief recess. When it's over, he stands and addresses the court. "Your Honor, I don't think it's any secret that the events of last night have cast a new light on this case. It has always been the policy of this state to treat everyone in a fair and impartial manner, and my office conducts this and all cases with that fairness as our primary concern."

I allow myself a look at Kevin, and his expression confirms my feelings. Tucker is about to give it up.

"With that in mind, Your Honor, we believe that you should order a directed verdict of not guilty, and all charges against Daniel Cummings in this matter should be dismissed."

There is an uproar in the courtroom, but my feelings, while I'm happy with the result, are unlike any I've experienced in my career. We've won, a client I believe is innocent is being set free, but I feel I've done little to accomplish that fact. Forces outside of my control intervened to provide this victory, and mixed in with my joy and relief is a slight discomfort.

It's possible that the actual mechanics of the event are causing my reaction. I'm used to the tension and buildup before a verdict; this opposition surrender has a bit of the surreal to it. But it's happened; I only have to glance at the press section to confirm that.

I look at Daniel, who seems stunned even though I told him this was a very likely result. He stares at me, questioning, and I smile and nod. Only then does his face reflect his joy.

Calvin dismisses the charges and it's over. Daniel hugs Kevin and me, and Tucker comes over to congratulate us all. It's a surprisingly gracious gesture from a man who is sure to face some difficult media scrutiny.

Vince comes down to the defense table. He hugs Daniel, then Kevin and me, and I think he's actually tearful. "Man, you did it," he says to me. "You did it."

It's not true, of course, but I don't bother to correct him. Someone else did it, last night, by strangling and mutilating Denise Banks.

• • • • •

OUR POST-TRIAL VICTORY celebration is at Charlie's. It's a tradition, and as always, we are given a private room in the back. In this case the privacy is more necessary than usual because the press and public somehow became aware of the location, and they've shown up en masse.

We limit the party to the core group: Kevin, Laurie, Vince, Daniel, and myself. We are more subdued than usual, possibly because there is no explosion after the tension of waiting for a jury verdict. Relief is etched on Daniel's face; he claims never to have been so scared in his entire life.

He raises his glass in a toast. "To the best legal team and the best lead lawyer a man could ever have."

There seems to be no dissent from that opinion, so I'm not about to quibble. I've gone from the worst lawyer on the face of the planet for putting Eddie on the stand, to

America's finest legal mind. All because a maniac committed a brutal murder.

The gathering breaks up fairly early, and Daniel gives us each a final hug as we leave. I tell him that we will need to get together to go over my final bill, and he smiles and says, "Anytime. No problem."

Vince comes up to me and for a moment seems to be readying for a hug himself. At the last moment he veers off, and it becomes a handshake, which is fine with me. "I knew you could do it and you did," he says. "You did."

The fact is that I didn't, but I don't bother saying that to Vince. Laurie and I head home, and when we're in bed, she asks, "You okay, Andy?"

"I'm fine. I'm glad it's over."

"Are you going to go away?" She's referring to my traditional post-trial break, where I take Tara and get away for a couple of weeks to decompress.

"I'm not sure. I'm not sure I need to."

"I thought maybe we could go together," she says. "The three of us."

"That sounds nice."

My reaction sounds less enthusiastic than I actually feel about her suggestion, and she picks up on it. "Unless you don't want to," she says. "I know you like to be alone."

"Laurie, getting away with you sounds wonderful. But not for too long. I was thinking under five years."

She smiles and kisses me, but we wait until morning to tell Tara the good news.

Kevin is in the office in the morning when I arrive. We go over the hours we put in, and prepare a final bill for Daniel. It's very substantial; Lassiter could have saved

Daniel a lot of money by committing another murder a couple of months earlier.

When we're finished, I call Daniel to set up a meeting to go over the charges. He's not yet back working at the paper, so he asks if we can meet at his house at six P.M., which is fine with me.

Kevin and I haven't really had a chance to discuss the sudden ending to the case, and I can tell he shares my rather disoriented feeling about it. He's more of a legal purist than I am and is very uncomfortable with the fact that the determining event of the trial happened in a back alley in downtown Paterson.

No matter what angle we look at things from, the actions of Lassiter make no sense. He went to huge trouble to frame Daniel for the murders, only to save him when his efforts were about to be rewarded. Even more puzzling is Lassiter's motive for the entire murder spree: Could someone be paying him to do this? And if so, why? Is it simply that he is insane?

Kevin thinks that Lassiter is a psychopath who gets off on making fools of the police and is unconcerned about how many people must die to make that happen. The fact is that the only way we are going to get any of these answers is if Lassiter gets caught, and hopefully, that will be accomplished before other women are killed.

I head home and take Tara for a long walk in the park. Laurie and I have decided to rent a house on Long Beach Island for a couple of weeks, and Tara seems fine with that. Tara and I have been there a number of times; it is beautiful and peaceful, especially outside the summer season.

I leave a note for Laurie, suggesting that we have dinner at Charlie's after my meeting with Daniel. I then drive over to Daniel's house, which is in a very expensive, heavily wooded section of Englewood Cliffs.

As I pull up to the house, I can see Daniel looking out at me through his front window and smiling. He is dressed casually and seems the picture of comfort, a far cry from the agony of confinement behind bars.

Moments later the front door opens, and he comes out on his porch to greet me. As I walk toward his house, I hear what seems like a small clap of thunder from behind me and to the right. I turn but don't see anything, then look back toward the porch.

Daniel is still standing there, but he no longer has a face. It has been replaced by a bloody mask, and I watch, transfixed, as he slowly topples over onto a small table and then to the floor.

It takes my mind a split second to process what has happened, and I realize that a shot must have been fired from the wooded area behind me and across the street. I dive behind Daniel's car, parked in his driveway, and try to peer into the trees. It's getting dark, but I doubt that I would be able to see anyone even if it were broad daylight.

In my panic I briefly consider trying to make it to those woods, in the hope of at least getting a look at the shooter, but it seems futile. If he has taken off, he's had plenty of time by now, and I won't be able to catch him. If he's still there, I'll be a sitting duck and his next victim. My logical decision to stay put does not have to overcome any latent heroic streak residing inside me, so I stick with it.

It is unlikely anyone in this sparsely populated area saw or heard anything, so I am going to have to make the next move, whatever that move might be. Staying low and under cover as best I can, I make it to the porch to check on Daniel's condition. It doesn't take a physician to know that he is dead; it is one of the most horrible sights I have ever seen.

The door to the house remains open, and I decide to go inside to get out of the possible line of fire. I make a break for the door and half dive, half trip into the foyer, sprawling on my stomach. It's not pretty, but unfortunately, no one around is alive to see it.

I find a portable phone and call 911, reporting the crime and making sure they alert Captain Millen. As I do this, I occasionally peek out the front window, though there is no sign of the shooter. Clearly, Daniel was the sole target; if the killer wanted to get two for the price of one, I was an open target as I approached the house.

The next thought to enter my stressed-out mind is that Vince must be told that his son is dead. I consider the possible ways to do this, and none seem right. I don't want him to hear it from the media or from the police, and it doesn't feel right to tell him over the phone, certainly not from here.

Instead, I call Laurie, and fortunately, she hasn't gone to Charlie's yet. "Laurie, it's me. Something terrible has happened."

I go on to describe my situation, and I'm not two sentences in before she's yelling at me to "stay down." I tell her that the shooter has gone, that there's no longer anything to worry about, but she keeps saying it, until I sit down on the floor to continue the conversation.

I bring up the subject of Vince, and she immediately says, "I'll tell him." I mention that Vince is usually still in his office at this time of day, but she cuts me off, telling me not to worry. "I'll find him and I'll tell him," she says. "You just be careful. And call me as soon as the police get there."

At that moment sirens can be heard in the background, so I peek out the window. "They're here. Thanks."

By the time I get outside, the street is filled with police cars, ambulances, and every flashing light in New Jersey. Patrolmen, with guns drawn, approach the house and order me to lie down with my hands outstretched. I let them search me, all the while identifying myself and telling them that I'm the one who called 911. In answer to their questions, I describe how this happened and where I think the shot came from.

I'm brought back into the house and led into a den near the back. As I go, I see medics rushing to attend to Daniel. If they can do something for him, we've made greater strides in medicine than I was aware of.

Two patrolmen sit in the den with me, but neither asks me any questions. My guess is that Millen has sent instructions that he wants to be the first to question me. It's a good guess, because Millen arrives five minutes later, with two other detectives.

I describe what happened in my own words, then answer a number of questions from Millen designed to bring out more detail. He's good at it; he gets more out of me than I realized I knew. Nothing earth-shattering, but maybe it will be helpful to him.

My assumption is that this was Lassiter, finishing up a deadly game with Daniel that I've never understood. I tell this to Millen, and rather than blowing me off, he seems to consider it. "Maybe," he says. "Or maybe some looney-tune citizen thought justice wasn't done in court and figured he'd take care of it himself."

I write out a detailed statement and sign it, promising

to make myself available to Millen. He tells me I'm free to go, and when I stand up, I'm surprised and a little embarrassed to find that my legs are shaky. This has been a rough night.

I go outside, and it's still just as much of a madhouse as before. I start to walk to where I left my car when I see Laurie and Vince, standing next to a police car. I instinctively look to where Daniel had been lying on the porch and am glad his body has been removed. I hope it was done before Vince got here.

I walk over to them and put my arm on Vince's shoulder. "I can't tell you how sorry I am, Vince."

He just nods, and Laurie hugs me as hard as I've ever been hugged. "Are you okay, Andy?" she asks.

I confirm that I am, after which Vince starts asking me questions, probably as many as Millen did. Laurie makes eye contact with me, and this time I know we're thinking the same thing: Vince is trying to attack this problem logically, trying to immerse himself in the effort to catch the killer, so that he will not have to deal with the emotion.

I patiently answer every question Vince has, until the crowd is starting to thin out and there's just no reason to stay there anymore. I ask him if he wants to come to my house and stay with Laurie and me, but he doesn't.

He wants to be someplace where he feels comfortable, but no such place exists.

• • • • •

THE CROWD AT DANIEL'S funeral could fill Madison Square Garden. Vince asks Laurie and me to sit up front with him, so it's not until it's over that I get a full appreciation for the size of the crowd. Daniel had a lot of friends, though the overwhelming majority of the attendees are there because of Vince. Vince knows everybody and everybody knows Vince, and it's apparent today that they like him as well.

Vince sits stoically throughout the service, much as he's been the last three days. Laurie and I are worried about him, but all we can do is watch him try to deal with this nightmare as best he can.

Vince invites about a dozen people back to his house afterward, and Laurie views this as a healthy sign. She and I are included in the group, and she has the foresight to call ahead and order some platters of food to be delivered there when we arrive. It's not something Vince thought of, and he's grateful for her thoughtfulness.

There do not seem to have been any developments in the search for Lassiter, and as I sit at Vince's, my mind wanders back to the circumstances leading up to Daniel's murder. There's got to be an answer to the question of why Lassiter would get Daniel off his legal hook only to gun him down. Hatred is not the likely motivation; it's fair to say that Daniel would have suffered more if the state had put him to death after years of miserable confinement on death row.

Vince's boss, Philip Brisker, comes over and sits down with Laurie and me. Philip is in his early seventies and has been publisher of the paper since taking over from his father twenty years ago. The paper has been in the Brisker family for as long as I can remember, and that family has been well respected for a lot longer than that.

Philip wants to discuss our mutual concern for Vince. He thinks it would be good for Vince to come back to the paper sooner rather than later, and Laurie and I agree. I say that I'll talk to Vince and gently suggest it but that he needs to do what feels right for him.

"It's ironic," Philip says, "all that time, with all everybody went through . . . for it to end like this. You win your case, and then . . ."

He doesn't finish his thought, but I wouldn't know if he did because my mind is racing. I'm realizing why I won my case and why Daniel lost his life.

Laurie and I stay for a short while longer and then say our goodbyes to Vince. I drop Laurie off at home, though she wants to stay with me.

Where I'm going I have to go alone.

I arrive at Dominic Petrone's house at about five in the

afternoon. I have no idea if he is at home, but I didn't think calling ahead would be possible or productive. I could have had Vince arrange the meeting, since Vince knows Petrone along with everyone else, but I didn't want him to know about it.

I pull up to the gate that we went through the night Driver and Gorilla brought Marcus and me here. Once again three enormous men are on duty, though I don't recognize them as having been there that night. It doesn't matter; any one of them could handle me quite easily.

"Yeah?" says one of them when I open my window.

"I want to see Dominic Petrone," I say.

"Who the fuck are you?"

"Andy Carpenter."

He picks up the phone and calls in, reacting with some surprise a few moments later when he gets an apparently positive response. "Park behind the house and wait," he says, and the gate opens.

I park where I'm told, and in less than a minute Driver and Gorilla come out to meet me. "This brings back a lot of memories, doesn't it?" I say as Gorilla frisks me. They don't answer, but then again I don't expect them to.

I'm brought into the same room as on my previous visit, except this time Dominic is not there when I enter. Gorilla, Driver, and I sit and wait for almost twenty minutes, without a word being spoken. It's not the most comfortable twenty minutes I've ever spent.

Dominic enters and comes over to shake my hand, ever the gentleman. "Andy, sorry to keep you waiting. You should have told me you were coming."

"I'm sorry," I say, "but I didn't figure things out until about an hour ago."

He seems amused. "Is that right?"

I nod. "Dominic, I just want you to confirm what I believe. We both know there's nothing I can do about it legally, so I give you my word it won't leave this room. I just have to know for sure."

He sits down at his desk. "I'm listening."

I lay it out for him. "You came to believe that Daniel had Linda Padilla killed, and maybe he did . . . I don't think so, but I don't know for sure. You wanted him dead, but you had promised me your help if I kept your name out of the trial. When I did so, you sent me Eddie as a witness, but that blew up in my face. To make good on your promise, you made sure I won my case by having another murder committed."

"Andy . . . ," he says, but I'm almost finished, so I continue.

"Once I had my victory, you got your revenge on Daniel for Linda Padilla's death."

He shakes his head in apparent sadness and looks at Driver, who mimics the shake. "Andy, you believe I would have an innocent woman murdered for no other reason than to let you win your case?"

I nod. "I do."

"You are entirely wrong. About everything. I would not and did not have that woman murdered, I doubt very much that your client had anything to do with Linda's death, and I did not have him killed. Now, if you'll excuse me . . ."

"I don't believe you," I say, and immediately regret it.

"You flatter yourself," he says. "You are not important enough to lie to."

"Then tell me the truth. All of it. Please."

He considers this for a few moments, then, "I'll tell you what I know and what I believe. And if any of it is spoken outside this room, you will long for a death as quick and painless as your client's."

There isn't much to say to that, so I just wait.

"Tommy Lassiter killed Linda and the other women. I believe he was out for revenge against your client, which is why he framed him. I also believe he shot and killed him."

"So Linda Padilla was randomly picked like the others? She was in the wrong place at the wrong time?"

He shakes his head. "No, she was killed because Lassiter knew how much I valued her friendship. He killed her to hurt me . . . to show he could."

I understand this completely; he also shot me with the paint ball on the street simply to show he could. But there is much I don't understand. "Why would Lassiter commit that other murder, the one that got Daniel set free?"

Dominic shrugs. "I have no idea. He's not the most stable of men."

"And why would he want revenge against Daniel?"

"Daniel," he says, pronouncing the name with distaste, "hired Lassiter to kill his wife and make it appear as if someone else committed the murder. The man Lassiter framed turned out to have an alibi that Lassiter failed to anticipate, and the case fell apart. Daniel was dissatisfied and withheld some of the payment." He shakes his head. "Not a smart thing to do."

My mind is spinning, a fairly common occurrence these days. I believe Dominic; he would have no reason to lie to me. He is saying that my client, Daniel, was a murderer all along, though he was not guilty of the crime for which he was on trial. He arranged for the murder of his wife in a business transaction and then was stupid enough to renege when it came time to pay up.

The more I think about it, the more incredulous I get. "Lassiter killed five women, strangled them and cut off their hands, to get revenge against someone who didn't pay him enough money? That's what this was all about? Money?"

Dominic smiles a slight smile. "That's all it's ever about."

● ● ● ● ●

LOGIC TAKES A BUM RAP. It is the way I live my life. I probably ask myself the question "Is it logical?" more often than I ask, "Is it right?" Because logic is almost always right, and as far as I'm concerned, it should be the primary basis for human behavior.

Yet I am often told that I am "too logical" by people who don't understand that there is no such thing. Those people worship emotion and passion, and that's fine. Their mistake is in thinking that such feelings are inconsistent with logic, when in fact they should be using logic to drive that fire within them. If you're desperately, passionately in love with a woman, you don't win her over by picking your nose. It wouldn't be *logical*.

I guess that's one of the reasons I'm so disconcerted by what I've been through these past few months. I've been trying to apply logic in order to figure it out, when all along it's been a madman calling the shots. People have been literally dying all around me while I have been figuratively hunched over my desk, trying to apply logical theorems to the work of a vicious psycho.

Lassiter was angry because Daniel reneged on a deal, and he wanted revenge. So far it makes sense. But then he went out and killed five women and got Daniel on and off a legal hook, before killing Daniel himself. Why go to all that trouble? Why not just go out and kill Daniel in the first place? There is just no logical answer.

It's been three days since my conversation with Dominic Petrone. I've shared what he said with Laurie, and while she couldn't provide any real insight as to Lassiter's behavior, she was less surprised by it. I suppose that comes from her years on the police force, during which she dealt with an unending list of villainous screwballs.

I also told Pete Stanton about the Petrone conversation. I value his advice, and I can trust him to keep it to himself. He was so interested to hear what I had to say that he didn't make me take him to an expensive restaurant to say it.

I call Vince every day, but he's still pretty much in a fog. He's not ready to go back to the newspaper and says he doubts whether he ever will. I know it's going to take him time to bounce back, and I'm frustrated that I'm powerless to speed up the process.

I've decided against sharing Petrone's revelations with Vince. I know he has a right to know, but right now I just can't see myself telling him that his son murdered his daughter-in-law. Maybe I'm looking for an excuse, but I know he wouldn't believe it anyway; he would assume that Petrone had some reason to lie. Since he knows Petrone, he also might confront him about it, thus demonstrating that I revealed what Petrone told me, despite his warning not to. It could result in my untimely and very painful death, which would complicate matters greatly.

I haven't been in the office since Daniel's death; what little productive time I've spent has been at the foundation. There's something comforting about taking care of those dogs. They absolutely need me to provide food and shelter and comfort and life, and I know exactly how to provide them. It's all very logical.

I've also gotten to spend a lot more time with Tara, which is always good. We go on extended walks in the park, just like the one we're on now. Tara seems to appreciate the world more than I do; each bend in the path provides new sights and especially smells that captivate her. I both admire and envy this.

We are passing the Little League fields, a place that holds countless pleasant memories for me, when my cell phone rings. It is an unwelcome intrusion, and I'm sorry I brought it with me. I see on the caller ID display that it is Vince calling.

His voice is crisper, more alert, and his message is to the point. "They found Tommy Lassiter."

I'm very pleased to hear this, but my primary reaction is surprise. I had become convinced that Lassiter would never get caught, and I also assumed he was long out of this area.

"Where was he?" I ask.

"In a motel on Route 4."

"Is he talking?"

"I doubt it," Vince says. "He's been dead for three days. Shot in the head. The maid saw the Do Not Disturb sign on the door, but the place started to stink, so she decided to disturb."

"Any idea who did it?"

"Someone who knew him . . . he was having a beer and eating a sandwich. Somebody else's beer was there also, but Lassiter's was mixed with a drug to knock him out. The coroner thinks he was unconscious when he took the bullet."

"So it had to be someone he trusted," I say.

"Damn straight," says Vince. "If Lassiter thought he was in danger, a marine division couldn't have killed him."

What Vince is saying makes sense, but I still think Petrone was behind it. "It's got to be Petrone," I say, since Petrone had said to me that if he found Lassiter, we'd be "talking about him in the past tense."

Vince shrugs. "I don't care who did it. I'm just glad it got done."

"Thanks for letting me know, Vince. You doing okay?"

"Yeah. I'm getting there. You up for Charlie's later? There's a college game on."

Laurie and I were planning to spend a quiet night at home, but I know she'd want to support getting Vince back into the world. This news about Lassiter seems to have given him a lift, and I don't want to do anything to discourage it. "Sounds great. Okay if I bring a date?"

"Only if it's Laurie."

We meet at seven-thirty, and by seven-forty-five the table is covered with burgers, french fries, and beer. The game is on ESPN 2; it's Boise State versus Fresno State. The NCAA claims to be against gambling, yet they don't complain when ESPN buys a game like this for national broadcast. Do they think there's a single person east of Idaho who would be interested in Boise State–Fresno State if they weren't betting on it?

I take Boise State minus seven points. For the entire

first quarter, Vince is yelling at the bartender to adjust the color, refusing to believe me when I tell him that the football field in Boise is actually blue. My mind is filled with interesting tidbits of knowledge like that.

Boise is up twenty-one at the half when Pete Stanton comes in. He tells the bartender he's going to run a tab, but the tab he's talking about is mine.

"I knew I'd find you losers here," he says, then turns to Laurie. "Female company excepted."

Laurie smiles. "Exception noted."

"What's the score?" Pete asks.

"Twenty-eight–seven, Boise," I say.

"Who'd you take?"

"Boise."

"Damn," he says, shaking his head. "Money goes to money."

Like most of his comments, I let this one slide off my wealthy back. "Anything new on Petrone?"

He nods. "Yeah, the word on the street is he didn't hit Lassiter. He wanted to, but somebody beat him to it."

"You believe that?" I ask.

"Yup. The people who told me would know one way or the other. And the word is that it had to be somebody Lassiter trusted. Also, the gun was a Luger. Not the Petrone group's weapon of choice."

"So who could it have been?" I ask.

"Come on, you want a list of the people that would want to see Lassiter iced?"

"I'd be at the top of that list," says Vince.

Pete frowns. "You're not confessing, are you, Vince? 'Cause I'm off duty."

"Nah. But if I had a clean shot at him, I'd have taken it."

I'm getting that disconcerting, "where the hell is the

logic?" feeling again, and Laurie picks up on it. "Let it go, Andy," she says. "You're out of it now."

But even if I wanted to drop it, Vince doesn't. "If someone else killed Lassiter besides Petrone, you think that person could have killed Daniel as well?"

I shake my head. "No, I think it was Lassiter that shot Daniel."

"Why?" Vince asks. "I still don't see what he had against him. I mean, to frame him like that and then kill him . . ."

I don't know what the indoor record is for quick, embarrassed eye contact, but Pete, Laurie, and I are certainly smashing it. The three of us know about Petrone's accusations against Daniel, but we've left Vince in the dark. Right now that doesn't feel right, and Laurie seems to agree. Her slight nod tells me she thinks we should come clean with Vince.

"Vince, there's something I've got to tell you, something Dominic Petrone said."

"What?" asks Vince, and he literally prepares himself for a bombshell by gripping the table with his hands.

"He said that Daniel hired Lassiter to kill Margaret and then reneged on the payment. That's why Lassiter did what he did; he was getting revenge on Daniel."

"He's full of shit." It's a knee-jerk reaction, made without thought. A defense of his son.

"I didn't say he was right," I say. "I just thought you had a right to know."

"He's wrong," Vince says.

"Of course he is," says Laurie.

"Did he say why he thought so?" Vince asks.

"No. But he didn't say it's what he *thought*. He said it's what he *knew*."

Vince takes a drink from his bottle of beer but finds it empty. He looks around for the waitress. "Whose ass do you have to kiss to get a beer around here?" It's Vince's way of ending this part of the discussion, and it's fine with me.

I signal to the waitress that she should bring beers for everyone. Telling a man his son is a murderer is thirsty work.

● ● ● ● ●

ANOTHER LONG-STANDING tradition goes down the drain. And in this case, the drain is where it belongs.

For as long as I can remember, at the conclusion of every major case I've had, I take Tara and head down to Long Beach Island, where I rent a house and spend two weeks decompressing. It seems like I've done this for twenty years, but I realize that it's actually only seven years since I rescued Tara from the animal shelter.

This time Laurie has come with us, and while I haven't discussed it with Tara, I can't believe we didn't bring her along before. It's really quite remarkable; Laurie is all plus, no minus. By that I mean that she is great company, terrific to talk to, and I love having her around. At the same time, there are no negatives; she doesn't intrude, doesn't make me feel like I have to entertain her or be anything other than myself. When I want to be alone, I can be alone, either literally or just with my thoughts.

And since Tara has twice as many hands petting and giving biscuits to her, I suspect she agrees with me.

At the ten-day mark, I'm trying to figure how to add another week onto the trip. And maybe another decade after that. A phone call from Willie puts an end to such fantasies.

"When are you coming home?" he asks.

"Why?" I evade. "Any problems at the foundation?"

"Nope. We're doing great. I just wanted to know if you'd be home by Saturday."

"I will if you need me," I say.

"Good. I need you."

"What's going on?" I ask.

"Sondra and I are getting married Saturday night. You're the best man."

"That's a real honor, Willie. I wouldn't miss it for the world." Laurie walks into the room at that moment. "And neither would Laurie."

"Good," Willie says. " 'Cause she's the best woman." I hear Sondra's voice correcting him in the background, so he corrects himself. "Maid of something."

"Maid of honor," I say.

"Right."

Willie goes on to tell us the location of the wedding, an Italian restaurant/pizzeria in Paterson. He's negotiated a private room in the back. I would venture to say that Willie is the wealthiest person ever to get married in a pizzeria, but I think it has a certain panache.

I hang up the phone and turn to Laurie. "Willie and Sondra are getting married Saturday night. We are the best man and maid of honor, respectively."

"That's wonderful," she says.

For a woman who thinks that every marriage is "wonderful," Laurie makes surprisingly little effort to have one of her own. "Jealous?" I ask, casting my bait and hook into the water.

"For sure," she says. "I've had my eye on Willie for a long time."

We stay at the house until Saturday morning, trying to make the vacation last as long as possible. Just before we leave, I take Tara for a walk on the beach, a departure tradition that I want to continue. I throw a tennis ball into the water, and she dives in after it, oblivious to the cold and the oncoming waves. It is an act of absolute joy, and I want to watch her do it for years to come.

Weddings for me are high on the list of things that I dread attending. They're generally fancy and boring, and the fancier they are, the more boring they are. I particularly hate "black-tie affairs," which is one of the reasons why Willie and Sondra's wedding is so much fun. It's not fancy, not boring, and very much a no-tie affair.

The ceremony is nondenominational and relatively brief. Willie and Sondra take their vows, kiss, and the fifty or so guests raise their beer bottles in salute. We are all led into another room, where huge bowls of pasta are on the tables, and buffet tables are set up with every kind of pizza imaginable.

As best man, I am called upon to make a toast after dinner. I'm not at my best in situations like this, but I do the best I can. I toast Willie and Sondra as two wonderful people who have turned their lives around and who deserve each other, and I speak of Willie as a cherished partner and friend.

I'm not much for dancing, so Laurie must find other

partners to satisfy her apparent need for public gyration. Fortunately, Vince loses all inhibitions after his fifth beer, so he is able to more than fill in ably for me.

It is while they are dancing that Willie comes over to me and sits down. "Man, I know you don't like to hear this, but I owe everything to you. Everything."

"Who said I don't like to hear it?"

Willie never likes to talk about his time on death row, and we don't do so now. But we do talk about the other things that have happened since, the money, the foundation, new friends, and finding Sondra.

"It's weird," he says, "all these things happenin', one after another."

"I don't believe in coincidences," I say. "They're happening because of who you are and the way you're living your life."

"You always say that."

"What?"

"That you don't believe in coincidences."

"That's because I don't," I say.

"Well, I've got one for you. I've been thinking about it a lot." His tone is uncharacteristically serious, maybe a little worried.

"What's that?" I ask.

"In just a few months, Sondra almost got murdered twice."

His words hit me right between the eyes. Sondra was shot and then almost strangled. I never connected the two; they seemed like isolated events. Coincidences.

"Maybe you should move out of this neighborhood," I say, but the words have a hollow, foolish ring to them. It may even be a sign of a bias I didn't know I had: This is a poor, mostly black neighborhood, so attempted murders are not such earthshaking events. If it happened in wealthy suburbia, they would be forming commissions to investigate it.

"Maybe," he says, but he doesn't sound any more convinced than I am.

"And with all the expensive jewelry you're buying her, it makes her more of a target," I say, grasping at more straws.

"What are you talking about?" he asks, annoyance creeping into his voice. "Add everything up, I ain't spent a thousand bucks. Sondra thinks I'm cheap."

"Come on, Willie, it's none of my business, but that locket alone is worth ten thousand. It didn't fall off a truck, did it?"

His look is one of pure amazement. "Ten thousand? Are you kiddin' me? For that thing around her neck?"

"What did you pay?"

"I didn't. It was her friend's . . . Rosalie. It was in her stuff. Sondra wears it all the time . . . it's kind of a good-luck charm."

"Let me get this straight," I say. "Rosalie, the . . . girl that was working with Sondra, she had an alexandrite locket?"

Willie calls out to Sondra, sitting across the room, and asks her to come over, which she does. She's wearing the locket, and Willie points to it. "That was Rosalie's, right?"

Sondra reacts defensively, her hand covering the locket. "Yes . . . it was hers . . . I didn't know anyone to give it to." Some defiance creeps into her voice. "I think she would have wanted me to have it."

"Can I see it?" I ask.

She takes it off and hands it to me. I'm not an expert, but I have no doubt that it's real. "Rosalie had this in her apartment?" The apartment was ransacked after the murder; it would take a stupid criminal to leave this behind.

"No, we shared a safe-deposit box. All the girls had them. The guys that would come around . . . let's just say we didn't trust them that much."

I nod, and hold up the locket. "Did she have anything else like this?" I ask.

"No, not really. Just some old clothes . . ." She points to the locket. "Is it worth anything?"

"Ten grand," says Willie, and Sondra makes a sound somewhere between a gasp and a shriek.

"Oh, my God . . . ten thousand dollars," she says, then points to the locket. "It opens. There's a picture inside."

She shows me how to open it, and there is in fact a picture of a quite attractive woman, maybe fifty years old. The woman is well dressed and seems to be wearing the same locket, or one just like it. In the background is a stately Victorian house; it does not take a genius to figure out that this is a wealthy woman. "Do you know who this is?" I ask.

Sondra shrugs. "She sort of looks like Rosalie, so I just figured it was her mother or grandmother."

"Can I borrow this for a few days?" I ask.

"Sure. No problem."

On the way home I relate the story to Laurie, who doesn't see it as so remarkable. "Most of these kids don't start out on the street, Andy. Some of them come from upscale families, and if they run away, they could take a piece of those families with them."

"But Randy Clemens said it was all about 'the rich one' and that the others were 'window dressing.' We all just assumed it was Linda Padilla. What if it was Rosalie?

What if she was the real target, and Linda Padilla and the others were killed to cover up that fact?"

"So we need to find out who Rosalie was," she says. "Without prints, that's going to be tough. Dental records don't help unless you know who it might be, so you can get them and compare. They—"

I interrupt her, slapping the steering wheel in my excitement. "Maybe that's why he cut off her hands! Laurie, this guy was out there committing these psycho murders, but he didn't fit the profile of a psycho. There was no passion, no sexual molestation. He was cold and calculating, but cutting off the hands didn't fit in with that. Now it does! Maybe he was cutting off the hands so we wouldn't be able to identify Rosalie."

Laurie asks me if I have any idea at all who Rosalie might be, and though I do, I'm still so unsure that I don't want to voice it yet. Instead, I pick up the phone and call Kevin, Vince, and Sam Willis and give them each an assignment. I ask them to come to my house at four P.M. tomorrow with whatever they find out.

In the morning, I'm going to call Cindy Spodek and ask her a key question. Other than that, I'm going to just wait until four P.M. and try to relax. Because if I'm right, that's when the shit is going to start hitting the fan.

• • • • •

I BELIEVE THAT ROSALIE was Eliot Kendall's missing sister. Eliot had said his sister had never been found, but I think he was lying and that he had learned where she was. I also believe he hired Lassiter to kill her, and to kill the others as a way of deflecting attention.

I have to wait until four P.M. to find out if I'm right. It's like waiting for a jury verdict. People are going to march in and tell me whether or not Eliot Kendall is guilty of murder. They won't be doing it as part of a decision they've reached, but rather with the information they've spent the day gathering. But I feel just as powerless as when I'm waiting for a jury verdict: The final result is in the hands of others.

By three-thirty Kevin, Sam, and Vince have arrived. Only Vince hasn't brought the answers with him; they are being dug out of the Cleveland newspaper archives and being faxed directly to me. Laurie puts out food and drinks, and we begin.

Sam has done his usual amazing job of digging information out of that bewildering world inhabited by computers and the geeks that run them. He has come up with a copy of the recently deceased Byron Kendall's will, which is part of the public record because it involved a significant transfer of ownership of Kendall Industries, a publicly traded company. Byron, whose wife, Cynthia, died eight years ago, split his entire fortune evenly between his two children, Eliot and Tina. It notes that Tina has been missing for seven years and that if she is not found within three more years, she is to be considered deceased for the purpose of the document. In that case, Eliot would become the sole heir. As best as Sam can tell from his computer snooping, the total value of the estate is six hundred million dollars.

Kevin's job was a lot easier: simply to get a list of all visitors that Daniel saw at the prison, as well as the dates he saw each of them. He shows that to us, and it's consistent with our theory, but now we have to wait for Vince's information to be faxed.

We sit by the fax machine, watching it and waiting for it to ring. This is not the most fun I've ever had, and by six-thirty I want to slam the silent machine against the wall. Finally, it rings, and the material from the *Cleveland Plain Dealer* starts to come through. As requested, they have sent all their stories on the disappearance of Tina Kendall those seven years ago. Included are the stories Daniel wrote, and as Eliot described them, they were compassionate and not exploitive.

Some of the stories included photographs, and one of

them shows the entire Kendall family, two years before Tina's disappearance and one year before Cynthia's death. In the picture are Tina, Eliot, Byron, and Cynthia. It is impossible to tell if the young Tina is the same girl as the one found slain behind the Dumpster. But there is no doubt that Cynthia Kendall is the woman whose picture is in the locket.

The group now turns to me to hear my theory on what has taken place. I caution them that there is much I don't know, but I lay it all out to see if they can poke holes in it.

"Vince, I'm sorry, but I believe that Daniel hired Lassiter to have his wife killed." Vince winces slightly when he hears this, but he doesn't answer, so I continue. "And when Lassiter didn't successfully frame someone else for the murder, Daniel withheld some of the payment. If you'll remember, Marcus reported that someone else was originally charged with the crime, but the case fell apart. I think this was because Lassiter was sloppy.

"Meanwhile, Eliot's father was dying, and Eliot wasn't about to risk sharing the six hundred million with a sister that ran away. He tracked her down and then decided to kill her.

"Cindy Spodek of the FBI told me today that Kendall Industries has long been suspected of having mob ties and that it's assumed they've laundered money. Eliot must have used these connections to hire Lassiter to murder his sister, cutting off her hands so she couldn't be identified. Eliot would then wait the three years to get her removed from the will.

"Lassiter, whether on his own or with Eliot's approval, murdered the other women to deflect attention from the main target, Rosalie. Then, to get revenge against Daniel,

Lassiter set him up to be the fall guy. I'm sure he found it fit together quite well."

Laurie asks, "So the entire time Daniel was communicating with the killer, he knew it was Lassiter?"

I shake my head. "I don't think so. I think he found out the night of the Padilla murder, which is why he didn't call the police when he got the cell phone call. I think Daniel went to the park hoping to kill Lassiter himself."

"So why did Lassiter kill the fifth victim, which let Daniel off the hook?" Kevin asks.

"Here I'm guessing, but I think it's a good guess. In court the day Calvin let in the murder scene pictures of the previous victims, Daniel asked for their files. I think that's the day he recognized Rosalie. The day he put it all together."

Kevin nods and quickly thumbs through the logs showing visitation to Daniel at the prison. "And he saw Eliot at the prison the next day." I can hear the excitement in his voice.

"Right. Daniel pieced it together and told Eliot that if he didn't get him off, he would reveal Rosalie's identity to the world. Eliot had Lassiter do another killing, which ensured Daniel's freedom."

"But Lassiter wasn't about to let Daniel walk away, so he killed him at his house," says Laurie.

"And then Eliot killed Lassiter so there couldn't be a link back to him," says Kevin.

I nod. "Except for Sondra. It's why Rosalie was killed in her apartment and the place was ransacked. Eliot was looking to eliminate any possible connections between Rosalie and her real family. It's also why there were two attempts on Sondra's life; Eliot was covering another base on the chance that she knew something."

As I'm talking, another piece clicks into place. "You know, Eliot met Sondra in my office, and Willie and I both noticed he was staring at her. What I think he was really staring at was her locket. He recognized it, and it was soon after that he tried to have her killed. Which is why the killer grabbed at her neck."

We continue talking, and I can feel myself, as well as the others in the room, grow more excited. Eliot wasn't here out of concern for Daniel; he was here to monitor the situation. It's why he offered help; he wanted to be as close as he could to the source of information.

We've figured it out, I'm sure of it, and it's a damn good feeling.

It's left to Sam Willis to bring us crashing down. "So what are you going to do about this?"

For a group with all the answers, we shut up mighty fast. Eliot seems to have covered all the bases; the only ones who could testify against him, Daniel and Lassiter, are gone. Through DNA we can conclusively prove that Rosalie was Eliot's sister, but we have no concrete evidence at all that he paid for her murder.

Laurie thinks we have an obligation to turn this information over to Captain Millen, and while I'm sure she is right, I want to think things through first. I feel like our advantage, slim as it may be, is that Eliot doesn't know we are onto him. As long as our information stays within our group, we possess the element of surprise, and I'm not ready to give that up yet.

The group leaves at a little after midnight, and Laurie and I stay up for another hour or so talking about the situation some more. As a longtime criminal attorney, I've seen some pretty awful things, but the fact that so many women were brutally murdered as nothing more than a smoke screen sets a new standard.

Eliot Kendall is a scumbag, the lowest of the low, and I am going to bring him down.

All I have to do is figure out how.

• • • • •

My PLAN IS NOT EXACTLY brilliant, but after twenty-four hours of intensive thinking, it's the best I can do. I've gathered our group together again this evening to present it, first asking if anyone else has come up with anything.

Vince volunteers to "kill the son of a bitch," but other than that, everyone seems to want to hear what I have to say. So I say it.

"I'll call Eliot, tell him I want to see him about something related to the case, but I won't let on that there is anything wrong. When we meet, I'll tell him what I know, make him believe I have evidence to go to the police, and try and blackmail him."

"Blackmail him?" asks Kevin, making no effort to hide his incredulousness at my plan. "Why would you possibly blackmail him?"

"So I can get him to incriminate himself," I say. "I'll be wearing a wire."

Laurie seems less impressed than Kevin. "Andy, this isn't a TV movie. You try wearing a wire, you'll electrocute yourself."

Next, it's Vince's turn. "Andy, this guy is responsible for at least six murders. He killed Tommy Lassiter himself. What if he decides to make you number seven?"

We kick it back and forth for a couple of hours. Nobody is crazy about my plan, not even me, but the advantage it has is that it's the only plan we've got. We decide to try it, with the understanding that if it doesn't work quickly and smoothly, we turn everything over to Captain Millen.

"And the press," Vince hastens to add.

Laurie is going to go to Cleveland with Marcus, where they will await my arrival. Their job will be to listen in on the wire, but more important, to protect me if things go wrong. Which they very well could.

I don't sleep much, trying to decide how I should approach Eliot. It has to be a matter significant enough to make me travel to Cleveland, but not ominous enough to alert him to any danger.

In the morning I walk Tara and then go to the office. It would seem more natural for the call to be coming from there. Eliot isn't there when I call, but he gets back to me within ten minutes.

"Andy," he says, his voice open and friendly, "I didn't expect to hear from you. What's up?"

"I didn't see you at Daniel's funeral, and I—"

His tone goes somber on me, the grieving friend. "I took it pretty hard . . . I just couldn't stay around anymore. I mean, after all that he went through, after all you did, after he got *off*, for him to die like that . . ."

"It was terrible," I agree.

"Any news about who might be responsible?" he asks, trying to sound conversational.

"Could be. That's actually why I'm calling."

"Oh?"

"I have reason to believe Walter Castle may have been behind it after all. I know you had your investigators checking into him, so I wondered—"

He interrupts. "They really didn't come up with anything important."

"Maybe so, but maybe it would look different in the light of the information I have. I'd like to fly out and sit down with you about it."

"It must be important to you," he says.

"I hate to see a killer go unpunished."

We make a plan to meet tomorrow evening, and he agrees to my request to maintain "discretion" by meeting at my hotel. I've already made a reservation, and Laurie and Marcus will be in the adjoining room. I chose the hotel Marcus had stayed in before; he knows the layout, it's near a Taco Bell, has no spa, but does have an ice machine.

Laurie and I go out to Charlie's for dinner, and we talk about everything but the trip to Cleveland. We've already worked out the arrangements, purchased the recording equipment, and made our plans, so there doesn't seem to be anything more to say. In any event, if there is, neither of us wants to say it.

It isn't until we get into bed that Laurie says, "I'm concerned about this."

"Don't be. If I'm too virile for you, I'll stop and give you time to rest."

"Let me see if I understand this," she says. "You're making a bad sex joke? Now?"

"I didn't think it was so bad, but it was definitely a sex joke. I thought it was pretty funny."

"Andy, I'm worried about you. This guy is dangerous."

"I can take care of myself," I say.

"Since when?"

That didn't go too well, so I try another approach. "You and Marcus will be there."

"I guess . . . ," she says uncertainly. "But there will be a wall between us. If anything goes wrong, if you suspect anything, you holler as loud as you can."

"I will. I promise."

She leans over and kisses me. "Good night, Andy."

She then rolls over to go to sleep, clearly playing hard to get. "You know," I say, "men can relax themselves by making love the night before they go into battle."

"Good for them. Good night, Andy."

"Good night."

Within seconds, I can tell by her breathing that she's already asleep. I guess women deal with impending battle differently.

Laurie and Marcus are on an eight A.M. flight the next morning, and I spend the hours before my three P.M. flight hanging out with Tara. I'm a little nervous, not too bad, and being with Tara calms me even more.

I get to the airport with plenty of time to spare, but I find myself sitting in coach next to a fat woman with a baby. The daily double of annoying. I had always said that if I ever became rich I still wouldn't fly first-class, that the much higher fare is a total rip-off. Now that I am rich, I think it's time to reassess my position.

I've checked a bag, since it seemed much easier than dragging it through security as a carry-on. When we land, I go to baggage claim, where the limo driver I had arranged for is waiting for me with a sign bearing my name. Wealth does have its privileges.

We get the bag and are in the car within fifteen minutes. I tell the limo driver the name of the hotel, and we're off.

"Have a good flight, Mr. Carpenter?"

I nod, since he's looking at me through the mirror. "Not bad, if you don't count the fat woman and the baby."

He laughs. "One of those, huh?"

"One of those."

I've never been to Cleveland before, but the little I've seen so far is unimpressive, so I turn to my notes, trying to anticipate the conversation with Eliot. My chances of leading him into an admission are small, and I'm only going to have the one chance. I've got to take my best shot.

I feel the car pulling into the right lane, apparently to make a right turn. I look up, and my first impression is that we don't appear to be heading toward the city. Suddenly, the door next to me is jerked open and another man gets in the seat alongside me.

As the automatic door locks shut, the new passenger says, "Hello, Andy."

"Hello, Eliot," I say as fear surges through my body. "What are you doing here?"

"The real question is, what are you doing here? Maybe to trip me up? Or blackmail me?"

"I don't know what you're talking about" is the lame

line I come up with. I'm finding that the petrified mind does not think too clearly.

"You're not here to talk about Walter Castle, that's for sure."

My mind processes the fact that no matter what he says, it's not going to help, because I'm not yet wearing the wire. But even if I were, it wouldn't help me, because Laurie and Marcus would have no way of knowing where I am. I look toward the limo driver, who's listening but not reacting; obviously, he's with Eliot.

"How did you find out about Tina, Andy? How did you know she was my sister?"

"Who's Tina? Come on, Eliot, I don't know what's going on, but I don't like it."

He laughs. "It's only going to get worse, I assure you. You see, here's your mistake, Andy. I am hot shit in this town; I know everything there is to know. So when you go to my hometown newspaper to get stories about Tina, then I know what you know. Get it? So don't insult me with any more of your bullshit."

"The problem for you is that the cops know where I am and why."

He shakes his head. "I don't think so; this doesn't feel like a police operation. I think you're the Lone Ranger here, Andy." He laughs again. "Except you forgot your silver bullets."

I look out the window and see that we're in the countryside, a run-down area of trailer homes and poorly maintained farms. This is where I'm going to die. The fear is so palpable that I am in danger of throwing up.

"There's a record of where I am. They'll piece things together."

He points to the limo driver. "He looks like you, doesn't he, Andy? He's going to fly back on your ticket.

His fellow passengers won't look closely enough; they'll say it was you. So you obviously got killed when you got back home."

The car pulls to a stop near what look like run-down warehouses, maybe farm storage buildings, I can't tell. For the life of me, and I mean that literally, I can't figure out what to do.

"Get out, Andy."

The door locks pop up, allowing me to open the door. I get out, then notice that the driver is already out and is pointing his gun at me. Eliot gets out after me.

My back is to an open field, and I steal a glance at it to judge whether I'd have any chance making a break for it.

Eliot reads my mind. "Think you can make it, Andy? There's a lot of open space."

I can hear the driver chuckling as I consider it. "I don't think so," I say. "I'd rather we could talk this out."

"Be serious," he says, then points to the field. "Go on, I'll give you a five-second head start."

I look at the field again. "No," I say, and then I take off running. I move in a ridiculous zigzag pattern, hoping to make them miss. Ray Charles couldn't miss from this distance.

I'm running, cringing, and audibly moaning all at the same time, waiting for the burst of fire that will cut me down. All I hear behind me is Eliot laughing, as he must be slowly raising his gun.

A burst of gunfire crackles in the air, and I tense, bracing for the metal that will tear into my body. I don't feel anything, and for one bizarre moment I try to figure out which is faster, the speed of sound or the speed of a bullet.

I keep running as fast as I can. If they missed once, they can miss again. But I don't hear any more firing. I'm not yet confident; there is no reason to think they've let me off the hook. But as long as I'm alive, I'm going to do all I can to stay that way.

"Hey, asshole, get back here!"

The voice isn't Eliot's but it sounds familiar. I continue running but turn at an angle where I can quickly look back to where the car is.

There are now two cars there, two men standing, and two lying on the ground. One of the guys on the ground is dressed like Eliot. I can't tell who the two guys standing are, but they called me "asshole," so they must know me. If they wanted to kill me, they could have easily done so already, so I hesitantly walk back toward them.

As I get closer, I can see that the other man on the ground is the limo driver. The two standing are Gorilla and Driver, the men who work for Petrone who took Marcus and me to his house that night.

"You saved my life," I say.

"No shit," says Driver.

"Petrone sent you," I say.

"No shit."

"How did you know I was here?"

Driver shrugs. "We didn't. We were after him." He points to the very dead Eliot.

"How did Petrone know about him?" I ask. Getting information out of Driver is not the easiest thing in the world.

"Your pain-in-the-ass friend."

I realize immediately whom he is talking about. "Vince."

"No shit."

Driver offers me a ride back, and we wait while Gorilla digs an enormous grave to put the two bodies in. He does so with a minimum of effort; Gorilla is one ~ong guy.

"You might want to avoid mentioning this to anyone," says Driver. "Or he'll be digging a hole for you."

"My lips are sealed."

"That's a first."

They drive me back to the city. Very little is said on the way, though Gorilla remembers, "Your fucking dog bit my leg."

"I'll speak to her about it as soon as I get back. I'm sure she'll send you a note of apology."

They drop me off on the outskirts of town, and I take a cab to the hotel. Laurie has been frantic with worry, but Marcus seems to have handled it well.

"Where the hell have you been?" she asks.

I tell them the whole story, though I come off somewhat more heroic in the telling than I did in real life. For instance, in my version I had thrown Eliot to the ground and was about to disarm him when Driver and Gorilla showed up.

She listens patiently, then asks, "You want to tell us the real story?"

"Not particularly."

Marcus doesn't seem mesmerized by my account. Midway through it he gazes out the window toward the Taco Bell that he insisted be near the hotel. "You guys hungry?" he asks.

●　●　●　●　●

ELIOT KENDALL'S disappearance is a major national story. It's been two weeks now, and speculation runs rampant on where the heir to the Kendall fortune could be. I, of course, know exactly where he is, and that he is permanently sucking dirt. It bothers me that I am aware of two violent deaths and haven't done my civic duty and gone to the police, but I'll get over it.

Vince was unapologetic about informing Petrone of Eliot's guilt. He wanted to make sure that Eliot got the punishment due him, and he had more confidence in Petrone's ability to make that happen than he had in mine. In retrospect, he certainly was right.

I've had three conversations with Vince since coming home, and he's probably mentioned that he saved my life a hundred and fifty times. The last twenty times I haven't thanked him, but that hasn't slowed him down any.

The incident in Cleveland has stayed with me. I was

literally running for my life, and I fully expected to die. I know it's a cliché to say that experiences like that put things in perspective, but they really do. The experience has changed me, and I've been trying to focus on that which is important, and that means focusing on those I love.

I've been spending as much time as I can with Laurie and Tara, and today we're hiking in the rolling mountains in northwest New Jersey. Nothing too arduous; I haven't changed that much. But the air is cold, and it feels good to be outside, especially with Laurie and Tara. There's an inch of snow on the ground, and Tara loves to roll around in it.

About a half hour into the hike, Laurie says, "Doesn't the fresh air feel wonderful?"

"You never talk about getting married," I say.

"That answer wasn't exactly on point," she says.

"The fresh air feels wonderful. Absolutely wonderful. Much better than stale air would feel, I'll tell you that. So why don't you ever talk about getting married?"

"It's not something to talk about. It's something to do or not do."

"But you never mention it. That's a little unusual, don't you think?" I ask.

"Andy, are you asking me to marry you?"

Uh-oh. The direct approach. This is not my strong suit. The fact is, it's not so much that I want to get married, but more that I want Laurie to want to. "Would you say yes if I did?"

She smiles slightly. "Okay, I'll let you off the hook and answer your question without you having to ask it. No, I don't want to marry you. Not now."

I feel like somebody just hit me in the stomach with a seven-hundred-pound snowball. "Why?"

"Andy, I love you. Right now I want to spend the rest of my life with you. I don't know if that will ever change; I hope it doesn't. But I've just never had a need to be married. If it's that important to you, I'll do it. But it won't make me love you any more, because I couldn't love anyone any more than I love you."

Tara barks, which I think is her way of telling me to keep my mouth shut and leave well enough alone. I can't stifle a smile as I look up toward the sky and take a deep breath. "The air really feels great, doesn't it?"

ABOUT THE AUTHOR

DAVID ROSENFELT was the former marketing president for Tri-Star Pictures before becoming a writer of novels and screenplays. For more information about the author, please visit his Web site at www.davidrosenfelt.com.

More
David Rosenfelt!

Please turn this page
for a preview of

SUDDEN DEATH

Now available
in hardcover.

● ● ● ● ●

I STEP OFF THE PLANE, and for the first time in my life, I'm in Los Angeles. I'm not sure why I've never been here before. I certainly haven't had any preconceived notions about the place, other than the fact that the people here are insincere, draft-dodging, drug-taking, money-grubbing, breast-implanting, out-of-touch, pâté-eating, pompous, Lakers-loving, let's-do-lunching, elitist scumbags.

But here I am, open-minded as always.

Walking next to me is Willie Miller, whose own mind is so wide-open that anything at all is completely free to go in and out, and often does. I'm not sure how thoughts actually enter his mind, but the point of exit is definitely his mouth. "This place ain't so cool," says Willie.

"Willie, it's only the airport." I look over at him and am surprised to see that he is wearing sunglasses. They seem to have appeared in the last few seconds, as if he has grown them. While he doesn't consider the airport "cool," he apparently fears that it might be sunny.

Willie has become a good friend these last couple of years. He's twenty-eight, ten years my junior, and we met when I successfully defended him on an appeal of a murder charge for which he had been wrongly convicted. Willie spent seven long years on death row, and his story is the reason we're out here. That and the fact that I had nothing better to do.

We take the escalator down to baggage claim, where a tall blond man wearing a black suit and sunglasses just like Willie's holds up a sign that says "Carpenter." Since my name is Andy Carpenter, I pick up on this almost immediately. "That's us," I say to the man, who is obviously our driver.

"How was your flight?" he asks, an opening conversational gambit I suspect he's used before. I say that it was fine, and then we move smoothly into a chat about the weather while we wait for the bags to come down. I learn that it's sunny today, has been sunny this month, last month, and will be sunny next month and the month after that. It's early June, and there is no chance of rain until December. However, I sense that the driver is a little nervous, because for tomorrow they're predicting a forty percent chance of clouds.

I have just one small suitcase, which I wouldn't have bothered to check had not Willie brought two enormous ones. I make the mistake of trying to lift one of Willie's bags off the carousel; it must weigh four hundred pounds. "Did you bring your rock collection?" I ask, but Willie just shrugs and lifts the bag as if it were filled with pillows.

I've lived in apartments smaller than the limousine that transports us to the hotel. The movie studio is obviously trying to impress us, and so far succeeding quite well. It's only been a week since they called me and expressed a desire to turn my defense of Willie into a feature film, and we are out here to negotiate the possible sale of those rights. It's not something I relish, but Willie and the others involved all coaxed me into it. Had I known we would be flown first-class and whisked around in limos with a bar and TV, it might not have taken quite so much coaxing.

The truth is, none of us need the money we might make from this deal. I inherited twenty-two million dollars from my father, Willie received ten million dollars from a civil suit which we brought after his release, and I split up the million-dollar commission from that suit among everybody else. That "everybody else" consists of my associate, Kevin Randall, my secretary, Edna, and Laurie Collins, who functions in the dual role of private investigator and love of my life.

I would be far more enthusiastic about this trip if Laurie were here, but she decided to fly back to Findlay, Wisconsin, for her fifteenth high school reunion. When I warily mentioned that it would also be a chance for her to see her old boyfriends, she smiled and said, "We've got a lot of catching up to do."

"I'll be spending all my time in LA with nubile young actresses," I countered. "Sex-starved, lawyer-loving, nubile young actresses. The town is full of them." I said this in a pathetic and futile attempt to get her to change her mind and come out here with me. Instead, she said, "You do that." I didn't bother countering with, "I will," since we both know I won't.

So it's just Willie and me that the driver drops off at the Beverly Regent Wilshire Hotel. It's a nice enough place, but based on the nightly rate, the fairly average rooms must have buried treasure in the mattresses. But again, the studio is paying, which is one reason the first thing I do is have a fourteen-dollar can of mixed nuts from the minibar.

Since Willie's release from prison brought him some measure of fame, his life has taken some other dramatic turns. In addition to becoming wealthy, he's gotten married, partnered with me in a dog rescue operation, and become part of the very exclusive New York social scene. He and wife Sondra are out every night with what used to be known as the in crowd, though I am so far "out" that I'm not sure what they're called anymore. He is constantly and unintentionally name-dropping friends in the sports, entertainment, and art worlds, though he comically often has no idea that anyone else has heard of them.

Willie's social reach apparently extends across the country, because he invites me to go "clubbing" tonight with him and a number of his friends. I would rather be clubbed over the head, so I decline and make plans to order room service and watch a baseball game.

First I call Laurie at her hotel in Findlay, but she's out. I hope she's in the process of marveling at how fat and bald all her old boyfriends have gotten. Next I call Kevin Randall, who is watching Tara for me while I'm gone.

Golden retrievers are the greatest living things on this planet, and Tara is the greatest of all golden retrievers, so that makes her fairly special. I hate leaving her, even for a day, but there was no way I was going to put her in a crate in the bottom of a hot airplane.

"Hello?" Kevin answers, his voice raspy.

I put him through about three or four minutes of swearing to me that Tara is doing well, and then I ask him how he's feeling, since his voice maintains that raspy sound. I ask this reluctantly, since Kevin is America's foremost hypochondriac. "I'm okay," he says.

I'd love to leave it at that, but it would ruin his night. "You sure?" I ask.

"Well . . . ," he starts hesitantly, "do you know if humans can catch diseases from dogs?"

"Why? Is Tara sick?"

"I told you she was fine," he says. "We're talking about me now. I seem to have developed a cough." He throws in a couple of hacking noises, just in case I didn't know what he meant by "cough."

"That definitely sounds like kennel cough," I say. "You should curl up and sleep next to a warm oven tonight. And don't have more than a cup of kibble for dinner."

Kevin, who is no dummy, shrewdly figures out that I am going to continue to make fun of him if he pursues this, so he lets me extricate myself from the call. Once I do so, I have dinner and lie down to watch the Dodgers play the Padres. I'm not terribly interested in it, which is why I'm asleep by the third inning.

I wake up at seven and order room service. I get the

Assorted Fresh Berries for twenty-one fifty; for that price I would have expected twin Halle Berrys. They also bring an *LA Times* and *Wall Street Journal,* which are probably costing twenty bucks apiece.

The same driver and limo show up at nine in the morning to take Willie and me to the studio. We arrive early for our meeting, so we spend some time walking around the place, looking for stars. I don't see any, unless you count Willie.

We are eventually ushered into the office of Greg Burroughs, president of production at the studio. With him are a roomful of his colleagues, each with a title like "executive vice president" or "senior vice president." There seems to be an endless supply of gloriously titled executives; I wouldn't be surprised if there are three or four "emperors of production." The lowest ranked of the group is just a vice president, so it's probably the pathetic wretch's job to fetch the coffee and donuts.

It turns out that the overflow crowd is there merely as a show of how important we are to them, and everybody but Greg and a senior VP named Eric Anderson soon melts away. Greg is probably in his late thirties, and my guess is, he has ten years on Eric.

"Eric will be the production executive on this project," Greg informs. "He shares my passion for it." Eric nods earnestly, confirming that passion, as if we had any doubt.

Willie's been uncharacteristically quiet, but he decides to focus in on that which is important. "Who's gonna play me?"

Greg smiles. "Who do you have in mind?"

"Denzel Washington," says Willie without any hesitation. He's obviously given it some thought.

"I can see that." Greg nods, then looks at Eric, whose identical nod indicates that he, too, can see it. "The thing is, Will, we don't start to deal with casting until we have a script and director in place. But it's a really good thought."

Eric directs a question at "Will." "I hope you don't mind my asking, but do you have a mother?"

Willie shakes his head. "Nah. Used to."

"Why?" asks Greg of Eric, barely containing his curiosity.

"Well," Eric says, looking around the room and then back at Willie, "I hope I'm not talking out of turn, and this is just me speaking off the top of my head, but I was thinking it would be really great if you had a mother."

"Interesting," says Greg, as if this is the first time he has heard this idea. My sense is that Eric wouldn't say "good morning" without first clearing it with Greg, even if it's just "off the top" of his head.

"Well, it ain't that interesting to me," says Willie. "My mother took off when I was three and left me in a bus station. I ain't got no family."

Eric nods. "I understand, and again, I'm just thinking out loud off the top of my head, but I'm talking about for the sake of the story. If your mother was there, supporting you the whole time you were in prison, believing in you . . ."

Willie is starting to get annoyed, which in itself does not qualify as a rare occurrence. "Yeah, she could have baked me fucking cupcakes. And we could have had a party in the prison. Mom and Dad could have invited all my fucking invisible aunts and uncles and cousins."

I intervene, partially because I'm concerned that Willie might throw Greg and Eric out the fifth-story window and they might bounce off the top of their heads. It would also necessitate getting two other passionate executives in here, thereby prolonging this meeting. The other reason I jump in is that they are alluding to an area in which I have a real concern, which is taking dramatic license and changing the characters and events. I've heard about the extraordinary liberties Hollywood can take with "true" stories, and I don't want to wind up being portrayed as the lead lawyer of the transvestite wing of Hamas.

We hash this out for a while, and they assure me that the contract will address my concerns. We agree on a price, and they tell me that a writer will be assigned and will want to go back East to meet and get to know all of us.

I stand up. "So that's it?"

Eric smiles and shakes my hand. "That's it. Let's make a movie."

• • • • •

THE FLIGHT HOME is boring and uneventful, which I view as a major positive when it comes to airplane flights. The movie doesn't appeal to me, so I don't put on the headphones. I then spend the next two hours involuntarily trying to lip-read everything the characters are saying. Unfortunately, the movie is *Dr. Dolittle 2,* and my mouse-lipreading skills are not that well developed.

Willie, for his part, uses the time to refine his casting choices. On further reflection he now considers Denzel too old and is leaning toward Will Smith or Ben Affleck, though he has some doubts that Ben could effectively play a black guy. I suggest that as soon as he gets home he call Greg and Eric to discuss it.

Moments after we touch the ground, a flight attendant comes over and leans down to speak with me. "Mr. Carpenter?" she asks.

I get a brief flash of worry. Has something happened while we were in the air? "Yes?"

"There will be someone waiting at the gate to meet you. You have an urgent phone call."

"Who is it?" I ask.

"I'm sorry, I really don't know. But I'm sure everything is fine."

I would take more comfort from her assurances if she knew what the call was about. I fluctuate between intense worry and panic the entire time we taxi to the gate, which seems to take about four hours.

As soon as the plane comes to a halt, Willie and I jump out of our seats and are the first people off the plane. Somebody who works for airline security is there to meet us, and he leads us to one of those motorized carts. We all jump on and are whisked away.

"Do you know what's going on?" I ask.

The security guy shrugs slightly. "I'm not sure. I think it's about that football player."

Before I have a chance to ask what the hell he could possibly be talking about, we arrive at an airport security office. I'm ushered inside, telling the officers that it's okay for Willie to come in with me. We're led into a back office, where another security guy stands holding a telephone, which he hands to me.

"Hello?" I say into the phone, dreading what I might hear on the other end.

"It took you long enough." The voice is that of Lieutenant Pete Stanton, my closest and only friend in the Paterson Police Department.

I'm somewhat relieved already; Pete wouldn't have

started the conversation that way if he had something terrible to tell me. "What the hell is going on?" I ask.

"Kenny Schilling wants to talk to you. And only you. So you'd better get your ass out here."

If possible, my level of confusion goes up a notch. Kenny Schilling is a running back for the Giants, a third-round pick a few years ago who is just blossoming into a star. I've never met the man, though I know Willie counts him as one of his four or five million social friends. "Kenny Schilling?" I ask. "Why would he want to talk to me?"

"Where the hell have you been?" Pete asks.

Annoyance is overtaking my worry; there is simply nothing concerning Kenny Schilling that could represent a disaster in my own life. "I've been on a plane, Pete. I just flew in from Fantasyland. Now, tell me what the hell is going on."

"It looks like Schilling killed Troy Preston. Right now he's holed up in his house with enough firepower to supply the 3rd Infantry, and every cop in New Jersey outside waiting to blow his head off. Except me. I'm on the phone, 'cause I made the mistake of saying I knew you."

"Why does he want me?" I ask. "How would he even know my name?"

"He didn't. He asked for the hot-shit lawyer that's friends with Willie Miller."

An airport security car is waiting to take us to Upper Saddle River, which is where they tell us Kenny Schilling lives, and they assure us that our bags will be taken care of. "My bag's the one you can lift," I say.

Once in the car, I turn on the radio to learn more

about the situation, and discover that it is all anyone is talking about.

Troy Preston, a wide receiver for the Jets, did not show up for scheduled rehab on an injured knee yesterday and did not call in an explanation to the team. This was apparently uncharacteristic, and when he could not be found or contacted, the police were called in. Somehow Kenny Schilling was soon identified as a person who might have knowledge concerning the disappearance, and the police went out to his house to talk to him.

The unconfirmed report is that Schilling brandished a gun, fired a shot (which missed), and turned his house into a fortress. Schilling has refused to talk to the cops, except to ask for me. The media are already referring to me as his attorney, a logical, though totally incorrect, assumption.

This shows signs of being a really long day.

Upper Saddle River is about as pretty a New York suburb as you are going to find in New Jersey. Located off Route 17, it's an affluent, beautifully wooded community dotted with expensive but not pretentious homes. A number of wealthy athletes, especially on those teams that play in New Jersey like the Giants and Jets, have gravitated to it. As we enter its peaceful serenity, it's easy to understand why.

Unfortunately, that serenity disappears as we near Kenny Schilling's house. The street looks like it is hosting a SWAT team convention, and it's hard to believe that there could be a police car anywhere else in New Jersey. Every car seems to have gun-toting officers crouched behind it; it took less firepower to bring down Saddam Hussein. Kenny Schilling is a threat that they are taking very seriously.

Willie and I are brought into a trailer, where State Police Captain Roger Dessens waits for us. He dispenses with the greetings and pleasantries and immediately brings me up-to-date, though his briefing includes little more than I heard in radio reports. Schilling is a suspect in Preston's disappearance and possible murder, and his actions are certainly consistent with guilt. Innocent people don't ordinarily barricade themselves in their homes and fire at police.

"You ready?" Dessens asks, but doesn't wait for a reply. He picks up the phone and dials a number. After a few moments he talks into the phone. "Okay, Kenny, Carpenter is right here with me."

He hands me the phone, and I cleverly say, "Hello?"

A clearly agitated voice comes through the phone. "Carpenter?"

"Yes."

"How do I know it's you?"

It's a reasonable question. "Hold on," I say, and signal to Willie to come over. I hand him the phone. "He isn't sure it's me."

Willie talks into the phone. "Hey, Schill . . . what's happenin'?" He says this as if they just met at a bar and the biggest decision confronting them is whether to have Coors or a Bud.

I can't hear "Schill's" view of what might be "happenin'," but after a few moments Willie is talking again. "Yeah, it's Andy. I'm right here with him. He's cool. He'll get you out of this bullshit in no time."

Looking out over the army of cops assembled to

deal with "this bullshit," I've got a feeling Willie's assessment might be a tad on the wildly optimistic side. Willie hands the phone back to me, and Schilling tells me that he wants me to come into his house. "I need to talk to you."

I have absolutely no inclination to physically enter this confrontation by going into his house. "We're talking now," I say.

He is insistent. "I need to talk to you in here."

"I understand you have some guns," I say.

"I got one gun" is how he corrects me. "But don't worry, man, I ain't gonna shoot you."

"I'll get back to you," I say, then hang up and tell Captain Dessens about Schilling's request.

"Good," he says, standing up. "Let's get this thing moving."

"What thing?" I ask. "You think I'm going in there? Why would I possibly go in there?"

Dessens seems unperturbed. "You want a live client or a dead one?"

"He's not my client. Just now was the first time I've ever spoken to him. He didn't even know it was me."

"On the other hand, he's got a lot of money to pay your bills, Counselor." He says "Counselor" with the same respect he might have said "Fuehrer."

Dessens is really pissing me off; I don't need this aggravation. "On the other hand, you're an asshole," I say.

"So you're not going?" Dessens asks. The smirk on his face seems to say that he knows I'm a coward and I'm just looking for an excuse to stay out of danger. He's both arrogant and correct.

Willie comes over to me and talks softly. "Schill's good people, Andy. They got the wrong guy."

I'm instantly sorry I didn't leave Willie at the airport. Now if I don't go in, I'm not just letting down a stranger accused of murder, I'm letting down a friend. "Okay," I say to Dessens, "but while I'm out there, everybody has their guns on safety."

Dessens shakes his head. "Can't do it, but I'll have them pointed down."

I nod. "And I get a bulletproof vest."

Dessens agrees to the vest, and they have one on me in seconds. He and I work out a signal for me to come out of the house with Schilling without some trigger-happy, Jets-fan officer taking a shot at us.

Willie offers to come in with me, but Dessens refuses. Within five minutes I'm walking across the street toward a quite beautiful ranch-style home, complete with manicured lawn and circular driveway. I can see a swimming pool behind the house to the right side, but since I didn't bring my bathing suit, I probably won't be able to take advantage of it. Besides, I don't think this bulletproof vest would make a good flotation device.

As I walk, I notice that the street has gotten totally, eerily silent. I'm sure that every eye is on me, waiting to storm the house if Schilling blows my unprotected head off. "The tension was so thick you could cut it with a knife" suddenly doesn't seem like a cliché anymore.

Four hours ago my biggest problem was how to ask the first-class flight attendant for a vodkaless Bloody Mary without using the embarrassing term "Virgin

Mary," and now I've got half a million sharpshooters just waiting for me to trigger a firefight. I'm sure there are also television cameras trained on me, and I can only hope I don't piss in my pants on national television.

As I step onto the porch, I see that the door is partially open. I take a step inside, but I don't see anything. Schilling's voice tells me to "Come in and close the door behind you," which is what I do.

The first thing I'm struck by is how sparsely furnished the place is and how absent the touches of home. There are a number of large unopened cardboard boxes, and my sense is that Schilling must have only recently moved in. This makes sense, since I saw on ESPN a few weeks ago that the Giants just signed him to a fourteen-million, three-year deal, a reward for his taking over the starting running back job late last season.

Schilling sits on the floor in the far corner of the room, pointing a handgun at me. He is a twenty-five-year-old African-American, six three, two hundred thirty pounds, with Ali-like charismatic good looks. Yet now he seems exhausted and defeated, as if his next move might be to turn the gun on himself. When I saw him on ESPN, he was thanking his wife, teammates, and God for helping him achieve his success, but he doesn't look too thankful right now. "How many are out there?" he asks.

Why? Is he so delusional as to think he can shoot his way out? "Enough to invade North Korea," I say.

He sags slightly, as if this is the final confirmation that his situation is hopeless. I suddenly feel a surge of pity for him, which is not the normal feeling I have for an accused killer pointing a gun at me. "What's going on here, Kenny?"

He makes a slight head motion toward a hallway. "Look in there. Second door on the left."

I head down the hall as instructed and enter what looks like a guest bedroom. There are five or six regular-size moving cartons, three of which have been opened. I'm not sure what it is I'm supposed to be looking for, so I take a few moments to look around.

I see a stain under the door to the closet, and a feeling of dread comes over me. I reluctantly open the door and look inside. What I see is a torso, folded over with a large red stain on its back. I don't need Al Michaels to tell me that this is Troy Preston, wide receiver for the Jets. And I don't need anybody to tell me that he is dead.

I walk back into the living room, where Kenny hasn't moved. "I didn't do it," he says.

"Do you know who did?"

He just shakes his head. "What the hell am I gonna do?"

I sit down on the floor next to him. "Look," I say, "I'm going to have a million questions for you, and then we're going to have to figure out the best way to help you. But right now we have to deal with *them*." I point toward the street, in case he didn't know I was talking about the police. "This is not the way to handle it."

"I don't see no other way."

I shake my head. "You know better than that. You asked for me . . . I'm a lawyer. If you were going to go down fighting, you'd have asked for a priest."

He wears the fear on his face like a mask. "They'll kill me."

"No. You'll be treated well. They wouldn't try anything . . . there's media all over this. We're going to walk out together, and you'll be taken into custody. It'll take some time to process you into the system, and I probably won't see you until tomorrow morning. Until then you are to talk to no one—not the police, not the guy in the next cell, no one. Do you understand?"

He nods uncertainly. "Are you going to help me?"

"I'm going to help you." It's not really a lie; I certainly haven't decided to take this case, but for the time being I will get him through the opening phase. If I decide not to represent him, which basically means if I believe he's guilty, I'll help him get another attorney.

"They won't let me talk to my wife."

He seems to be trying to delay the inevitable surrender. "Where is she?" I ask.

"In Seattle, at her mother's. They said she's flying back. They won't let me talk to her."

"You'll talk to her, but not right now. Now it's time to end this." I say it as firmly as I can, and he nods in resignation and stands up.

I walk outside first, as previously planned, and make a motion to Dessens to indicate that Kenny is following me, without his gun. It goes smoothly and professionally, and within a few minutes Kenny has been read his rights and is on the way downtown.

He's scared, and he should be. No matter how this turns out, life as he knows it is over.